BULLETS BEFORE DAWN

Murder in Chinatown

Featuring
Homicide Detective
Johnny Vero

fred berri

Bullets Before Dawn
Copyright © 2019 frederic dalberri
ISBN: 978-1-970153-02-6

Cover art: Shutterstock

La Maison Publishing, Inc.
Vero Beach, Florida
The Hibiscus City
www.lamaisonpublishing.com

Dedicated To

My childhood lifelong friend and former neighbor,
Anna Bocskay Allen, for helping me become a better
writer with her suggested directives and encouragement.

Thanks also to Ellen Gillette, editor,
and
Janet Sierzant of La Maison Publishing
for their expertise,
and to all of my first readers.

This story is fictional. Any names, places, or situations are a 'fougasse.'[1] They are purely coincidental with the exception of historical events, historical names, historical dates or any actual location(s) and facts.

Reader Awareness
The story herein is for a mature audience containing adult material that includes coarse language, sexual content and violence.

---

[1]   Fougasse /fuːˈɡɑːs/ is a term used for "fake" or not real. The word originated back in the seventeenth century to describe a fake rock that was filled with explosives during wars. Soldiers would step on these fake rocks, exploding the bomb and causing serious injury or death. So the rock being fake or not real was termed a *fougasse*. This novel is a fougasse.

Prologue

The crowd chants in unison... TEN-NINE-EIGHT-SEVEN-SIX-FIVE-FOUR-THREE-TWO-ONE...

"*Happy New Year!*" shouts Benny Roberts into the microphone as confetti falls from the ceiling. The dance floor is crowded, many blowing into their noise makers wearing silly New Year's hats. Everyone is caught up in the moment. Once a year, at the stroke of midnight, celebration overtakes the city.

Benny waves his baton for the orchestra to begin playing "Auld Lang Syne," already queued up for the downbeat. His mind drifts. He's given up a night with his wife of twenty-five years for this ... again ... so that others can enjoy the festivities, turning to whoever is near for a New Year's kiss and an embrace, while she waits patiently at home for him to drag in at 5 a.m. Wearing a sheer negligee, she'll have the champagne chilled. Benny smiles at the thought. *Like I tell folks, I always start the new year off with a bang!*

The soft melody strikes a pensive aura, filling the hearts of everyone. Whether in the arms of a one-night-stand, someone who'll be around a long time, or marking the end of a relationship, there is something about the tune that tugs at the ole' heart strings, bringing tears to many. Most people don't know what the lyrics mean, but when did that stop anyone from singing along?

Benny looks back at the crowd on the dance floor, everyone stopped for the song. Waxing philosophical, he wonders how many are thinking of the past, of good times or hardships, love lost and gained, disaster, or the disappointments when life got in the way of their plans. *Everyone's hoping for a better, happier, and prosperous New Year. Myself included.*

Out on the floor, one movie-star-handsome man in the crowd caresses a particularly beautiful woman. Johnny Vero, six feet of muscle topped with thick blonde hair just beginning to gray holds an armful of curves as her soft brown eyes get lost in his blue green ones. They are frozen by each other's gaze. "Happy New Year, Detective," she says. "I…"

Johnny kisses her softly to stop her words and tenderly pulls her even closer. Everything comes to a complete stop, it seems, even the confetti. *How strong his hands are.* She sighs sensuously, as he lifts her to her tiptoes and off the floor.

A New Day, a New Dawn, a New Year

CHAPTER 1

"Johnny, I can't believe it! Can you?" Molly sat up, shuffling the sheets, and rubbed the sleep from her eyes as the morning sun radiated the room. Molly's enthusiasm was just one of the qualities men loved about her. She had instinctively pulled the sheet modestly up, but as she turned to look at him, she let it drop, showing off a few more of her assets.

"Believe what? How beautiful you are or that I'm really here with you?" Johnny Vero stroked her back in a way that made her wriggle with delight. Her tawny complexion, smooth as silk, seemed to invite his touch. He was used to seeing her hair up; loose and flowing was a definite improvement. "Do I believe that the new year is starting yet again with cold, damp, snow? Or maybe that I haven't gotten a call yet for the first homicide of the year?"

"Silly, I mean it's 1949 already. The war's been over for years; people are getting their lives back together. The Budapest Hotel murders are safely in the past." Molly lay back down to snuggle close. "You and Billy got your promotions from hunting that maniacal serial killer and bringing him to justice all the way from France. There have been a lot of good things, Lieutenant. And besides, New York has a special persona, a magic in the air, no matter what time of year it is. Like you, Johnny," she whispered. "Electrifying." Molly looked up and smiled. "By the way, I like your tattoo, which somehow I'd missed until last night."

"Yeah. Lady Justice. She knows her stuff."

"I like that it has the word wisdom across the bottom. She does, you know. Have wisdom I mean. Did you get that tattoo in the Navy?" Molly stroked the curly hair on Johnny's chest as she spoke. This was nice, just lying here together.

Johnny chuckled. "I got it on 48th Street in a little place behind a barber shop. Very hush-hush," he explained. Tattoos were beginning to grow in popularity, but to many "respectable" citizens, they only belonged on the Tattooed Lady at the circus. "I'd just been accepted to the police academy." He kissed the top of her raven head. "I'm happy you stayed the night, Molly."

"Me too."

"I guess you're my Lady Justice, being the District Attorney," he whispered, turning himself and Molly so that he could feel her length against his. "And Lady Justice is about to make a wise decision," he murmured, kissing Molly's neck below her ear. *I'm in bed with the fucking DA*, he thought, grinning at the literal meaning. *Amolia Penett. Miss Elegance and the top of her class. In my bed. About damn time, too.*

"What decision is that?" In response to the movement of his hands under the sheet, she giggled. "Mmmmm, never mind. Ohh! Yes! *Yes!* Lady Justice does likes that!"

Molly's quite the fine instrument, he thought, as he rolled her gently onto her back. Like the cello he played, her sounds were euphoric, finely tuned. As she shuddered against him, he knew that she was his. He just wasn't entirely sure what that meant.

One year earlier...

Every morning newspaper had the picture of Detectives Vero and Bradshaw holding serial killer Jean-Paul Vincent's hands, handcuffed high in the air, as they departed the airplane that had brought them from France back to the United States.

The bold print headlines summed it all up nicely: *BUDAPEST HOTEL KILLER FOUND IN FRANCE, BROUGHT TO JUSTICE BY NEW YORK DETECTIVES. MAYOR TO BE RE-ELECTED!* **Speedy trial anticipated. Full story page six.**

Byline: Grace Tilly.

A New Year, a New Homicide

CHAPTER 2

Angie answered the telephone in a whisper, trying not to wake her father. Hearing the water running in the bathroom, however, she raised her voice. "Hold on. I hear him. Let me tell him," she said as she held the receiver out into the hallway. "Oh, Lieutenant," she sang, "It's Molly. Telephone! Can you take a call?"

Home from college for the winter break, beautiful auburn-haired Angie had no idea that her father and Molly had spent New Year's Eve and most of New Year's Day together at the Budapest Hotel, but she'd always admired Molly. It had been many years since her mother Simone had left him to pursue the somewhat shocking lifestyle of an artist in Europe. Molly would be a good fit for him. At a dinner the year before, Angie had observed them together. He'd been professional, of course, but underneath it all there was something going on. More like a college boy, Angie had thought. Although reluctant, he'd even agreed to play the cello for her. She was proud of her handsome father, but worried, too. A man like that shouldn't be alone.

Now Johnny tweaked his daughter on the nose as he took the receiver from her. "Good morning, Molly. It *is* morning, isn't it?"

"I'm sorry to bother you," Molly's voice said. "I know Angie's there and you were going to spend some time together –"

"It's okay," he said, remembering suddenly the silkiness of her skin. Angie was still standing there, so he couldn't exactly say anything about it. Hopefully he could keep an erection in check, but her skin ... "It's her last year of college and she's becoming completely independent, always making plans with *her friends*." When he glared at his daughter, she rolled her eyes on cue and pivoted away just in time.

"You should be proud of the job you did all these years as a single Dad. Angie's lucky to have you."

"Thanks, Molly." He lowered his voice a notch. "She reminds me of you, actually."

"Oh?" Molly cooed. "That's nice to hear. I'm flattered. And curious. How so?"

"She's independent. She knows what she wants and how to get there. She's intelligent." Johnny stretched his head to make sure his daughter wasn't eavesdropping before continuing. "She's also beautiful. And respectful. And she would never fall for just any guy." *Careful. Keep your thoughts in check. Angie could come back any minute. Plus, you don't want to show your hand, now do you?*

Molly's silence spoke volumes. "I'm very flattered, Johnny. If Angie and I are all that, we should be considered kindred spirits."

Johnny's mind was not on his daughter, however. "I'm really happy –"

"Me too, Johnny," Molly interrupted, "but I'm not calling about ... that. There was a shooting on Mott Street, south of Canal. Here's that New Year's homicide you mentioned, and we're not even 48 hours into it."

7

"Shit! Five Points. I hate that place." A notorious slum, Five Points was governed unofficially by Chinatown's underground. Businesses, disputes, anything that went on whether legal or not, the underground manipulated it for their own benefit. "This will be one hell of a case to get into."

"I know, Johnny."

"Was it the On Leong or the Hip Sing Tongs? Do you even know yet?" The rival gangs had ongoing bloody battles for control of the streets and everything that happened on them: gambling, protection, prostitution, opium. Johnny knew all too well how closed-mouth everyone would be; most homicides eventually got swept under the rug.

"Doesn't look like a gang hit this time. A single murder."

Johnny grinned with an epiphany. "Molly!" he said. "South Central's jurisdiction ends at Canal Street. That means this is the 5th Precinct's debacle, not ours!"

Molly groaned. "That would be nice. Canal's the dividing line, but the body's on our side. Mott."

"Can't we drag him across the street?"

Molly tried not to giggle, but couldn't help it. She could picture Lt. Vero doing that very thing. "Sorry, Johnny. I've called for a squad car to drive me. The MEs already on his way."

"I'll meet you there."

Click.

CHAPTER 3

The wind coming off the East River dropped the temperature to 18 degrees. Huge chunks of ice appeared in a river that all but cried out in pain. The weather wouldn't get better for some time.

Uniformed police corralled people away from the crime scene, but not before it was compromised. A few curiosity hounds gawked from behind glassed store and building entrances or from windows, but only a few. It was much too cold to lean out into the morning to get a better view of the body lying in the street. Murder was such a regular occurrence at Five Points that most people were conducting business as usual, scurrying about unconcerned, ignoring the police work for the most part.

A uniformed officer moved wooden barriers to block off scene perimeters, as Johnny arrived, parking around the corner on Mott Street. Since the crime scene was secure, he wouldn't have to draw his .38 from its holster; that was one advantage, anyway. *It is too fucking cold to be spending a lot of time over a body. Where's the fucking ME?*

He got out of the car and walked toward the scene. Molly had just arrived from the looks of things, still studying the victim. Even with woolen trousers covering those long,

Rockette-quality legs of hers under a heavy coat, she was stunning. Hearing footsteps, she turned around; now he could see the ME kneeling on the sidewalk, carefully inspecting the body. It was so cold, little puffs of air made it clear that he was talking, calling out observations for his assistant to jot down in a little notebook nearby. You could hardly tell it was a tall, thin woman, so bundled up she was, a thick scarf revealing only her eyes.

At this temperature, every breath actually hurt. "Good morning, Miss Penett."

"Good morning, Lieutenant," she answered with her usual professional demeanor. Business is business, friends are friends, lovers … Molly pursed her lips to him in a quick air kiss, away from everyone else's sight. Johnny smiled ever so slightly in reply.

Peering down into the lifeless face of an adult male was Dr. Christopher Michaels, New York City Medical Examiner, with almost as lifeless face himself. "Lieutenant, help me roll him over?" he asked. He would love to get him back to the lab, out of the damn cold, but he needed to note as much as he could at the scene that would help them get started – evidence, cause and time of death, signs of a struggle, rigor mortis.

"What've you got so far, Doc?" Johnny asked, his breath mingling with the doctor's in a little cloud as they rolled the body over.

"He doesn't look Chinese. A gunshot caused this poor bastard's unfortunate demise," Dr. Michaels said, always appreciative of an audience. "The bullet traveled from the cranium through the brain tissues, causing a laceration to the brain parenchyma and also producing multiple high energy fragmentation damaging the brain parenchyma before –"

"Whoa! Doc!" Johnny interrupted. "Speak English. I only wanted to get a time frame for when he bought the farm, not a lecture."

Dr. Michael shrugged off the rebuff, slipping back into the cadence of conversation he'd often shared with his friend Johnny over a beer. "It's colder that a witch's tit out here. I can't tell if this is rigor or he's frozen." The doctor shook his head. "I'll know better once I get him on the table and he can defrost. At the moment, all I'm sure about is that this is a tall thin man, reedy you might say. With a bullet in his head."

Molly interrupted, "Detective, I have to leave. I'll be in my office by noon if you need anything." She was already walking briskly toward the car that would take her back to a warm room. "Doc, I want the autopsy ASAP!"

"I'll need at least a week," he called. "My refrigerators are full! We're shorthanded and back logged from last year's carryover ..." His voice trailed off when she stopped and turned around. He knew that look.

"Make this a priority, Doc. Detective, when will Bradshaw be back from vacation?"

Next to Vero, Bradshaw was the best detective on the squad. The Budapest Hotel killer hadn't been a match for the two of them. "Not soon enough, Miss Penett, not soon enough," he replied and continued, not really to her at all. This was going to be one shit show of an investigation. "Look around. Whispers lurk in every shadow. Whispers with answers. They pretend not to pay attention, but they know." Aloud he asked, not even bothering to mask his hope, if the good doctor had seen anything that might land the case with another precinct.

"Sorry, Lieutenant, but this one's all yours." The ME gave his friend a little bow. "He was murdered right where he was standing, not offed somewhere else, and dumped here."

"How can you be sure?"

"Dead man's fall. His legs are crossed at the ankles. You've probably witnessed it before but didn't give much thought to it." He had an audience again, and he knew it. "It's a spinal reflex when the body becomes brain dead and the body falls. Automatically, the ankles cross. Crazy phenomenon, huh?" He grinned. "When you're finished with your own look-see, my assistant can bag and tag him for the ride."

Johnny examined more carefully, searching the dead man's coat and pockets. *No shell casings, no exit wound. Had to be a revolver, probably a .22. Up close and personal. A professional hit? But why? He's dressed to the nines. Still has his gold watch, gold lighter – initials D G. No wallet but cash in a money clip, same initials. Not a robbery.*

As he moved the man's sleeve to check for possibly identifying cuff links, a small gray object escaped, fluttering against the curb. He picked it up before the wind could carry it away. Placing it in one of the envelopes he always kept inside his coat for just such occurrences. *A feather. What the fuck is a feather doing next to a dead man lying in the street?*

He stood there, holding the feather in his hand and happened to look across the street, then down the street, both ways. A second ago, people had been hurrying to and fro. Now, the streets were virtually empty. He still saw faces at windows. Was it the feather? The cold? You never knew in this business, what might set a person off, or scare him off.

Removing the victim's watch, Johnny was pleased to find an ascription. *Deshi Garner. Love, Mom.*

Johnny called to the uniformed police office. "Sergeant, have your men start canvassing. You know the routine. Find me some witnesses, anyone who's willing to talk." He directed his orders to the doctor's assistant. "Get him out of here," and turned back to the sergeant without missing a beat. "Be sure your men check garbage cans on the corners and alleys. His wallet, maybe the weapon if we're lucky." He looked again at the watch, clip, and lighter, as if some new clue might reveal itself. "Bag these and get them to evidence."

"Sure thing, Lieutenant. Another John Doe?"

"No," the detective frowned. "This one has a name. And a mother." *But don't they all?*

13

A Conscious Inattention

CHAPTER 4

Johnny hated Five Points, not just because of the Chinese underground, not because of the poverty or the crime. This is where his father was killed as a beat cop when Johnny was in the Navy. Just being there brought it all vividly to mind. He'd read the reports over and over. Without trying to, it flooded back as he stood on the corner, looking up and down Mott Street, looking for anything and everything, and at nothing at all.

His father was so proud to be a policeman. He walked his beat every day twirling his nightstick with the rhythm of a drum major leading a parade band, people said. He was a good cop and a good man, people said. People. Eyewitnesses gave a detailed account which Johnny had practically memorized.

Officer Vero, tall, friendly, walks into the First American Savings and Loan Bank on Eight Avenue and Thirty Seventh Street. He walks in like he does every day of the week, heading straight in, as if to greet the manager at the front desk by the door. Today's different, though. The manager, assistant manager, and secretary are standing on their desks with their hands in the air.

People lay on the floor, arms over their heads; the tellers were standing on the counters. In the split-second he realized what was happening, before he could draw his weapon, yelling, "Mary, Mother of God!" he was shot twice, killed as two bullets pierced his chest.

Mother of God, indeed. Johnny came back to the present. *That's a good place to start the investigation.* The Church of the Transgression, the oldest Catholic Church building in the city, sat on the corner of Mott and Mosco Streets. *I haven't been to church since Angie's baptism.*

Priests don't lie. Or shouldn't. Maybe someone saw something, went to church to light a candle and pray for protection in fear of being seen as a witness. It was worth a try.

At least he'd be in out of the cold. Entering, Johnny recognized the musty smell from so many years ago. Walk in, dip hand into the holy water hundreds of others have dipped their disgusting fingers into, make the sign of the cross. His footsteps on the hard floor echoed through the vast empty space. Only a few faithful were there, kneeling, clutching rosary beads in prayer. The priest preparing the altar for the next mass noticed Johnny standing in the back of the church. Just standing. No movement toward a pew or confessional, no clink of coins for candles. The priest turned to the cross overhead and genuflected before making his way to Johnny.

"Greetings," the priest said genially as he approached Johnny. "You look lost. Once you enter God's house, you need never be lost again." He gestured to a nearby pew. "Come, sit here. It's cold outside. Tell me what's troubling you, my son."

Johnny was touched by the priest's genuine concern. "Thank you, um, Father. My name is Lieutenant Vero, a detective at South Central," he said as he held up his badge. "I'm investigating a homicide on Mott Street, near the corner of Mosco. Happened during the night." The priest shook his head sadly, but said nothing. "Do you know anything about it?" *Dammit, this is a murder investigation, and I'm tip-toeing around.* "Are you hiding anyone that may be connected to this murder?"

The priest was horrified. "Detective, you *are* lost! Anyone in this neighborhood that would commit such a sin against God would flee far from these doors. They would probably knock on Satan's doors to escape. He has many doors close to here."

"Any particular doors?"

"The Old Brewery," the priest said softly, and then smiled. "Would you like me to hear your confession, Lieutenant? You seem to have a lot on your mind. How long has it been?"

Johnny shot to his feet. "No. No, *thank you*, Father. You've been a great help." Suddenly he felt trapped; he walked to the door as fast as he could, back into the chill air.

CHAPTER 5

The Old Brewery was five stories of dilapidation, just southwest of Five Points at Anthony and Orange Streets. Detective Vero knew the building well. So did *Johnny* Vero. He'd played in this neighborhood as a boy. It was infamous, as well-known to Chinatown as the Labyrinth was to ancient Greece. The Labyrinth and its inner mazes and tunnels was said to have housed Minotaur, the monster of Crete, half man and half bull, eventually killed by the Athenian hero Theseus.

The Old Brewery was reportedly every bit as impenetrable with 75 different chambers, "home sweet home" to 150 men, women, and children. It had been turned into a *gong si fong*, communal apartments where Chinese immigrants slept in shifts. In a word, the entire premise was the equal of the Minotaur, monstrous and unkillable because this was reality, not myth. Residents of the *gong si fong* would work at anything for very little, sometimes honest jobs, sometimes less so.

The living conditions were abhorrent. The American Dream may be just a few feet away, geographically, but for most of the *gong si fong*'s unfortunate residents, they might as well stayed in China. Johnny often wondered how they had enough money to pay off their traffickers and open a business.

Tunnels running through the Old Brewery's basement made it easy for anyone to hide or escape. Over the years, rumors surfaced about the maze of passageways, some leading to the East River and as far north as Washington Heights' Fort Tryon Park.

The priest was right about this being the devil's door, Johnny thought, looking up at the forbidding building. It would take weeks of gumshoe work to properly canvass the place. Even then, he anticipated a case of "monkey see no evil, hear no evil, speak no evil."

Johnny decided that it might be better to wait a few days. Give "things" a little time to settle down, catch someone off guard. Taking out his pad, he made notes and sketches of what he saw, counting the doorways, stairwells, apartments on each floor, windows, whatever information that might be of value down the line. Any seasoned cop would do the same; Johnny had certainly used enough salt over his years to tenderize many investigations. *Now it begins,* he thought grimly. *How to cut through this one, though?*

Partners in Crime

CHAPTER 6

"Well, beat me daddy, eight to the bar. Welcome back *Sergeant* Detective Billy Bradshaw." Johnny was happy to see his partner.

"Heh, heh, heh," Billy laughed quietly, in good spirits after an extended vacation – more of a honeymoon really, since he hadn't been married long. "Good morning, *Lieutenant.*" The men shook hands, congratulating each other on their promotions for capturing Jean-Paul Vincent just months before. Vincent had terrorized the city, luring dance hall girls from the Flamingo Room to the Budapest Hotel, where he brutally murdered them. It had been the case of a lifetime. Or perhaps not.

"I don't know about you, Johnny, but I'm definitely enjoying the raise we got with our promotions. Oh, and Nancy said to tell you congratulations and Happy New Year, not that we were here to ring it in. Me too, Johnny. *Thank* you. I really owe you one. I don't know if we have *bupkis* on the board, but there's got to be something for us." The tall, athletic redhead walked over to the nearest wall of the squad room. "Let me see for myself."

Johnny leaned against his desk and waited for it.

"Fuck!" Billy exclaimed. One murder standing out like the Christmas tree at Rockefeller Center. *Chinatown.* "What a way to start the year." He turned to Johnny and held up his hands. "Don't tell me. We've got it, right?"

"Right as rain, buddy-roo. Just consider Chinatown as job security." Johnny chuckled. "If only he'd gotten popped across the street, the 5th would have been blessed instead of us. We're going to earn our pay on this one, Billy."

"What've we got so far?"

Johnny handed him a sheaf of papers. "Catch up with these. I've got to brief the captain before getting all these other flatfoots to work." From around the room, other detectives groaned good-naturedly. The bureau worked well together. As he headed for Captain Sullivan's office, he spoke over his shoulder. "There's a copy of the autopsy there too. Give me your two cents' worth."

Reading carefully and quickly, Billy finished just as Johnny returned. "This is bad for business right here. So soon after we got that Frenchy, we'd better get this one in our satchel so it doesn't come back to bite us. We better solve this one even faster, or they'll think he was a fluke. Above our pay grade. Could they bump us back down?" He looked worried. "A .22 caliber to the back of his head. That makes a statement."

"Agreed. This was a contract. Not much hard evidence at the scene, either. Now, the question is –"

"Who put out the hit on Mr. Garner? And what kind of name is Deshi, anyway?" Billy interjected. "I see you found a feather. So, maybe a pillow to help quiet the shot?"

Johnny shrugged. "Maybe. Maybe it's nothing. At the scene it was business as usual. Like nothing happened. The uniforms had put up barriers, but no one seemed to care.

Mott was buzzing like a beehive, all the workers going about their business. Then it got eerie."

"What do you mean?"

"Everyone stopped all at once. It was like a signal went out. I think somebody knows something."

"What does our lovely District Attorney have to say?"

If Billy only knew what she liked to say, *during*. Johnny frowned to stop the automatic smile at the thought. "Actually, Billy, we're headed there right now. Her office got some information from the narcotics bureau that might help. Activity in that area."

"I hope it's good. We need a jump start."

Johnny patted him on the shoulder. "Yes, Sergeant. I know Sergeant. But we know that –"

Billy chimed in with Johnny for the well-rehearsed mantra. *"Every murder has a motive. Every motive has a reason."*

Johnny gathered his overcoat and paperwork. "Unfortunately, it's our job is to find out the reason."

CHAPTER 7

Molly's gal Friday, Louise, greeted Detectives Vero and Bradshaw happily, winking at Johnny as he turned his head to give her a glance and a nod. "Congratulations on your promotions," she whispered provocatively. Bradshaw might be a happily married man, but there was always hope. And Vero ... well, that man was just crying out for feminine attention.

"Come in, come in," Molly eagerly called out. "Welcome back, *Sergeant* Bradshaw. Congratulations on your promotion. I'm sure you've been brought up to date on the Chinatown homicide. We've got a lot of territory to cover in-house. Out in the field, well, that's your domain. Johnny, you've been holding out on me," she let her words slow to a lingering gloat. Her lips were slightly parted, and she purposefully ran the tip of her tongue across her top lip, never taking her eyes off Johnny.

Billy noticed. How could he not? He just stood there, staring at his partner with raised eyebrows. He hadn't been gone that long. *When did* this *happen?*

"I, um, I'm not sure what you mean," Johnny said, ignoring Billy.

Molly gestured for the men to sit down. "Your military record indicates you've worked with the Chinese. On the *USS Monrovia*. Didn't you think I'd find out?"

Given their brand-new relationship, Johnny was visibly relieved – there was so much in his past she might have brought up! – But also a little confused at the context. "Nothing gets by you, Molly! Yes, we had some Chinese on board. Nothing spectacular. We were a transport assault ship. It was before the war and our policy with China was simple: non-interference. The goal of our policy makers was to secure economic interests in China. We entertained some of the higher Chinese naval officials. I picked up some of their lingo, if I can remember the dialect. They've got a lot of them."

"Well, brush off the dust. You've got to be the one," Molly nodded at Billy, "you and Billy. I need you to get into that hellhole – the Old Brewery building, the shops on Mott. We only need one person to be willing to give us a lead. On the street, you spoke of whispers in the shadows."

Johnny nodded, but was surprised she had even heard him. It had been so windy. He was impressed.

"If we send a detective that understands them better than most, it may open some dialog. Can't hurt, anyway. I'm also requesting some Chinese officers from the 5th precinct to join South Central for the investigation. I already spoke with Captain Sullivan. He's on board, pardon the pun…"

"Maybe we should get Lamont Cranston from *The Shadow*," Billy suggested with a chuckle. It was one of his favorite radio shows. "'The Shadow knowssssssss….'"

Smiling, Molly pointed at Billy with an expertly manicured finger. "*That* would be too simple and we'd all be out of a job. Let's stick with the problem at hand. Did you both catch the Medical Examiner's time of death in his report? Somewhere between 3 a.m. and sunrise?"

"Sunrise was at 7:20, so I'm going with just before dawn. The shopkeepers wouldn't have been hustling before sunrise. The streets would've been empty. We think it was a professional hit," Johnny said, glancing over at Billy. "I'm going to say he was probably popped between 3 and 5."

While Johnny spoke, Molly had trouble staying focused. It had been days since they were together. Too many days. Between work and Angie's visit – *focus, Molly, focus. There's a murder to solve.* "Okay, Johnny. I'll go with your gut on this. Dr. Michaels was also wrong about the victim's ethnicity, part Chinese, part American. We traced the inscription. Undercover vice tell us that Deshi Garner was a Chinese-American raised in China by his Chinese mother. Here, though, he infiltrated an organization that runs gambling and prostitution. Why, we don't know yet."

Johnny was taking notes. Things were getting murkier, not clearer.

"We also have information that leads us to believe that drugs, mostly opium, are coming right into the East River Basin along with Chinese women. We're going to meet with a couple of undercover vice detectives in a few minutes. Did you get the report back for that feather you found?"

Just then, Louise buzzed her boss on the intercom: *"Miss Penett, the vice detectives are here."*

"Thank you, Louise. Send them in."

27

Collaboration

CHAPTER 8

Molly made simple introductions, purposefully leaving off everyone's titles so no toes were stepped on. "Detectives Johnny Vero and Billy Bradshaw, homicide ... meet Detectives Jimmy Pan and Ru Chang, undercover vice."

The office was getting a little crowded, but the men rearranged chairs so that they could all sit. Pan started. "What we have from our snitches is this: There's a smuggler bringing in narcotics, mostly opium but also young women, Chinese illegals, for prostitution. He's from Guyana, a small country on the northern shoulder of South America. It's the only country in South America that speaks English."

Johnny cut in, "Yeah, I remember from my Navy days. Guyana means 'Land of Many Waters.'"

"Exactly," continued Pan. "The Atlantic's right *there*. That's why it is so accessible for our smuggler to maneuver around. Guyana to Panama, to British Honduras, to Cuba, to Miami. From there, up the coastline to New York. He knows his shit," Pan said.

Chang took it from there. "It appears he was born and raised there. Our snitches say that when he was a ship's captain he brought in bauxite and sugarcane but lost his credentials when inventory went missing. At first, it was a small amount and could've been an accounting error." Chang held up his hands for effect. "After the sixth or seventh time? They never proved it was him, but his status and captain's license were stripped. It's rumored that he sold the missing inventory to foreign countries. Bauxite's expensive – and used for things countries at war need. It was good timing." He paused and looked at a little notebook for reference. "After the war, he was running fishing charters out of Miami for a while. He could have made a lot of contacts doing that."

"He's smart, too. Stealing a small amount at the time, it took a while before it caught up with him. Lotta guys would've gone for the whole tamale at once," Billy commented.

"Let's not lose sight of why we're here," Chang pointed out. "The bauxite's history. Now we've got to worry about the women and narcotics."

"So what do we know about our mystery captain *now*?" Johnny asked.

Pan consulted his notebook, although he had memorized the facts. "He's in his early 40s, said to be good looking, very dark complexion. The people from Guyana don't consider themselves to be 'colored' but you'd say so. Six feet, maybe 180, 185? He has a distinctive scar about eight inches starting from the bottom of his left ear, down his cheek to his chin," he said, tracing a similar path on his own face. "Pretty easy to spot, I'd think. Apparently, someone tried to cut his throat but missed. And we believe whoever missed is now miss-*ing*, probably at the bottom of the ocean."

"Jesus Christ," Billy muttered, his own hand reaching for his throat in sympathy.

"Yeah, he's one lucky son-of-a-bitch. There's also a doctor–" Chang began.

"Not a regular doctor, though," Molly interrupted.

Chang nodded at her. "That's correct. At least our information right now points to him being a veterinarian. We haven't located him yet, but we've heard that he removes bullets, stitches people up, even uses anesthesia. He performs any medical procedures the women or the underground need, so he must be pretty good – and also one tough bastard or he probably wouldn't still be alive. If he's patched up goons from the underground, he could identify them."

Molly wrote something on a paper on her desk, a question to ask Johnny later? Johnny was watching her every move. "Whoever this doctor is," she said, "he's involved, probably the one that saved the smuggler's life. That could be another reason he's still alive...*quid pro quo*. Great. Two more names added. Four."

"Four?" Pan asked.

"The shooter and his victim, the smuggler, and the doctor," Johnny added.

Molly cleared her throat. "Okay, detectives. This is what we have. You know where to reach each other …

and me," she said, looking directly at Johnny. "Go hit the pavement."

Old Acquaintances

CHAPTER 9

Awakening from a long night of endless booze and sex, Johnny's eyes were on Grace Tilly's unembarrassed nakedness as she sashayed past him to find the kitchen. His thoughts were not. Thirsty, longing for a glass of water to sooth parched lips that had touched every inch of his body during the night. She could feel his eyes follow her. There was no way she could guess that he was full of regret, thinking only of Molly.

How did this happen? Grace had covered the Budapest Hotel murders, and had worked closely with Johnny. Very closely. But it was over! Where Molly was elegant, Grace was … accessible. Yes, infinitely accessible. She didn't make a man work for it, that was for sure. But he wanted Molly. He wanted to work for her, wanted to do it right this time. *Got to get rid of Grace.* He'd seen her at his favorite bar last night. She'd had a rough day, he'd had a rough day. *Too many shots. And lately, too little Molly.* It had been weeks. *A man has needs …*

On the kitchen table were books and a haggard leather notebook with a broken clasp that lay open. The pages were filled with scribbled writing; Grace couldn't just leave it alone. Always the reporter, she turned a few pages, raising inquisitive eyebrows as she read. Pages were stained with what looked to be coffee and whiskey; some of the ink had run on a few dog-eared pages. Alongside was a book: *The Student's Chinese-English Dictionary*. She called back to the bedroom.

"I see something here we can play, Johnny."

"What are you talking about, Grace?"

Glass of water in hand, she saucily stopped at the bedroom doorway, her round face framed by short brown bangs. "A game. I'll be a Chinese spy and you arrest me." She pouted a little and then broke into a smile that was pure dynamite. "You better handcuff me for the, um, interrogation."

Shit. He should've moved his books. Being a reporter for the *Daily Globe,* of course she'd know he was working on something. Maybe he could distract her. *Shit!*

Johnny slowly got out of bed and approached her, but not before grabbing his handcuffs from the bedside table drawer. A little roughly, he turned her around and pushed her back into the kitchen. Turning her around, he took the glass from her and set it by the sink, then held both her hands in front with his left, while slipping one cuff around her right hand, closing it ... *click, click, click.*

Grace's breathing was getting faster as he placed her other hand into the twin cuff and slowly squeezed it shut, never taking his eyes off hers. *Click, click, click.* If she'd been a cat, she would have purred. As it was, a little moan of pleasure escaped her lips. Heart pounding, she noticed that her nipples were already hard. In one dramatic motion using both cuffed hands, she pushed everything off the kitchen table to the floor, too excited to care about the mess.

Lifting her and laying her down onto the pathway in the table she'd just cleared, Johnny held her wrists above her head with one hand as he worked her breasts with his mouth.

fred berri

With his other hand, he placed two fingers gently into her joy spot. Grace's raw groans inflamed him, *Molly be damned,* he thought as he slipped himself inside. *A man has needs.* Each thrust moved the table slightly.

"My legs," Grace gasped. He lifted her slightly off the surface so that she could wrap her legs around him, pulling him more deeply into her. As his thickness filled her completely, bringing her to orgasm, she let out a high-pitched shriek of pleasure just as he exploded inside her.

Spent, Grace sighed. Her legs hung over the table's edge. Johnny withdrew from her and stood up, looking at her, looking at the ridiculous position of the table after its ordeal. Gently, he picked her up and carried her back to the bed.

CHAPTER 10

Things seemed to be at a standstill. With nothing new on the case in several weeks, Johnny wasn't hopeful when he heard his named called. "Lieutenant, there's a wacky dame on line three. Says it's important. Something about you running out and taking a powder and that you owe her," bellowed the desk sergeant, howling with glee.

Johnny shrugged his shoulders and waved his arms, questioning the air rhetorically. "Why do I get all the swiggers?"

"Lieutenant, they're not all drinkers," Billy said. At South Central, he tried to acknowledge Johnny's rank for the sake of the other guys.

Picking up the receiver, Johnny raised his eyebrows and mouthed the word *asshole.* "Lieutenant Vero. How can I be of assistance?"

"Johnny, it's Monica." That *had* been a while. "I haven't seen you since your last pleasure visit." When he said nothing, she continued. "I came across some information about, let's just say, *women.*"

"Monica, that's your entire business! Women, pleasuring men." At the mention of her name, he knew Billy would be listening, so he made a show of swiveling his chair away from him. "Which, I know about first hand." He wasn't proud of it, but in their early days as cops, he and Billy had "visited" her establishment quite often. True, they'd gotten good information in the process, but …

"No need to thank me, Johnny. My girls took care of you and your partner. Happy to be of, um, service. But I have some information you might be able to use."

Johnny swiveled back to face Billy. "Go on. I'm listening." He gestured for Billy to pick up another receiver and held up three fingers for the right line.

"I heard you're looking for Chinese prostitutes. News of competition flows downstream rather quickly. C'mon over. You and Billy can buy me a drink."

"Be there shortly, Monica….Okay, Billy, let's go. A lead from the Nostalgia Café."

"Ah, Monica. Definite nostalgia there." Billy grabbed his coat. "She's just like a broken clock that tells the correct time twice a day."

"No setting her clock, today, my friend. Gotta stick with police business. Besides," he looked shocked, "what would the little missus say?" Billy hadn't been married long. *Is there already trouble in paradise?* A stab of pain shot through him, remembering that in Molly's eyes, if she ever found out about Grace … but he couldn't think about that right now.

"Some days are diamonds, some days are pearls. Some days it's nice to have Monica's girls," Billy sang off-key something vice had come up long ago. "But not today!"

CHAPTER 11

The Nostalgia Café at the Budapest Hotel brought back a flood of memories, most of them unpleasant. But now, from her bar stool, Monica greeted Johnny and Billy with the warm smile of a mother welcoming her prodigal sons. A little past her prime, her hair dyed a shade too dark, she was still attractive even with a cigarette dangling from her bright red lips.

"Hello, boys, take off your coats! Sit a spell!" she said in a raspy voice. "Always a pleasure to see you." After they settled on either side of her, coats still on, she put the cigarette out on the bar and leaned conspiratorially toward Johnny. "I have a little, very little, information. But I owe you for getting the vice cops off our backs back then." She laughed huskily. "Although, I wouldn't mind them either way, front or back!" She grinned at Billy. "They were kind of cute. Not as cute as you but –"

"Monica." Johnny tapped his watch.

"Okay, okay. You're looking for Chinese prostitutes being smuggled into the country? Buy me a drink, will you?"

Billy put a sawbuck on the bar. "That's right, Monica. Lay it on us, so to speak."

"I'll show you mine, if you show me yours first." Before he could answer wittily, the bartender set a shot glass of whiskey in front of Monica. Greedily, she downed it in one gulp, tapping the bar for a refill. Another gulp, and the glass was empty again.

Monica would loosen up only after the third round, Johnny knew; he nodded to the bartender. Monica owed a lot of people, not just the cops. He wouldn't tell her any more than she needed to know. "We've got a dead man in Chinatown, and a smuggler from South American bringing in drugs and women. That's what *we* know. What do *you* know?"

"Well, Detective," Monica slowed down to a sip, "that's not all of it, according to what's on the street." She set down the glass, warming to the coming speech. "Your dead man is, or was, a high stake gambler within the Chinese faction. So one of two things," she said, holding up two fingers for emphasis. "He owed a shit load of money to the Chinese *or* he knew too much about your smuggler." Monica dropped her voice. "But *my* sources say he was paying for information on the smuggler and using his gambling to cover his tracks. A *ruse* so he wouldn't *arouse* suspicion," she said, wiggling her eyebrows up and down in self-satisfaction. When the men didn't join her for a laugh, she smirked and went back to sipping her whiskey. "Either way, he paid the price. You *also* might want to visit the No-It Awl Jazz Club on 52nd Street. Owner's Leelee Gaye. She's another one."

"Another one what?" Billy asked

"Your dead man was Chinese-American. Leelee too; mother was Chinese. They had a lot in common, see? Puts on a great show. Oh, and be sure to tell her you're a friend of mine." Monica shimmied a little closer to Johnny. "You're a bright guy, honey; connect the dots. I got nothing else for you, unless …"

"Thanks for the tip, Monica," Johnny interrupted.

"Don't you want to know the 'unless'?" she purred, not hiding her disappointment. Some women worked for money, others for money *and* pleasure.

"Monica, your 'unless' means 'more ' and I've got nothing more to give." Johnny and Billy stood up, forgetting their manners because, well, this was Monica.

"My door's always open, boys," Monica said, giving them each a little salute. "Carry on. Protect and serve. If you don't wanna do *me*, do what you do best." She turned to her drink, murmuring as they walked out. "Although, as I recall, you were both pretty damn good …"

CHAPTER 12

"Homicide, Lieutenant Vero." Back at his desk, Johnny answered the telephone by rote, prepared to listen carefully and take notes during the call, if necessary.

"*Mièjuè.*"

"English only, please," Johnny replied.

"Man killed! Man killed!"

Thank God for his Chinese cramming. "*Zài nail, Zài nail,* where?"

"*Gong si fong, gong si fong.*"

"*Mingzi, mingzi?* Name, name?" He heard only a dial tone in response. It would have to be enough. The Old Brewery building. The devil's front door. *Gong si fong!* "Billy, we've got another one! Let's move!"

"Chinatown?"

"The Old Brewery. We'll use the car radio to call Molly."

Minutes later, the men were en route. "*South Central Dispatch, go ahead.*"

"This is Lieutenant Vero, 4225. Patch me through to District Attorney Penett." After the night – and morning – with Grace, he was nowhere near being ready to see Molly, but given the circumstances, what choice did he have?

CHAPTER 13

The bees in the Old Brewery hive were trying to save their queen from attack, but the plan didn't seem to be working. *Another dead bee in plain sight,* Johnny thought grimly. *Who the fuck is the queen bee here, anyway? Who and what are they protecting?*

It hadn't taken them long to reach the body. A dead male lay in the first floor hallway, gunshot to the head. Still making his way down the hall with Billy, Johnny yelled to the uniformed officers at the scene. "Stop everyone from moving around. Nobody leaves. Nobody."

Molly was a little out of breath from the brisk walk to catch up to him. She'd beat the ME there. "I'll get a search warrant for every inch of this place."

Johnny shook his head. "Don't bother. Look around! Searching this place won't turn up a damn thing. Silence is golden. 'No speakee English.' They sure know how to say *that*, clear as a bell."

A uniformed officer approached. "Lieutenant, there's a guy, says he saw someone running down to the basement through those doors. Speaks a little English."

"Bring him here. Molly, can you have your office get one of the Chinese officers here on the double? I don't want any time to slip by."

"Done and done. They should've been here by now."

Johnny saw the officer leading a small Chinese fellow in his direction, and met them halfway. "What's your name? *Mingzi, mingzi?*" Johnny was excited. Maybe they'd finally get a break,

"Chin, Chin."

"Your name is Chin Chin?"

Molly called down the hall. "The interpreter's here, hang on."

"I heard the conversation, Lieutenant. I'm Officer Fang." Fang was slender, young, barely old enough to be a cop. "You asked for his name twice, so he answered you twice out of respect. That's the correct way. Chin is his last name."

"Do your magic, Officer Fang. Anything will be better than nothing."

Fang questioned the man in melodic dialect for several minutes before signaling for Johnny to join them, some distance from the body. "Lieutenant, Mr. Chin heard what he thought was a firecracker and knew it was a little early for the Chinese New Year celebration. Niù, the year of the Ox, doesn't start until January 29." Studying Johnny's face, Fang quickly understood that it wasn't the proper time for a culture lesson. "I'm sorry, sir. When Mr. Chin opened his door to investigate, he saw a man of medium height, a little taller than himself, turn to the stairs and go down. He heard loud bangs of each door that closed."

"Description?"

Fang turned back to the old man. "*Miáoshù rén.*" The man jabbered something in reply. To Johnny, Fang explained that it had been dark, but that the man was about "this tall," indicating with his hand. "He only saw the man's back."

"Clothes, color, anything else?"

"*Yīfú, yánsè, shénme*? Sorry, Lieutenant. He says he was scared and closed his door before the man could see him."

"Ask him what time." Johnny sighed. This might be harder than he'd hoped, after all.

"*Dāngshíjǐdiǎn*?" Fang asked, and respectfully waited for the man to stop talking, nodding his head in encouragement before turning to Johnny. "Very early. Before sun rise."

"Assuming he's the one who called me," Johnny said, reaching into his pocket, "he sure waited a long time before he called from the corner phone booth. Fear. Here," he said, handing the man a five-dollar bill.

"That's an awful lot of money to give him, Lieutenant," Fang said.

"Thank you for your help, Officer Fang. We want them coming back. You'll learn. If I have anything else, I'll call you. For now, get your men to start opening those doors Mr. Chin heard clanging shut. Gunfire that sounded like firecrackers and left no shell casings? Had to be a .22 revolver again." Johnny squinted down the dark hallway. "Where the hell's the ME? The longer this body lies here, the less people will want to remember. They don't want to end up like this guy."

"He's on his way. Caught in traffic," Billy answered. "Just got off the radio with him."

"Doesn't he have fucking lights? A fucking siren? Jesus Christ!" Drawing his .38 special, Johnny headed down the hallway to the stairwell. Let the ME deal with the body. They needed to see what Officer Fang had found behind those doors.

Cold Nights and Warm Hearts

CHAPTER 14

Hailing a taxi on a cold night in New York City was never easy, but persistence paid off. "52nd Street. The No-It Awl Jazz Club, and try not to make every red light, will ya? Don't worry, I'm a cop."

"That's what they all say, sir."

As the cabbie turned his meter on, Molly smiled and linked her arm through Johnny's, leaning into him for warmth, and something more. The bitter cold had been biting at her legs and toes, but no self-respecting woman would go to a jazz club in boots and trousers. "Ah! That feels better, Johnny," Molly exclaimed. "What kind of information do you think this woman will have?"

"I just know what one of my sources told me. 'Go see Leelee' because she and Deshi Garner have something in common." Johnny looked out the window as he talked. Those big brown eyes of Molly's scared the shit out of him. *Funny how guilt works. But why should I feel guilty? One night, weeks ago.*

The cabbie spoke up over his shoulder as he slowly pulled over to the curb. "Here we are. That'll be one-twenty-five."

Still chilled, the couple was reluctant to yield their heavy coats to the hat check girl. The Maître d' escorted Johnny and Molly to a table. When Johnny handed him a tip, the man thanked him. "Let's move you to the table Leelee keeps for the VIPs." He might not know who the DA was, but they were every inch a movie star couple.

Just as they sat down, the emcee approached the microphone. "Ladies and gentlemen…the moment you've been waiting for. Miss *Leelee* Gaye!"

The house lights went down as a gorgeous almond-eyed woman walked onto the stage in a spectacular flowing white gown. She wore a simple white orchid in her long jet-black hair, opening with a song from the sold-out Broadway play *South Pacific*. Her voice would have fit right in on Broadway, too, the voice of an angel as she sang "Some Enchanted Evening."

Leelee put on a wonderful show that lasted for almost two hours. After her final bow, she made her way to Johnny's table. When he stood to introduce himself, she stopped him. "No need, Lieutenant, please sit. I've been expecting you. You know… Monica," she smiled as she spoke. "And this must be Miss Penett." The three sat down as the band began playing softer dinner music.

"I know you're here about the Chinatown murders. Let me explain why you were sent to me." Leelee's English was perfect. "I have a similar background to the dead man, Deshi Garner. My mother is Chinese, and was a nurse in Hawaii. My father is American, an army captain stationed in Hawaii as a surgeon," she said, obviously proud of her heritage. "I was born at Schofield Barracks on the military base; I am an American citizen." She laughed softly. "That's one of the reasons I love *South Pacific*. It deals with the social

49

consequences of mixed marriages, as with my own parents. It was not always easy for them."

A waiter came to pour glasses of wine, and Leelee discreetly stopped talking until he had left. "I knew Deshi and what he tried to do. His mother's Chinese, but he never knew his father, an American war correspondent. Deshi's mother and his half-sister were smuggled here years ago. My mother's sister was also. We're trying to find Deshi's family and figure out how the underground works. Chinatown has its own culture, as you know. Its' own set of rules."

Molly frowned. "Do you know what happened to Deshi?"

"I know that he was paying for information. But what he bought, sadly, was his own death certificate." Leelee straightened her back. "We know the smuggler is paying for his entry into New York," she said with a scowl. "You may not like what you hear, as time goes on. This is dirty business. And there's someone called the Janitor that cleans up the messes."

"Our sources mentioned a veterinarian," Molly said.

"Maybe he is, I don't know. But he is known as the Janitor. That is all I know at this time," said Leelee. "If I learn more, I will call and give my first name only. Leelee. And I will not speak with anyone except you, Lieutenant." She stood, and Johnny stood with her. "I must greet other tables so as not to look suspicious. Enjoy your drinks and the music. I'll bet you make a lovely couple on the dance floor."

They hadn't danced since New Year's Eve, but as they sat and finished their wine, the night grew awkward. Clearly, there would be no dancing tonight. Helping Molly with her coat shortly thereafter, Johnny mulled over Leelee's information, but also wondered if he was ready for A Talk. Did he want to open that can of worms?

Molly buttoned her coat. "Johnny, I only live a few blocks from here. Turtle Bay Gardens. Grab a cab, though, will you? It's too cold to hoof it."

"Turtle Bay, heh, heh. What made you move into *that* neighborhood?" With a hand guiding her at her back, they moved out into the frigid February air.

"It's quiet, mostly. A respite from the hectic, sick world we work in every day," she said in her best "elect me" voice. "It has a community garden I can work in during the summer on weekends. Relaxing. You've got your cello, I've got my garden." She shivered. "If summer ever comes."

"What about the new United Nations building?" Construction had recently begun. The noise must cut down on the quiet. As Molly chattered about the progress, Johnny signaled to the doorman, handing him a bill.

In answer, the man blew his shrill whistle and waved his hand at the curb. "Taxi!"

CHAPTER 15

The ride in the elevator was still tense, but in a decidedly better way. They'd talked about nothing but business lately but now, standing close, Molly could feel the heat of Johnny's erection pressing against her from behind. Despite herself, she let a low sigh of passion escape her lips. The elderly couple in front of them turned to give a look of disgust before stepping to the side so that they could get off at Molly's floor.

As the elevator door closed, the two of them burst into childish laughter and frolicked down the hall like teenagers about to lose their virginity. Molly fumbled for her keys as Johnny, suddenly thawed out after...weeks?...kissed her neck. *I can't believe I'm doing this. I thought New Year's was it, over, done. What am I doing?* It felt like walking into a blazing building, not caring if she got singed. *He* is *the fire.*

With weeks of restrained foreplay behind them, the evening had advanced quickly. In the cab, Molly had boldly laid a gloved hand on his leg, forcing him to look her in the eyes. Once they locked eyes, nothing else mattered. And they both knew what happen next.

Clothes lay around the room in little piles, hastily pulled off or stepped out of, respectively. Naked on the sofa together, Molly enjoyed her own noises of pleasure as Johnny plundered her, controlled her, licked her body with his tongue. It all felt *very* nice, but she'd waited long enough. Taking charge, she reached for him, grabbing hold tightly as she guided him inside her. Groaning, he thrust once, hard, and raised his head to see her reaction. *Yes,* she whispered with her eyes.

This was not the time for gentle lovemaking, apparently. This lady wanted to *fuck*. He thrust again and again, but Molly still wanted more, needed him to be even deeper. Feeling as though she had invented something new, she flipped over on top of him. *Well, this is a first. I like, I like! Oh, yes.*

He was both surprised and pleased by her aggression. Holding his hands down, Molly positioned her hardened nipples so that they danced across his lips as she swung them back and forth. When he tried to grasp them with his mouth, she pulled away, teasing him, his penis growing even harder. Molly pushed down and up, down and up, everything moving, two bodies flowing rhythmically as one. Shuddering against him as her excitement mounted, Molly looked down at Johnny's face as he lifted his hips for one last powerful thrust. Another first: simultaneous, overwhelming climax.

They fell apart for just a few seconds before entwining in a more relaxed configuration on the sofa. As Molly drifted off to sleep, she thought, *How complete and satisfied this man makes me feel. It's more than the sex. Which happens to be mind-blowing. But it's more than that...Please, God, let it be more than that.*

CHAPTER 16

Looking out at the East River the next morning as they enjoyed coffee together, Molly waxed philosophic. "You know, Johnny, viewing the ships out there as they forge through the winter ice is kind of warming in a poetic way."

Johnny snorted. "What's poetic, sweet Molly, are thoughts of you, last night and on New Year's Eve. You are poetry in motion. And what's warming," he stretched across the table to plant a kiss on her lips, "is the direction our relationship is going." After last night, it was easy to forget that Grace Tilly even existed.

"Thanks, Johnny, I kind of like it myself."

She got up to turn the record player on, Lowering the needle onto an album by Coleman Hawkins, she said, "I know you like classical, but let's mix it up with some light jazz."

"That's nice, Molly." He nodded in time, appreciatively. "A good sound. It has soul."

She walked over to him and put her arms around his chest. "I'm glad we went to the jazz club, Johnny."

"I see why you enjoyed it so much. I like knowing that about you. Finding out what makes you tick puts soul into my soul," he said, kissing her arms.

"Outside of New Year's Eve, and last night," she said, blushing a little in the morning light, "it's been far and few between since college that I –"

Johnny stopped her, pulling her around to his lap. "You don't have to tell me anything about your past. I don't need to know 'nothin' about nothin.'" He smiled. "We're here and that's all that counts." *I think I'm off the hook about Grace.* He took a sip of coffee. "And of course, the case counts. What Leelee said about the Janitor is much more of a concern than who banged who before *us.*"

"Us. I like the sound of that, Detective." She stood to clear the table and get things washed up. She liked things neat and tidy, and this case was anything but. "How does someone get involved in cleaning up *under*ground, *black* market, *bloody* messes?" said, punctuating each word with another clatter of dishes. "I'm calling in Dr. Amiric Misak. I've used him on other cases we prosecuted."

"Never heard of him," Johnny answered, confused. "But we don't even have a suspect in hand, much less a prosecution."

Molly reminded him of those bees again, but she was a delight to watch as she cleaned. "He's a renowned psychiatrist, able to look at unusual homicides and piece together analyses of certain behavioral patterns to determine the kind of person we're hunting. He's done a lot of work in Europe," she stopped, as if that was the crowning glory. "He tells the cops certain characteristics to look for in a person capable of the most horrific crimes. He's published lot of papers about his work."

"Sounds like hocus pocus to me, but if you say he's worthwhile, I'll keep an open mind. And I'd love Angie to meet him. She'll be getting her degree in criminal psychology this year and who knows? Maybe there's something to it."

Kitchen in order, she sat back down on his lap smelling of pine cleaner. "I'll see what I can do."

"Great!" he nuzzled her close. "Angie won't be back until summer, probably, what with internships and boys and trips, but she might come back for that. You know, now that you mention it, I think Angie was talking about something along those lines too, some new concept to help piece together someone's thought process, figure out why he does what he does. They must be talking about it in class. So count me in."

He didn't notice that Molly had untied her bathrobe until she stood and straddled him. She nodded her head toward the record player. "He's playing 'Smoke Gets in Your Eyes.' I love that. And I'll definitely count you *in*."

"There's no smoke in my eyes when it comes to you, Molly Penett."

"Shh," she whispered, quieting Johnny's lips with hers.

CHAPTER 17

Johnny stuck his head inside Captain Sullivan's door, more of an afterthought than a requirement. Things were pretty loose around South Central, which he liked. "Captain, I'm heading to the DA's office. Molly has some psycho doctor from Europe who analyzes people – why they do what they do." When the captain said nothing, rolling his eyes at the latest alternative to good police work, Johnny grinned. "Bradshaw's got the squad today. And we're making progress," he said, knocking on the wood frame of the door for luck. *I think.*

"All right, Lieutenant. You know what's coming down the pike with the press and the mayor. We don't want hysteria like last time." Between Grace's paper and the radio, the city had been whipped into a frenzy while they tried to catch the Budapest Hotel serial killer.

"We've got a few strong leads. Undercover vice is squeezing some of their snitches to see what comes out. I'll keep you updated, Captain. Can't have anyone blowing a fuse."

The captain was tired, overweight, and hung over. "This may be my last hoorah, Vero. I'm thinking of retiring soon. Eighteen months, tops. Maybe go to Florida," he sighed at the thought of palm trees and warm weather. "My sister and her husband are there."

"My mother retired there a years ago. It had always been my father's ..." Johnny couldn't go on.

The captain nodded in sympathy. "That was a damn tragedy, Johnny. He was a cop's cop. But you certainly made up for his murder with all your arrests. You gotta know he's proud of you."

Johnny thought to himself, *Maybe, maybe not.* His father had understood his own childhood dream of playing with the Philharmonic. *Would he be glad I followed in his footsteps instead?* "Yeah, Ma loves it. Said she'd never come back to the city *or* the winters. Retirement, eh. You can relax, get a boat..." *I'll miss you, you bastard.*

"A boat? Well, who knows? Stranger things have happened. Now get going! You got a crime to solve."

Doubt

CHAPTER 18

"Ahhhh, Dr. Misak, I presume," Johnny introduced himself to a bald gentleman perhaps 20 years his senior, also arriving at the DA's main door inside the enormous brick building. The men shook hands and Dr. Misak made a correct presumption as well.

"Lieutenant Vero. I'm pleased to meet you."

"Tell me Doc … may I call you 'Doc'?" Johnny asked.

"If you wish, Lieutenant."

"Before we go in, I've got to ask. How can you characterize people just by their behaviors? Don't different people behave the same way, but with completely different agendas?"

Dr. Amiric Misak smiled and adjusted his briefcase so that he held it in front, with both hands. "I see you like to get right to the point. Shall we?" The doctor opened the door, and greeted Louise, who pointed vaguely toward Molly's office.

"She's waiting."

Johnny nodded and continued his train of thought as they walked. "I have to get to the point, Doc. Every moment that's lost is a moment our killer gets farther away. It's been a month, already."

Molly's door was open, and she welcomed them inside. She was about to speak when Dr. Misak silenced her with a finger. "Just a moment, Miss Penett. I need to finish our conversation first." The men sat down across from Molly's desk, and the doctor turned to Johnny. "I understand your desire for speed, but let me answer your question about different people first. Your premise is possible, Lieutenant, but rarely do agendas differ with certain behaviors. For example," he said, warming to his subject, "I observed that Molly spoke highly of you when telling me of the case. I observed how she measured you with her eyes when we entered the room." As Molly started to object, his finger silenced her again. "And you, Lieutenant. Your slightly parted lips, wet slightly with your tongue as you held eye contact with Miss Penett. That indicates to me that the two of you have, shall we say, feelings for one another? That you either have had or are having a relationship outside the scope of police business." As Molly and Johnny squirmed a little in their chairs, he continued. "Furthermore, you asked to call me Doc. By diminishing my credentials, you revealed that you are skeptical of my findings."

Johnny knew when to call and when to fold. "I'm starting to see the light."

"So, I am correct, am I not, Lieutenant?"

"Let's just say, *Dr. Misak*, that I'm grateful for your help with the case."

Dr. Misak smiled and took a notebook from his briefcase. "Then let's begin. Tell me everything you know and everything that you do *not* know about the murders in Chinatown." Out of deference to her title, he looked to Molly first. After all, she had reached out to him.

"You're the Lieutenant. You go first," Molly said, a little hesitant to reveal more of herself to the good doctor's scrutiny.

Without leaving out even an iota of detail, Johnny began at the scene of the first murder, ending with the latest information from Leelee. Dr. Misak made notes throughout. Molly followed up with her observations and thoughts.

"That's a lot of information," he said. "You know, Miss Penett, from what you've both said, I'm feeling that someone knows too much about the smuggler and his associates, not too little. It sounds as though they may want you to think that they are cooperating, feeding you information, when in fact they may be the ones paid to smuggle the smuggler in to the East River port in order to keep the police away from *them*."

Molly's heart sank. "Dr. Misak, some of our information came from within. Are you saying that – ?"

"I'm not saying anything, Miss Penett. What did one informant say? 'Connect the dots.' This killer is not a serial killer as was that—that Budapest Hotel killer all over the news, and you with it, Lieutenant. Let me explain." Dr. Misak gave a full medical psychological profile describing the difference between a serial killer and a killer for hire. Johnny had to admit, it made sense.

"I must have missed that class in law school," confessed Molly.

Johnny glanced at Molly with furrowed eyebrows. "We have a lot to digest here. I don't think I'll be sleeping easily any time soon."

Dr. Misak pulled out a pocket watch and checked the time. "You know where I can be reached. Good luck to you with the case. And in the future," he said, nodding with a warm smile toward both Molly and Johnny.

Johnny waited until he heard Dr. Misak leave the main door. "Molly. Dr. Misak is an ace in his field. And that ace just told us that our murderer isn't a serial killer because serial killers select their own victims. A professional hit man's motivation is strictly financial. A serial killer is meeting an emotional, spiritual, or psychological need. A hit man wants to get paid. Does that sum it up?"

"I think so. Opium plus prostitutes equals a hefty financial reward. A lot of people are getting stinking rich with a lot of do-re-mi. And to throw more into the mix, Misak said the smuggler may be paying off someone – or several someones – to get into the harbor undetected. Our informants could be feeding us information just so we don't suspect them."

"Which means that our killer may be or may not be the smuggler. And we probably have people on the take helping this all go down?"

Molly groaned. "I don't want to think any member of the department is dirty."

"It doesn't necessarily mean it's coming from within our own inner sanctum, Molly. Let's not jump the gun."

Molly picked up a newspaper from her desk and threw it at him. "Today's headlines in the *Daily Globe*."

CITY IN PANIC... ANOTHER SERIAL KILLER IN CHINATOWN. CHINESE-SPEAKING TASK FORCE BROUGHT IN. WHO WILL BE NEXT?
Page 3
Byline: Grace Tilly

Johnny mumbled every word aloud through pursed lips until he came to the byline, wondering what he should say, what he shouldn't say. At the sight of Grace's name, though, he couldn't hold back. "That bitch!"

Molly walked around the desk and sat by him while also closing the door behind their chairs. "Are you all right? Do you know her? Grace Tilly?"

Johnny sighed, then stammered, "No, not really. Well, sure An old acquaintance of sorts. She worked with us on the Budapest Hotel stories. She interviewed me when the Mayor gave me that award." He scowled. "She always knew how to get her information and did whatever she had to do to get it." *Including me.* "Ignore whatever she writes, Molly. She gets lost in her reporting, following lies, questioning explanations, that's all." Johnny cleared some phlegm from his throat. "Has the Medial Examiner had any updates on our victims?"

Interesting reaction. "Yes. Victim two was Chinese, dead a few hours before we got there. He's still working on the body. Two murders, one half Chinese, one full-blooded."

"Two murders before dawn," Johnny said. "Which still leaves us nothing."

CHAPTER 19

Johnny picked up the phone on the first ring. "Homicide, Vero."

"This is Leelee. You saw the headlines in the *Daily Globe?* Go to the classified section and look under 'jobs.' " *Click.*

Johnny scrambled for the newspaper he'd picked up from the newsstand that morning, almost tearing the pages to get to the classifieds.

"What the hell are you doing?" Billy asked, watching his frenzy.

Johnny scanned the columns, running his finger over the print. *There.* His finger came to a stop. "Remember what I told you about meeting Leelee Gay? She just called. Look at this."

"'Janitor wanted for upcoming cleaning job,'" Billy read aloud. "So? Your apartment's a mess?"

"Billy, the *veterinarian*! He's known as the Janitor because he cleans up the messes. *For the smuggler.* This must be how he's contacted when his services are needed," Johnny said with growing excitement. "The needle in the haystack may be getting easier to thread. If we find the right thread. There's no address or telephone number, no day and time. He must already know who to call or where to go."

"Maybe they go to *him*," Billy said.

Johnny nodded. "That may very well be. And this ad means that he's needed soon." He was already heading for the captain's office when he stopped to bark at Billy. "Call the newspaper and find out who placed this ad and how they paid for it. Maybe we can get a break there, get something that links him to the organization."

The captain didn't look up from what he was doing, which happened to be perusing boat brochures. "What do you need, Johnny?"

"Captain, I need to speak to you about detail uniforms to canvass the Old Brewery." He paused as he just got a new idea. "And I need the SABSO.[2]"

That got Sullivan's attention. The boats were forgotten for the moment. "The Saber Blue Society? What about it? They only get called in for special details. *Very* special details." The SABSO had, in fact, met Johnny and Billy on the plane when they extradited Jean-Paul Vincent back from France just months before.

Johnny sat down, almost pleading. "Captain, what we've pieced together may be corruption in the harbor. The harbor patrol, longshoremen, or … one of our guys. We need to infiltrate. The SABSO could do it."

"It won't fly, Johnny. You know as well as I do that we'd have to bring in Internal Affairs to investigate any allegations." The captain didn't get upset easily, but he was upset now. "I'll… maybe…this is serious, Johnny."

Johnny let out a long breath. "I know, Captain. I know. But we need to cover every angle, every resource that's giving us information. Even the information that comes from within.

---

[2]   SABSO; Saber Blue Society. See reference page

My snitches have always been very reliable in the past, but now I don't know."

"I'm going to need more than hearsay before I act on this," Sullivan said, punching the desk with his big beefy fingers.

"Shit! Sir. We're not getting anywhere," Johnny said, disappointed. As each calendar page turned, the case seemed to grow colder and colder, even as the air began the slightest of warming trends.

CHAPTER 20

As soon as Johnny left South Central headquarters, he headed to the US Coast Guard station on South Street, pulling his overcoat tighter against the wind. *Those poor saps out on the water.*

It had been a while, but the commander's face lit up as he walked in. "Well, well, *Lieutenant.* I don't remember the last time I caught sight of you! What brings Detective Johnny Vero to my fine headquarters?" Commander Fred Cunningham and Johnny had been in school together all the way up. They'd played a few games of stickball in their day, too. "I heard about the promotion. What can I do you for? A utility boat and crew? All my cutters are still patrolling the three-mile demarcation."

Not so long ago, enemy ships had come perilously close to the eastern seaboard. The Coast Guard had done a great job during wartime, and Johnny had the highest respect for Fred and his guardsmen.

"I wish it were that simple," said Johnny, taking a seat. "We've caught wind of a smuggler that's bringing in opium and women from China for prostitution." Johnny sat back in the metal chair, his eyes scanning the office. "We believe he's from Guyana, South America, and is capable of entering the harbor unnoticed. Doesn't he have to check in with someone?

Fred lit up a cigarette and offered one to Johnny, who declined. "Small vessel reporting's voluntary for eligible, frequent, pleasure boat operators and passengers if they're US citizens, or LPRs – lawful permanent residents. That bypasses the need for port-of-entry, face-to-face inspection. Saves us a lot of time and grief, I'll say that much. Boaters are still supposed to phone in their arrivals, however." Fred turned to look out the window, grateful to be behind a desk. Command did have its privileges, but he'd earned them the hard way.

"And if he's neither of those? Could he still come in undetected?"

"It's possible, *Lieutenant*," Fred grinned. Johnny had razzed him for moving up the ladder, so now it was payback. "We miss one here and there, I'm sure. To get past us, though, this guy must be familiar with our waterways, all 150 miles of them." His was one of the busiest harbors, with year-round movement of ferryboats, ocean liners, freighters, tankers, tugs, barges, scows, sightseeing cruisers, commercial and party fishing boats, all plying their trade daily. Fred pointed to a chalkboard on the wall, filled with yellow writing. "That's only one day's activity. Along with the Harbor Patrol, we scour the waterways 24 hours a day. It's even more crowded when it warms up."

"Holy shit!" Johnny whistled. "No wonder he gets in and out undetected. With all those boats on the water, he could play hide-and-seek with you all day, if he knew what he was doing."

Fred smashed his cigarette into a glass dish on his desk and leaned against the edge of it, crossing his arms. "Why am I just hearing about this now, Johnny?"

"We're just putting the pieces together ourselves. It's news to us too. If we come across any more info, we'll get it to you pronto."

Fred was a family man, and the idea of drugs and prostitution coming into his harbor didn't sit well. "I'd love to catch this son-of-a-bitch for you, Johnny. We don't have any tolerance for this coming into the United States. Not on my watch."

"Thanks, Fred. I knew I could count on you. I'll keep you posted," said Johnny, thinking to himself *I'm glad murder, mayhem and river pirates are not among the listed tourist attractions for New York.* "Before I go, let me ask you about my theory I came up with…"

CHAPTER 21

As Johnny gently slid her panties down her thighs, maneuvering around one foot and then the other before tossing them aside, she found her mind exploring new territory. They'd been doing this for over a month now, but she still felt exposed at that first moment of nudity. *Do whores feel as exposed as I do? What do they do? Maybe they ignore it like this...* She cupped her breasts in her hands, rotating her nipples between her thumbs and forefingers, never taking her eyes off of him, as he pulled his boxer shorts off, freeing his magnificent erection and straddled her on his knees. *Now this is a great way to spend Valentine's Day.*

As he knelt over her, she pushed her feet against the bed in a ballet dancer's *en pointe* move, lifting her pelvis into the air as a less-than-subtle invitation. But she didn't quite reach high enough. He didn't thrust his considerable length into her. *Damn.* Remembering that he'd liked her hard nipples to graze his lips, she pulled his face down to her chest, willing him to kiss her breasts, suck them hard, kiss her everywhere. Still, nothing. *He's not going to. Why is he hovering over me? Can't he see that I need him?*

"This way," he whispered, pinning her hands over her head. He didn't want her to use her hands. Not this time.

Once he entered her, though, there was no stopping her hips. They moved involuntarily in response to his new rhythms. He thrust hard and fast, and then deliciously slowed down, pulling back, almost withdrawing himself completely before filling her again and again. It was agonizing; it was perfect. At last he reached a frantic, greedy state, trying to get as much of her as he could, driving himself harder into her.

Crying out in pleasure, Molly climaxed more quickly than she'd ever experienced. Johnny slowed himself, placing his hands behind her knees to pull her legs higher. He was at his peak, ready to explode, and so was she for the *second* time. There! Quivering from a massive, pulsating ejaculation, Johnny's sighs deepened as Molly felt him melt inside her.

Molly suddenly needed him to be off of her, just holding her in his arms. Kissing her, not fucking her. She needed to make sure that she wasn't being used. She needed to know that this was about more than toe-curling, exhilarating sex. If she didn't pull away a bit, she knew it would be too hard to say no again – *I couldn't do that* – and so very easy to say yes – *I would do that* – and then she still wouldn't know.

At his brief frown as she pushed him off, she said, "I'm still here, Johnny. We need this time, too. It helps clear the mind."

"And the soul, if you let it Molly." He lay back on the pillow, behaving himself while still stroking her leg.

For a few minutes, they let their thoughts stray wherever they might roam. Molly was surprised by the route her own thoughts took. But she felt so comfortable with this man. So right with him. "Do you remember when we were hitting a wall during our investigation of Jean-Paul Vincent?"

"Of course. We hit lots of walls. Serial killers are such pieces of shit, the worst."

"The Commissioner said he wanted an arrest, toot sweet, and you said –"

"I said 'and I want a girl named Lola.' I remember."

Molly turned to face him. "I'll be your Lola, Johnny," she said kissing him softly, "if you'll be my valentine."

CHAPTER 22

Monday night's kisses, flowers, and candy gave way to Tuesday morning reality: Crimes to solve, people to murder, bees to buzz. Captain Sullivan couldn't care less if Johnny was falling for the DA. He was on the warpath. "Vero! Bradshaw! Get in here," he barked, continuing in one breath, "we can't have another serial killer on the loose like that Frenchman! First I had to send you to France, now the Chinese are fucking with me. Sure as shit, you're not going to *China*!" His face was getting hot and red, a sure sign he needed to let his blood pressure lower for a few seconds.

Vero and Bradshaw sat and waited. Sullivan was just getting warmed up.

Sullivan inhaled deeply and blew it out. "We all saw the headline and article a few weeks ago, with the letters to the editor and fucking op-ed pieces that followed. Sensationalism, pure and simple. But we do have two bodies still tied to Chinatown." He shook his head. "I'd like to squash that Grace Tilly dame like a cockroach!"

Johnny pushed the visual of the kitchen game with Grace out of his mind. "We're working on the leads we've got, Captain," Johnny answered quickly, not wanting Sullivan's temper to escalate further. "What about our discussion about

SABSO?" Johnny held his breath, hoping for a positive response.

Captain Sullivan shook his head. "No go. I told you. The Saber Blue Society only handles specialized assignments. I can get Internal Affairs hooked in."

Johnny set his jaw. "Captain, we need new faces. Every officer in the precinct can smell IA a mile away. If SABSO's out, I may have someone else who can handle it."

This was news to Billy. "Who?" he said.

"Officer Fang at the 5th. He interpreted for us at the Brewery." He looked at the captain. "Guy who called in the number two victim didn't 'speakee.' Fang got through to him."

Sullivan liked the idea, but he didn't love it yet. "Get him in here. I want to interview him before I put my balls on the line."

Back at their desks, Billy was tasked with calling Fang in. "What about the ad for the Janitor?" Johnny asked. "What's taking so long?" Sullivan had called them in so early, they hadn't had a chance to say much more than "'morning."

"The woman at the ad desk was out sick with the flu for weeks. When I finally got a hold of her, she said she didn't remember anything about the person who placed the ad, not even if it was a man or a woman. People walk in all day long, she said, and just about all, except for the businesses, are –"

Johnny's phone interrupted him, but as Johnny answered, Billy whispered, "– paid in cash." *So. Another dead end.*

"Hello, Detective. Did you miss me?"

Oh, crap. "Grace. What do you want?"

"I assume you saw the headlines. And all the rest."

"Grace, you have clearly succeeded in –"

"Oh, I like to succeed, Johnny." Her voice was pure musk.

75

"– being a royal pain in my ass." This had been brewing for weeks, and Johnny let it all out. "You *don't* care about facts. And you don't give a *shit* whether your precious headlines stir up the city or not. Or if it causes problems for anyone else because you *took* information from them." Johnny lowered his voice as he hissed, "That book on the table was personal, Grace. Not for you. I trusted you as a person, as my friend, and as a professional. You sorry –"

"Oh, shut up, Johnny, I hadn't caught a story in months. My boss was ready to let me go if I didn't come up with – not a good story, but a *great* story." She purred. "I have some terrific memories of that table..."

"Grace, you were always able to get a by-line. You're respected for your journalism." Johnny thought, *and for being a great lay, it's true.* "But you could have jeopardized our investigation."

"Johnny, I *had* to. You know me. I'll do whatever it takes, not only to keep my job, but to keep doing what I love. And I love being a journalist. I guess I'm like the scorpion that asked the frog to take him across the pond."

This woman was maddening. "Grace, what the *fuck* are you talking about?" He swiveled around to face Billy, who was clearly enjoying the one-sided conversation. Billy twirled a finger around one ear, mouthing *Grace is cuckoo.*

"A scorpion stings its prey, so when one asked a frog to carry him across the pond, the frog was hesitant, as you might imagine," she babbled. "The scorpion assured the frog that he wouldn't, because if he stung him, they'd both drown, so the frog agreed. Half way across, the scorpion stung the frog and the frog cried, 'Why did you do that? You said you wouldn't sting me. Now we'll both die!' And the scorpion said, *'Because that's what I do. I'm a scorpion.'* " Grace stopped to take a breath. " Get it, Johnny? *That's what I do.* I'm a journalist and sometimes I sting." Her voice softened again. "Let me make it up to you. Come over to my place this time for a belated Valentine's Day celebration. I'll make us dinner and we'll have wine and –"

Click. Johnny had had enough. In one conversation, Grace had been concerned, angry, and sultry. The quintessential narcissist. He had neither the time nor the stomach. "Billy, what were you saying?"

"The classified ad for 'janitor needed' was paid for in cash. So, all we know – or think we know – is that someone's going to need a doctor to be cleaned up, stitched, or have a bullet removed. Maybe some of the women smuggled in need medical attention. We don't know the who, when, or where. It could have been done already, for all we know, which is *bupkis.*"

"Well, the Janitor has to check the ads every day to see if his services are needed," Johnny suggested.

"Do you think he does … whatever he does … at the same place every time?"

Johnny sat back in his chair. "Yeah. Because his medical supplies would be there. I'm betting he does a lot of surgical procedures, big and small. Get back over to the newspaper and talk to the editor. Make sure he understands that everyone taking janitor ads needs to get a description."

"Sounds like Grace owes you a favor, big guy," Billy said, raising one eyebrow. "Why don't you sic her on it? I'm sure she wants to be back in your good graces. Ha! Grace in good graces." He always enjoyed his own jokes.

"Ehhh, no. Just do it, Billy. I'm going to the DA's office. I can't believe it's taken so long, but she finally has the autopsy report on our second dead guy."

CHAPTER 23

Johnny rode with his coat on as he hummed along to the classical radio music. His ears picked out the cellos without his even being aware. *That could have been me.*

Louise greeted him, but not flirtatiously. *Does she know?*

Molly was all business at the moment, too. "Johnny, come in, shut the door, Officer Fang was finally able to ID the second man. Hèng Lìwùshì. He was a numbers runner for the Fafi game, whatever that is."

Johnny nodded. "I know the basics. Participants choose the number they want to gamble on by interpreting their dreams. The man running the game chooses the winning number based on self-interest, with full knowledge of the bets placed. A runner brings the bag with all the bets to a central location at the same time every day. Then the head guy holds up his fingers to designate the winning number. There's a little more to it, but that's the gist. The runners go back to their territories to tell everyone the winning number, and whoever had the winning number on their little piece of paper wins. Everyone else loses."

"So. It's all fixed," Molly said.

"Yeah, I can see why you would think that, smart lady." Johnny smiled. "There will always be winners and losers. What makes the world go 'round."

Molly smiled back. "Damn. I was hoping it was love." She consulted her notes again. "So, maybe this runner, this Hèng Lìwùshì – jeez, what a name – was murdered because the smuggler wants a piece of the Fafi pie? Or it was just a robbery for the cash that went with the paper slips?"

Johnny frowned. "Our smuggler's got enough to deal with hauling women and opium. Maybe the Fafi people weren't paying for protection, and this Fafi fellow took the fall." He was rather pleased by the sound of that.

Molly had an idea. "What if all the bets in the bag will be used as a ransom for the port entry?"

"Or for a no-hassle drop-off or escape route? Oh, by the way, Sullivan wants to interview Officer Fang before putting him undercover with Detectives Pan and Chang." *Pan, Chang, and Fang. The guys at the precinct would have a field day.*

"I heard, I heard. The wheels of justice turn just as slow in 1949 as they did in '48. I already had his personnel file pulled. Take a look before I send it to Captain Sullivan. Better yet, deliver it to him yourself. Here."

Johnny flipped through the file she handed him. "Jeez Louise, he's right on the nose for this."

Molly giggled. "Shh! don't say that too loud, or Louise will think you're calling her. She eavesdrops all the time. As a matter of fact –" Molly punched the proper button. "Louise, its 4:30 and it's Friday. You can leave. I won't need you any longer today."

"Thank you, Miss Penett. Good night. Enjoy the weekend, *Detective*." Molly and Johnny shared a look. *Yep. Louise knows.*

Reading aloud, Johnny continued with the file. "Former Army Police, Military Intelligence, two years of college. Why is he still in uniform?"

"Not interested in moving up, I guess? I would've sworn he was younger than that. Hit a wall, pissed off an LT, who knows? One man's loss – victim number two – is another man's gain, Officer Fang. This may get him moving up the ole' ladder again." Molly looked at Johnny sitting across the desk from her, and suddenly he was much too far away, and Valentine's Day had been much too long ago. *What is it about this man?*

First, she slipped out of her shoes under the desk while he had his attention on the file. Then she rose quietly, walking around the desk and behind him to lock the door. Without a word, she slipped his suit jacket off and began undoing his tie, then unbuttoning his shirt. When he started to protest, her kiss silenced him. Running her tongue gently around his inner lips, she guided him to the leather couch along a side wall.

Johnny found himself shaking his head involuntarily. It wasn't that he was unwilling, but he didn't want to be responsible for getting her into trouble. He grabbed her hands to stop her from unbuckling his belt, a task already encumbered by his growing erection. "Jesus, Molly, won't somebody walk in? Should we do this here? I mean, is it safe? You could lose your job!"

"Why, Johnny Vero, as I live and breathe. You're nervous! I'm flabbergasted that such a big strong, gun-toting man like you is afraid of getting caught. Or are you feeling guilty?" With each phrase, she went a little further: the belt undone, the zipper down, her hand inside his shorts. "Or is it that I'm taking advantage of you? Guilt can be such a hindrance, you know. You weren't raised by a Jewish mother, were you? Let me fix that for you. Now lie back, shut up, and do what you do best."

New Information

CHAPTER 24

Billy was clearly excited. He slammed down the phone just as Johnny rounded the corner to his desk. "Johnny, I just heard from Fang! His men completed the search of the Old Brewery and he wants to show us something." Initially, the men had been interrupted by more pressing matters at the 5th precinct, but they'd been going at it hard for several days.

Within minutes, they were headed that way. "Fang's now undercover with vice, and assigned with Pan and Chang," Johnny said as they sped down the street.

"I hope he knows what he's doing. He can't let anyone know who or what he's looking for. Is he clear that we don't know if anyone is on the take?" Billy had reason to be concerned.

"He's clear. So you know, word is out that he discovered a gambling ring that led to some big arrests up in the Bronx. Nobody will ever know the difference. Hey, pull onto Mott Street," Johnny directed. "Did Fang say where we should meet up?"

Billy nodded toward a spot nearby, putting the car into Park. "He's right there, Johnny. Let's go."

Fang was waiting with his hands in his pockets. He nodded at both men as they approached.

"What do you have, Fang?" Johnny wasn't beating around the bush. "What's your first name? I read your file, but I already forgot."

"It's Jin, with a J, not the liquor," Fang said with a smile. "Speaking of which. This place certainly was used to the full as a brewery, especially during Prohibition. Wait until you see this."

Johnny and Billy followed Fang closely down the staircase into a dank sodden corridor. Even with their flashlights, they couldn't avoid puddle after puddle of stale water. "Watch out for the rats," Fang said.

It didn't take long for Johnny to switch over to first names. "Jin … Jin … Jin … where are you? Billy, did you see where Fang went?"

"Shh!" Billy hissed.

"Can you see me?"

"I see you, Billy."

In the darkness Billy grunted. "That wasn't me, Johnny." In the pitch black, Johnny heard the sound of Billy's revolver coming out of its holster.

"Do you see me?" repeats the voice.

"Jin, where the fuck are you?

"Billy, put it away."

"Point your flashlight toward my voice."

"Okay, now what?" Johnny inquired.

Jin's voice was quiet, but excited. "Push the stone wall inward using your left hand."

He pushed, and the wall moved easily. "Holy shit!" A tunnel was suddenly in view.

"Look at this, Billy" Johnny whistled under his breath. "Jin, how did you find this?"

Following the tunnel, Jin took the men to the end. The tunnel opened onto a platform to the East River. Taking a deep breath, Johnny exhaled loudly. "Well, would you look at this?! Right in front of our noses." They had been down here just after the murder, but no one had noticed the secret passageway.

An easy boat ride south would take anyone from where they were standing to a condemned government building, once New York City's chronic health care facility for the insane on Labrè Island. [3] Later, the War Department had conducted research there on human tolerance for food starvation, and malaria.

"I can call for a boat, but it will take an hour," Jin looked up and wrinkled his nose. "It's starting to drizzle. While we wait, let's see what is left inside the place."

No sooner than he'd spoken, the heavens opened with a torrential downpour with such strong gusts of wind that they barely made it inside before the heavy steel door slammed behind them. If they hadn't gotten inside quickly, they would have been locked out in the storm.

"Whew! Good timing1 We'll set aside another day for that boat ASAP, Jin. I want to see what the hell is in that building."

---

[3]   Labrè Island . See reference page for details.

CHAPTER 25

When the storm eased a bit, Billy and Johnny dashed for their unmarked police car. Johnny had been so intent on seeing what Jin had found that he had hardly glanced at his partner. Now, as they patted the rain from their sleeves, he said, "Billy, you look like shit on a shingle.[4] What the hell did you do this weekend?"

"Oh yeah? I feel like shit too!" Billy grimaced. "I was on a bender. Me and Nancy were fighting."

"All weekend? We're not even to St. Patrick's Day, and you're drinking like a goddamn Irishman?" Johnny asked, puzzled.

"Well, yeah. Maybe you never got there with Simone, I don't know. Fight, make-up sex, drink, fight, make-up sex, drink."

Johnny just shook his head, unwilling to revisit his years with Angie's mother. "We need to go to 52nd Street. You can get a coffee."

"What's there? Besides coffee."

"The No-It Awl Jazz Club."

---

[4]   The US military adopted the term for its WWII chipped cream beef on toast.

"Open now, Johnny?" Billy slid in and out of traffic, knowing all the shortcuts, but going a little too fast.

Johnny checked his watch. "No, but we're going to see Leelee Gaye. She called again, and said there'd be someone there by now setting up for the night. She's a great singer; probably does a run-through about this time." Billy wasn't listening, though. And he was getting reckless. "Billy! Slow down! What gives?"

Billy sighed, easing off the gas. "I'll be okay, Johnny. I'll get my head around it."

"Around what?"

Billy glanced over at his partner and friend. "You remember Nancy's first husband was found dead in the rehabilitation pool?"

Johnny's face was grim. "I do. His unit was pushing forward to stop the Japanese from taking the Aleutian Islands, right? He stepped on a land mine. Roger, right?"

"That's right. Blew both legs off. He was at Walter Reed Medical Center looking at months, more likely years, to get his shit together physically. And mentally," said Billy. "He had a rough time accepting his fate. Talked about it a lot to the hospital chaplain. To Nancy." Billy closed his eyes briefly, as if wrestling with something he wasn't ready to say, but needed to.

"Were you already –"

"I'd met her. We had – well, yeah," Billy said. "But she'd been unhappy with Roger before he left. Before the land mine. And I think Roger knew in his heart that Nancy wasn't happy. He probably knew she was seeing me." The stoplight gave Billy more opportunity to face Johnny. And his feelings. "That would make a guy even more depressed. I think he knew in his heart Nancy was not happy and she was seeing me. I think he truly loved her. It … could have been suicide, although that's not the way the report reads." As the light turned green, Johnny let out a little gasp.

"We think he did it so Nancy would wind up with his military benefits and part of his family's business. They all love her."

Johnny mulled it over. He knew that Nancy ran the factory for Roger's family's and made, in Billy's words, a "shit load of money" making ladies' clothes. "So? That should make you happy."

"Her in-laws – ex-in-laws – want to retire. Since she's part-owner, she wants me to quit and come to work with her." Billy was miserable. "I *have* a job, dammit. I'm a detective and I love what I do. Don't you, Johnny?"

Johnny nodded, staring out the window at the crowded sidewalks, briefly wondered what his life would have been like as a concert cellist before dismissing the notion and enjoying the view. God, he loved New York at this time of year, when the winter began to melt into spring. Soon, anyway. Just on the brink. He wished they were on the brink of solving the murders. "I love being a homicide detective, Billy. This is where I want to retire."

"Me too. I have some years left before retirement, too, but this is where I want to retire *from*, not from some stuffy office in a factory. I knew you'd understand, Johnny. We'll work it out." Billy seemed more relaxed now. "So why are we going to see this dame again?"

"Jesus, Billy. I need you to focus. Leelee Gaye is the one who told us about the ad for the Janitor. Put the bubble light on and flip a 'U'. There's a space on that side of the street. Then cut the light."

Leelee's instructions were clear: Come in the rear, through the kitchen. The NYPD on the premises, plain-clothed or not, wouldn't be good for business. Walking in the back door, they were virtually ignored by the chef, sous chefs, dish washers, and staff prepping for the night's activity. If they knew they were detectives, they didn't let on.

Inside the main room, Leelee was on stage, not yet in costume, going over arrangements for the evening's performance. As they approached the stage she was singing "Good Morning Heartache" in her pure sweet voice. Her long black hair was down, almost to the waistline of the simple dress she wore. Billy recognized the fabric as one of his wife's.

"That's exactly what Nancy said to me: *Good morning heartache,*" Billy whispered to Johnny. He was trying to make light of their problems, at least.

"Okay guys. I like that arrangement. That's a rap. See you back at eight," Leelee dismissed the band. Spotting Johnny and Billy, she pointed to a table as she headed for the little side stairs. "Can I get you gentlemen anything?

"Coffee, black," Billy said.

"Same for me, thanks," Johnny smiled at her. "That *is* a nice arrangement."

A server was polishing silverware to one side, and Leelee put in the coffee order, adding a cup for herself. "Thank you. It's one of Billie Holiday's hits. I thought we'd add it to the show."

"So, Leelee, you asked us here. What information do you have"? Johnny asked as the trio sat.

"I told you that my mother was Chinese, and so was Deshi Garner's mother."

"Our first victim," Billy stated.

"What I didn't tell you is that our mothers were sisters. That means that Deshi and I were first cousins fighting for the same cause, trying to stop an evil man from smuggling in Chinese women, even very young girls. To me, the opium is secondary," Leelee said, starting to cry. "My connection is now dead. Deshi was getting great information until..."

Johnny patted her arm. "We're really sorry, Leelee. Tell us what you can so we can nail this son-of-a-bitch."

Leelee waited until the server set down three steaming cups of black coffee and returned to his task. "We wanted to build up more information before we gave it to the police, but Deshi told me that this piece-of-shit boatman comes into the East River port maybe four times a year. Sometimes he has as many as 10, 12 women per shipment. Girls, really, some only teenagers. He gets paid per head, big money, as much as $500 to $1,000 per person," Leelee's eyes narrowed as she spoke of it. "A bonus if they're young. Or virgins. The women are transported all over the place to whore houses run by organized crime. New Jersey, Boston, San Francisco, Canada." Leelee was angry, but also sad. "You know as well as I do that these women aren't coming in by boat without someone getting paid off. Deshi was getting so close, then –"

Johnny handed her his handkerchief to wipe her tears.

Leelee recovered quickly. "Come back with Molly. She is a beautiful woman." Leelee smiled at Billy. "You too, detective, and of course bring someone as my guest." She stood, holding out her hand to them. "Now I need to get some rest before tonight's show. Thank you for coming."

The men stood as well. "This is powerful information, Leelee," Johnny assured her. "We'll find this bastard, dead or alive."

Billy raised his eyebrows but said nothing until they were leaving, again through the kitchen. As soon as they reached the alley behind the club, Billy said, "Johnny, that was a heavy promise to make. We've got nothing solid yet, and it's been months."

"I know, but we have to be Deshi's voice for him."

CHAPTER 26

One of the squad detectives popped his head into the office Johnny shared with Billy. Their door was always open, though, so it felt more like an extension of the entire detective bureau than anything. "Lieutenant, I've been checking the classifieds every day for an ad for a janitor, like you asked. I don't know if you saw it. It's in Sunday's classified; *Janitor wanted for upcoming cleaning job*. I have it here," He handed Johnny the newspaper.

"Good job, Frank. Thanks. So, Billy, there's going to be another cleaning job."

"Which still tells us shit! Who, what, when, and where is the Janitor going to do the deed?"

Billy scurried over to grab the ringing phone on his desk. "Sure thing," Billy said, grinning like a loon as he placed the receiver back into its cradle. "Harbor Patrol's finally got a boat ready. That was Fang."

In less than a half hour, the men were once again trenching down the stairs to the antediluvian sodden tunnel, the beams of each flashlight directed ahead. The sewer-rats down here were the size of cats. Johnny stepped into what he thought was a shallow puddle that got him wet up to his ankles. "Goddamn it! There goes a good pair of Florsheims."

"The tunnel seems longer than the last time we were here." Billy's words reverberated off the walls.

"It is," Fang chimed in. "You didn't even notice. I took you through a different doorway. That's another reasons our shooter escaped. I got drawings from the building department. Believe me, it was not a labor of love. Those guys don't make it easy. And they take forever."

Fang swung the heavy metal door open. A Harbor Police boat was waiting as promised. Once aboard, the boat commander revved the engine, yelling, "Hang on, detectives. We'll be there shortly."

The morning March air was still chilly. Holding a pair of binoculars in one hand and trying to keep his balance on the rail with the other, Johnny watched his field of view quickly approaching. A lot of good had been done there in the past, maybe, but now it was just another condemned building. A building, which he hoped, had stories to tell.

"Can't imagine what you're going to find in there, Lieutenant," yelled the boat commander as he pulled up to the shoreline. "The Coast Guard dismantled the dock years ago to try and keep out vandals. You better take these." He handed Fang bolt cutters for any locks or chains they found. "I have no idea what you'll be walking on, so use caution. Lower the walkway," he hollered out to one of his crew. "We'll wait here. Good luck."

CHAPTER 27

Making their way to the front entrance with weapons drawn, all three agreed that Labrè Island was once a thriving asset to the city and the surrounding areas, helping hundreds of mentally ill people that would have otherwise been living under bridges, or worse.

"War closed this," Billy lamented "It's the curse of Labrè."

"To the victors go the spoils, "added Jin. "Wars cost money; to win, the US had to siphon its resources. People suffered and sacrificed for the cause. But we won the war."

"There is that!" Johnny said with a knowing smile. "I heard they moved experiments and research to a more remote area. So, I guess the 'spoils' are those who got fucked out of help."

Jin swung the door open letting it bang against the wall. What had once been a massive marble lobby with elaborate furniture was now a hellhole. They stood there staring at holes in the ceiling, water leaking from the roof, and writing on the walls. The smell of urine was strong enough to indicate recent use; garbage was strewn all around. What furniture had been left behind had likely been used as firewood by the first winter's homeless that squatted there before finally being forced out.

"How do you want to do this? Stay together, or split up?" Jin asked.

"At this juncture, let's stay together," said Johnny. "We don't know what we might find, or who. So keep it quiet."

It wasn't as dark as the tunnel, but they turned their flashlights on. There could be holes that would break an ankle, or traps that would do God-only-knows-what. Every so often a beam would stray off to scan the walls and ceiling.

"Lieutenant, is there any particular clue you're hoping to find in this shit hole?" Jin asked. He'd just spotted a spider in a corner. Jin did not like spiders.

"I was hoping that we might find –"

A harsh, disagreeable cry interrupted him from a balcony just above them.

"What the fuck?" Billy cried. "That made the hair on the back of my neck stand up!"

Walking in front, Jin didn't wait for a command. "Let's go!" he hissed. He pointed his light to the horrible sound, illuminating a pack of wild dogs. It looked as if one of the dogs may have been old or injured, because the pack had turned on its own for food. His revolver already out, Jin fired a shot toward them as they scattered through a broken window. Another bullet mercifully ended the half-mutilated dog's suffering. The pack would be back to finish their meal.

"Holy shit! What a horrible sound," Billy commented.

"Nothing up here," reported Johnny, who had gone up to search the second floor rooms while Jin took care of the situation. "Let's check the basement."

Stepping over assorted debris and human waste, the men made their way down the stairway without incident. There were large vacant rooms at the bottom, but nothing besides a few signs of being used sporadically for a shelter or toilet.

"Ah, just as I thought. These were the operating rooms," he sighed, "but not what I'd hoped."

The dog's screams had given Billy a major case of the willies. Grumpily he asked, "What the hell were you hoping? This dump is where hope goes to die."

Johnny gestured impatiently. "I thought this might've been the Janitor's base of operations. For his clean-ups. Bring in some equipment, water, lights, it has the room."

"Yeah, space, privacy, off the beaten path. But surgery would be hard in this shit hole. Infection waiting to happen." A howl was heard, perilously close.

"Do you hear that? They're back already." Jin was on high alert, his weapon ready.

"Let's get the fuck out of here, Johnny," Billy demanded.

As the three climbed back aboard the police harbor boat, the commander stopped them abruptly. He'd had time to think a few things over. "I know you didn't have a warrant for this visit, Lieutenant. And I don't care what you were looking for or what you found, I owed Jin a favor. Me and my crew and whatever this is here –" (motioning his hand in a circle indicated the three of them) – "never happened. *Capisce?*"

"We read you loud and clear, commander. I have no idea of anything you're talking about. We don't even know you," Johnny agreed. Billy and Jin nodded as well. "Could we take a quick swing around the harbor? I'd like to observe what happens this time of day."

"Sure thing, Lieutenant," he said, barking instructions to the crew.

Feelings

CHAPTER 28

The night and the wine were uncompromising while Molly listened in solitude to Coleman Hawkins playing his saxophone. The haunting music only added to her overly pensive state of mind. Her mind raced as she sat in the darkened living room alone.

What am I doing with Johnny? It's crazy. I worked so hard for my career – am I going to lose it all over a man? Dr. Misak saw it right off the bat. I spoke highly of Johnny, measured him with my eyes. Good grief. And what was it he said about Johnny? Something about wetting his lips with his tongue – oh my God, I love the way he wets me with his tongue. Eye contact. 'All of which indicates a relationship.' 'Ya think?

Molly took another long drink. She wondered how long it would be before others noticed. Louise, she could handle, because the girl's job was at stake. She knew what she *didn't* want in a relationship. At her age, and at this stage in life, she didn't want to be part-time. She didn't want to be a party girl, either. *Where is this going? He aroused such feelings – does he share them? I need some assurance, some commitment, not a five-and-dime fling.* There were political aspirations she'd only just begun to explore. What would a relationship mean there?

If Johnny had been there, of course, there would have been no second thoughts. She would have let herself be lost in his eyes and arms. *I need to plan this out. See where it leads.*

A Discovery

CHAPTER 29

Jin Fang walked into South Central's squad room looking for Johnny. He knocked on the open doorway and stepped in to Captain Sullivan's office. "Good morning, Captain."

"Good morning, Detective Fang. I'm glad you accepted the assignment." Sullivan put the boat brochures down, and covered them discreetly with a more official document. "I'm hearing good things about your work. What brings you here?"

"Thank you, Captain, my pleasure. I've got some information for Lieutenant Vero. Is he around?"

Sullivan shook his head. "He should be in shortly. He's briefing the squad with the Day Sergeant and the uniforms."

"Thank you for your support and trust in me, Captain." Detective Fang stepped backward out of the office and pointed. "I'll just wait in his office if you don't mind."

"Be our guest. Help yourself to coffee."

Jin was sitting in one of the extra chairs when Johnny walked in about 10 minutes later, enjoying one of the worst cups of coffee he'd ever tasted. "Jin! I'm glad you came to visit our house."

"It wasn't for the coffee, I assure you," Jin grimaced. "I have more information about victim number two."

"Billy's getting coffee, hold on," Johnny said, grinning at Jin's expression as he stuck his head out the doorway. "Hurry up, Bradshaw!"

The three men were settled soon, and Johnny closed the office door. "Blast away!"

"Hèng Lìwùshì, the second Chinatown victim, was second in command for Mò zhōngguó, better known as Mo China. Short for Monarch of China. No ego there! He's the top boss in Chinatown for the Fafi game and controls the Hip Sing Tong faction. He was not just a runner carrying betting slips to Mo China. This hit was a message for Mo China. Word is that Mo China and his gang members are up to their eyeballs in murder, drugs, and other illegal shit but they are *very* fearful of whoever killed Hèng Lìwùshì."

"Holy shit! The Tongs are as crazy as they come and *they're* scared? It doesn't make sense. If both Mo China and the Tongs are scared, why was victim two killed? Wouldn't they be scared *before* he got popped?" Billy asked.

"Yes and no. Again, I think this was a message. Word is, the Tongs were going to confront the smuggler the next time he came into port, demand protection money from them instead of whoever he's currently paying off to get in safely. The plan backfired. Apparently before they could see him, someone else – whoever that is – found out and struck first. Now the Tongs and Mo China realize they're dealing with someone or something even stronger than they are. Plus it looks like they have a leak within the ranks. That's *really* surprising."

"Why?" asked Billy. "Stool pigeons are everywhere."

"Mo China was top boss in the entire region of Shandong, China, along the coast line of the Yellow Sea. Our snitches paint a grim picture. Rumor has it that he'd send wood coffins to the homes of those he planned to kill. He was a rice patty farmer who became a policeman, but he branched out into crime shaking down the opium trade for protection. That's why we have a hard time bringing him to light – he knows the police way. He has connections to the opium trade working with this smuggler, someone he's probably known for a long time. I would think that a leak wouldn't last long in his organization."

"If things were going so well in China, what's he doing in New York?" Johnny asked.

Jin laughed. "This is crazy, but Chiang Kai-shek put him in charge of the Bureau of Opium Suppression. When Mo was caught skimming money from the Bureau, he had to flee the country."

"Why don't we let Chiang Kai-shek's men find him and kill him? That would take care of Mo China for us," Billy snickered.

"Too simple, Billy. Mo China is an intelligent man. He chose New York because of the 1943 repeal. When we said bye-bye to the Chinese Exclusion Act, he knew immigration would rise. It also clogged the system. He seized the opportunity to bypass the red tape, smuggling people in for money. 'Course none of the poor suckers handing over their cash realized they would be forced into prostitution and servitude." Jin sighed. And smiled. Everything to that point was the appetizer. Now, for the main course. "Wait until you hear this! The ME found something we all missed, a piece of paper in the dead man's mouth."

"What fucking piece of paper?" Johnny questioned angrily. *How could we have missed that?* "And why are we just now learning about it?"

Jin grinned like the proverbial cat that swallowed the canary. "The ME – actually one of his co-workers – found a piece of paper stuffed in Hèng Lìwùshì's mouth which read; *Zhōngguó zhī xià*. He thought it was one of the Fafi slips the victim didn't want found. Figured he'd stuck it in his mouth rather than put it in the bag with all the bets and money. Which were never found, by the way. No surprise there."

"Translation?"

"*Mo China next*." Jin was excited. A real clue! "Somebody wants Mo China to back off!"

Johnny took a few notes, frowning. "And Mo China and Friends are scared. But it doesn't make sense. Mo China has all the Hip Sing Tong firepower at his disposal. If he's scared, we're dealing with somebody absolutely evil. I can't wait to get my hands on that son-of-a-bitch smuggler to see his face when we bring him down along with Mo China and the Janitor." Johnny's voice had risen progressively; now his fist hit the desk.

Detective Fang was less emotional, but just as committed. "Keep in mind that whoever the smuggler is; he's paying someone off too. We may have to settle for him and the Janitor. Mo China will probably never be caught. If Chiang Kai-shek hasn't found him, I doubt we will. But if we can get the others, it will be a great collar."

Billy chimed in, waving his hands. "Let's not count the chickens before they hatch. Who knows? Maybe Mo China is a myth."

Jin was a little offended. "Detective, I can assure you that Mo China is no myth. His reputation is spoken of throughout China still. And it is repeated by Chinese families here in New York. The only hope of catching him is that there really

107

is a leak within his organization. That's why I believe victim one, Deshi Garner, was killed. He found out too much."

CHAPTER 30

Billy waited for Detective Fang to leave before bringing up a nagging question. "How the hell does he find out all this information?"

"That's what undercover does," Johnny said. "You know that. They can't divulge where they get it from. Not at this point in a case."

"Yeah, well. I know you drove undercover a while back, so you would know. But it eats at me sometimes."

"Don't let it. They do what they do best, with a lot more risks than we encounter most of the time, and we do what we do best. Both branches are important," Johnny chewed on a pencil. "Keep in mind, Jin said Mo China may have a leak in his organization. That would be a gift."

"I know. You're right," Billy said as he slipped a file folder back into the tall metal cabinet. "I'm just really disappointed. I thought for sure we'd find some sort of updated medical, or surgical room in that shit hole of a building on the island. It would be a perfect spot for the Janitor to do his clean up. It's condemned, it's out of the way, and you need a boat to get there."

Johnny put the gnawed pencil down. "Billy! I think you just hit on something! That's been my theory for a while."

"What?"

"Needing a boat to get to the island. What if the smuggler's boat is big enough to hold a three-man crew and women *and* have a small medical room? Think about it. If the Janitor can't clean up what's needed, they dump 'em in the drink right then and there. No fuss, no muss," he said as he slapped his hands back and forth. "It would also put the fear of God into the women onboard: *This could happen to you!*"

"This *honcho* smuggler and the Janitor are really hard-boiled." Billy sat down at his desk facing Johnny's. "Frenchy killed one person at a time. These guys are wreaking havoc throughout Chinatown." Two victims in as many months wasn't exactly a crime spree, but knowing that the deaths might be the tip of the iceberg – that was unsettling,

"The question is, who are they in cahoots with and what makes Mo China and the Hip Sing Tongs scared shitless of the smuggler?"

Billy made a show of shaking his head while lifting his hands in disbelief. "A floating hospital, no less! Where do you come up with this shit?" he groaned.

"Billy, grab the binoculars. Let's go back to the Old Brewery. This time I want to spy out the river from an aerial view. What do you think?"

"Why not? You're the boss!"

110

The Unexpected

CHAPTER 31

Climbing five stories to the roof, not knowing what they would come face-to-face with as they did, the men had their suit jackets open, hands ready to pull out their weapons. When they finally reached the metal door to the rooftop, Billy held up a hand and bent over. "Wait, I need to catch my breath. Five stories is serious shit."

Billy opened the steel door slowly as they stepped out cautiously, walking back to back with pistols in hand. Their search of the rooftop came up empty.

"Billy, hand me those binoculars, I want to take a gander." Walking to the edge, Johnny scoped out the harbor carefully, stopping periodically to focus on different locations.

"What are you looking for?"

"Somewhere a forty-foot vessel might dock without suspicion."

Billy whistled, "That's a lot of boat, Johnny. A lot bigger than the police boat that took us to Labrè."

"I spoke with Commander Cunningham about my theory. ' You remember Fred?"

"Sure, the commander at the Coast Guard station."

Johnny let the binoculars hang from the neck strap, squinting in the bright sunlight. "He said that's the size vessel needed, forty feet, when I described what I thought was onboard. Let's go back to the dock where Jin's police boat was waiting. I want to get a different angle up close of the river and harbor."

It was a lot easier going *down* five flights to the basement. They were standing at a juncture, trying to remember which tunnel would be the best to take, when they suddenly heard a great crack in the air as loud as the loudest thunderclap. Both Johnny and Billy knew the sound all too well, a noise that heralded the message: *I'm coming for you.*

The odor of gunshot residue was thick as fog in the narrow tunnel as the speeding lead projectiles cut through it, oblivious, not caring that they brought death and destruction. Under different circumstances, the pinging and whining of ricocheting bullets might be reminiscent of a carnival shooting gallery as a shooter successfully made contact with a metal target. Under different circumstances. Now there was nowhere to hide; Johnny and Billy hit the ground, covering their heads. And then, a ghostly silence.

"Johnny, are you alright?" Billy nervously whispered.

CHAPTER 32

Johnny's adrenaline was pumping so hard he hadn't yet noticed the loud ringing in his right ear or the sensation of a hot fire poker pressing into his head. As yet, he felt no pain. But he could hear Billy's muffled voice over and over. *Johnny are you alright? Johnny are you alright?* Johnny didn't mean to ignore the voice, coming as it seemed from across the harbor, but then he felt Billy's strong arms lifting him to his feet. Only when Johnny felt the blood running down the side of his face through his shirt collar down his side did he realize he'd been shot.

"Jesus, Johnny. Your ear's bleeding like a stuck pig," Billy cried, picking up the call radio from where it had fallen in the scuffle.

Struggling not to pass out, Johnny mumbled, "Don't call in a 10-13, Billy." A call of "officer in need of assistance" would bring every cop in the city, leaving too many streets unprotected.

"Johnny, you're losing a lot of blood. Half of your fucking ear is shot off, for Christ's sake! Are you hit anywhere else? That's an awful lot of blood."

Johnny knew that shock was beginning to set in. Weakly, he took a quick inventory. "I don't think so. What about you?"

Billy walked around his friend, holding the radio. "I'm okay. You don't look like you've been hit anywhere else. Don't move."

As soon as the static was quiet, Billy blatantly disobeyed orders. "Bradshaw here. 10-13, 10-13, officer needs assist. Gunshot wound to, to…to the right side of the head. Location is the Old Brewery basement, Mott Street south of Canal."

The dispatcher's voice was confident. "Units and medical are on the way, Detective."

With Billy's help, Johnny sat slowly down to lean against the damp wall of the tunnel. Billy joined him on the floor and pressed his handkerchief against Johnny's ear in an effort to curtail the bleeding. From outside, a boat's horn mournfully called. A seabird squawked. *The bees buzzed everywhere. Bees buzzing,* thought Johnny, *bees. Spring is in the air.* He tried to stay awake.

CHAPTER 33

Awakening the next morning to see Molly, Angie, and Billy by his bedside, Johnny lifted his head from the pillow to see where he was. "What happened?"

Billy was concerned his injuries were more serious. "Don't you remember? We were at the Old Brewery and you got shot. Half of your right ear is gone."

"Oh Daddy," Angie sighed. Her eyes were red from crying as she stepped closer and took his hand. "Thank God, you're okay." She'd caught the first train out as soon as she heard.

Molly's voice was husky, but business-like. "Johnny, there's a ton of uniforms in the hallway. The Chief and the Captain, too. The PC was here earlier, and told us to get the son-of-a-bitch that did this," Molly's voice broke slightly, and she cleared her throat. "Our units scoured the building from top to bottom and turned up nothing. Not even shell casings. The slugs they did find were so damaged; the caliber couldn't be identified."

"I'm not surprised," Johnny said. "If it's only half an ear, why am I still here? Get my clothes."

Just then a nurse in a starched white uniform walked in, hearing Johnny's order. "You had surgery, Lieutenant Vero.

You'll have to stay for a day or two. The doctor wants to be sure you're stable and needs to verify your hearing in that ear."

"A malediction and a blessing in disguise. I won't have to listen to the Captain's bullshit, anyway." Johnny's voice was a little louder than necessary. "I sure hope the bandages are cutting off sound on that side." *What about my music,* he thought. *A good cop has two good ears, or he winds up dead.*

The nurse was brisk. "That's what we have to check. Okay, everyone out. If you want him home, he needs to rest."

CHAPTER 34

After four weeks of R&R, punctuated by multiple doctor's visits and a precious few stolen hours here and there with Molly, Johnny walked into South Central one fine March morning, ready to get back into action.

"Well hi-de-ho," Billy greeted him as he filled a cup of coffee at the community urn.

Captain Sullivan was beside him. "Lieutenant!" he screeched through retracted lips that exposed his gritted teeth. "You're not supposed to be here. You're not scheduled to return for another two weeks. Jesus Christ, Vero," he snarled. "how am I going to justify this? You could've taken off until Easter, for that matter."

It was good to be back. "Captain, don't bust my chops. You won't be on the hook. I'll just stay at my desk and review everything we have to refresh my mind."

Sullivan rolled his eyes. "I better see you every time I look for you."

"No fooling, Captain. I've got you covered," Johnny responded, making a show of shuffling files on a nearby desk.

Billy was not convinced. "I know that look, Johnny. You've got something up your sleeve. Does Angie know you came back to work?"

"Stop flappin' your lips, Billy. She went back to school after a few days. And I made her promise not to call my mother, but yes, she knows I was coming in." Johnny said, sidling up to Billy and lowering his voice. "Keep an eye on the Captain, though. He should leave soon and then so will we. I have to use the *head*. Keep an eye on him."

When Johnny came back from the rest room, he noticed the captain's office was vacant. "You're not ready yet?" he razzed Billy.

"Where are we headed, Johnny?"

"To finish what we started, where and when I got shot."

Billy grabbed his coat. "I'll drive. How did you get here?" he asked.

"I called for a squad car."

Uniforms, thought Billy with disgust. *Leave it to the uniforms.*

CHAPTER 35

"Well, Johnny, it's been over a month. Let's take a look once more," said the doctor as he slowly unwound the bandages one more time.

"Well, Doc?"

"Not bad, Johnny. Not bad at all. I thought it would be a lot worse. Doc, you did a hell of a job," Billy commented as he leaned in close to get a better view.

The doctor beamed. "Thanks, Detective. Here Johnny," he said, handing his patient a mirror. "We were able to reattach the partial piece that was hanging. Mind you, it's only a piece. The important thing is that you didn't lose any of your hearing. You've just got a new look. It'll take some getting used to. You might get some stares," admitted the doctor, "but it'll make a great story for the ladies. Not that you'd need one. One more follow-up in a month –"

Johnny interrupted, "Thanks, Doc, but I need you to sign off on me now so I can get back to active duty and away from the desk. I'll come back for a check-up on my own, I promise."

The doctor was skeptical, but finally agreed. "Okay, Detective. I'll take you on your word."

No sooner had the men returned to their car than they heard the crackling and squelch noise of the police radio. *South Central to Detective Bradshaw, over.*

Billy picked the radio up. "Bradshaw, go ahead, over."

Dock workers pulled a body from the Hudson, over.

Billy all but dropped the radio, turning to Johnny excitedly. "We've got a floater, Johnny!" Scrambling to regain control of the device, he said, "Dispatch, we're on our way. Give me the 10-20."

He was back in the game now. "Shit!" exclaimed Johnny.

"Sure as shit!" replied Billy.

The Floater

CHAPTER 36

Billy flipped on his siren to move the crowds of onlookers gawking at the body police divers had pulled from the waters at Pier 36.

"Billy, where do you think our floater came from?" Johnny asked, stepping from the car. It was a short walk to where the ME was doing his thing. "What do we have, Doc?"

"We have a dead body, Detective."

"Very funny, Doc. 'You went to school for that?"

"Twelve years, including my residency at Boston General and my fellowship in forensic pathology at the New York City's ME's office. All to tell you with expert precision that this person is definitely dead."

"Twelve fucking years?"

"How long did it take for you to be standing next to me looking at the same dead body as a Lieutenant?"

"Touché, Doc."

"Wow, you even speak French," Michaels said, tilting his head for a better look at Johnny's ear job. "You are one lucky son-of-a-bitch. I could've been looking down over you just as easily." Johnny pointed to the body; he didn't need a reminder about his close call. "Right. Just look here, Johnny. Faces of the dead are always a lot alike, except this one. She's bloated, but a woman that's been nibbled on with fish, turtles, and who knows what. Bounced around, in other words." Michaels pointed to a chewed up stump of a leg. "Leg probably got caught in a propeller, which helped bring her to the surface. Bodies dumped here during winter don't usually surface until spring." Michaels stood straight, stretching his back. "I presume your killer knew that, and also and knows the water, the tides, and the thaw. Bacteria and yo-yo temperatures are thrown into the mix. Rigor mortis is altered by the water current, too. Unless you find a witness who can tell you when she was dumped, your time frame is generally fucked, in my *expert* opinion." Michael twisted from side to side. *They don't tell you how hard this job is on your back when you're in med school.* "Female, bullet in the forehead. There's no exit, probably a .22 again. Anything else will be in my report, but I wouldn't hold my breath for much more."

"Thanks, Michaels. Billy, get what you can from the scene. I'll have a uniform drive me – need to see the DA."

Heading to Molly's office, Johnny's mind went over all the facts and theories thus far. *Gotta be the work of our smuggler from Guyana, or the Janitor, but why a woman this time? With all the damage, I wonder if they can tell if she's Chinese.* The warm day reminded him of Florida. He decided to make time to give his mother a call in Florida.

Anxiety

CHAPTER 37

"Oh, Johnny," Molly cried as she shut her door behind him. "You don't know how happy I am you weren't killed."

"Me too! But that was a while ago –"

She shuddered in his embrace. "I know, but I was thinking about it just now. And I'm sorry we couldn't spend time together during your recovery. I mean, first Angie was there, and then the job..." She brushed his hair aside. "Let me have a look...mmmm, not too bad." Molly took his face in both her hands. "I can get used to that. A little less to nibble on, but that's okay. Are you feeling well?" She led him by the hand to sit with her on the couch. "I heard the department's psychological profile for you came back with flying colors." She took a breath. He was alive, he was here. And they still had a case. "Do you think the floater has anything to do with the other two Chinatown murders?"

"Your office is on top of things like always, I see. I just left the pier."

"We got the call immediately to see if I or one of the ADAs could be on the scene. We were all in court."

Johnny still got tired more quickly after his ordeal, and sat back on the couch now. "I know you won the election on the platform of being hands-on, Molly, but you can't be everywhere at once. The people will remember all you've done, come election time again." She leaned her head on one shoulder; he'd missed that. "No one will forget your campaign slogan, either: *there's no Folly with Molly!*" They sat together, close, not talking, for a few minutes. "I don't know if the floater is involved or not. The dead usually talk to us, though."

"What do you mean, Johnny?"

"They tell us something about themselves and they tell us something of why they were murdered. That's when we become their voice." Johnny sighed, remembering other cases. "Most floaters are jumpers with identification to follow up, so we've got the 'who.' That almost always leads us to the 'why.' I've only seen one other floater in all these years that was murdered, a mob hit similar to our floater with a bullet to the head. Only he also had two slugs to the chest. Shooter left his ID in his pocket and stuffed money in his mouth and all the way down his throat, just in case anyone missed the point: *Here's what happens if you skim from the mob.*"

"Maybe our floater was involved with all of this Chinatown business and was skimming off the top along with victim two?"

"Possible, Molly, but not likely from the details and the note stuck in Liwùshi's mouth. There's a lot involved here - prostitution, opium, gambling. We're talking a lot of lettuce in their pockets. Remember we met with Leelee Gaye just before I got shot? She and Deshi Garner were first cousins, which explain her wanting to help us. But we don't have a clue how the floater ties in."

"So now we're getting the skinny on some details. I wonder why she didn't mention it when we met the first time?" Molly sat up and her eyes shone with excitement.

129

"Johnny, let's not forget what we are finding out little by little. Jin Fang is doing a hell of a job since he joined Pan and Chang in undercover. There's also the hint of payoffs."

Johnny scowled. "That's especially disturbing. There may be a possible leak in Mo China's organization."

"How is that?" Molly asked. "A leak would have to be certifiable!"

"If our information's correct, the leak was to let whoever it is with the power to get the smuggler into the harbor, know that Mo China was going to try to rub him out. Or her." He sighed.

"The details are becoming more skewed as we go along."

"Not really," Johnny sat up. "It's actually helping us to put it all together. How about dinner Saturday night?" With one finger, Johnny stroked her throat above a matronly bow. "We can piece it together."

Molly's breath caught. "I can't. My cousin Charly is flying in from California late Wednesday night for the parade on Thursday and here through the weekend." Over a million spectators would flock to 5th Avenue for the St. Patrick's Day event, but she knew better than to ask if Johnny planned to attend.

The pupils in Johnny's eyes narrowed. "Charly, huh? I don't remember you mentioning him, but I'd like to meet him. He can come along."

Molly's smile softened. "We *do* have a lot of catching up to do." *He's not sure Charly's my cousin, but I'll play along. No harm giving him a little food for thought. Maybe I'll tell him about Charly next time. Maybe not. Men!* "Thanks, but I'll take a rain check, Johnny. I'm sure you understand."

Not giving Johnny a chance to kiss her more passionately, Molly picked up the files she'd left on the nearby chair, rose and looked down at him. "I'm due back in court. Walk me out?"

CHAPTER 38

Thoughts of Molly blowing him off for her "cousin" Charly distracted Johnny somewhat as he made a hasty exit through the courthouse lobby. He had seen her infrequently over the last month. He'd almost gotten killed. Catching up with the cousin? Sounded fishy.

Passing the newsstand, the headline on the *Daily Globe* stopped him dead in his tracks:

COP SHOT IN CHINATOWN BACK ON THE JOB:
IS OUR CITY SAFE?
Page 3
Byline: Grace Tilly

That bitch is one sly fox! It took her a while, but now she's getting back at me for not taking her up on her offer for dinner and a roll in the hay. I'll bet she *doesn't have a cousin in town.*

Walking back inside the lobby and making a beeline for an empty phone booth, Johnny dialed as fast as the rotary dial would allow.

"Grace, it's Johnny. Is that invitation still good?"

CHAPTER 39

"Lieutenant!" Captain Sullivan's booming voice pulsated through the squad room. "In my office. Now!"

Sighing, Johnny answered, "Aye, aye, Captain."

"Here's the ME report on our floater. Read it. Where the fuck are we with these Chinatown murders?" Sullivan's blood pressure was through the roof. "The goddamn mayor's all over me with this, to say nothing of the chief and PC. These fucking headlines are not good for re-elections or for the city's tourists. They read too, you know!"

Sullivan stood up and rubbed his jaw. Then he started to pace behind his desk. This was not a good sign. "That reporter, what's her name? Tilly. Tilly seems to have it in for us. I know she's just trying to sell more newspapers, but it gets the suits pretty crazy. Every headline coming down the pike makes my phone light up like it's Christmas."

Johnny leaned against the doorway. "Don't mince words, Captain. Why don't you tell me what's on your mind?"

Caught off guard for a moment, Sullivan squinted his eyes. "If you weren't such a good detective, Vero, I'd have your ass put in the boon docks. Decorations be damned."

Johnny flashed a grin. "I hashed it out with Grace Tilly already. She agreed to dial it back with the chilling headlines." *For the time being.*

"Good." From personal experience – years of it – Johnny knew that Sullivan just needed a few words to dial it back, himself. Sullivan's color was already better. "I read this report, and the similarities are here. Chinese female, shot with a .22 same as the other two. She was too mutilated to get an ID. But there has to be a tie-in somewhere." He handed the report to Johnny.

"It certainly looks that way, Captain. There are a few more things we're working on."

"Such as?"

"Such as the connection between victim number two and …"

When the phone rang, Sullivan reached for it. "This is Captain Sullivan."

Pivoting, Johnny took his cue to leave.

CHAPTER 40

St. Patrick's Day came and went, with nothing ominous occurring so far as Johnny could tell. The Charly discussion tabled for the moment, Molly asked to tag along with him for another meeting with Leelee at the club, hoping for new information that could tie the three murders together in a neat package. She liked neat.

The DA was used to front doors and grand entrances. Johnny felt bad for dragging her through the alley. "I'm sorry Molly; we have to use the kitchen door. Leelee can't take a chance being seen talking to the police, and if we waltzed in at this time of day, someone might notice. And talk. It was different when we came for dinner and the show; we blended in with everyone else. Right here, Molly, this door."

Molly wished Johnny didn't feel the need to explain everything. She was the DA, for cryin' out loud. She knew what was what. *Does he respect me?* She wondered. *Does he have any idea what I hope to accomplish one day?*

Leelee greeted them in the kitchen and led them to a table, again asking an underling to bring coffee. Easter was just around the corner, but coffee was welcome any time of the year. "It's good to see again, Miss Penett. You, too, Detective." She smiled a bit sadly, causing her eyes to crinkle. "I have some information for you. The floater's name is…was, Shui Li Yong. Ironically, her name means 'from water, upright, and courageous.'"

Leelee looked so child-like that Molly felt the need to encourage her, putting her hand on the woman's arm. "It seems that she was all of that and more. I am sorry for her family's loss."

"Thank you, Miss Penett. Yes, she was very brave. Just as there is an underground for smuggling prostitutes and drugs, there is another, fighting against all illegal activity. Shui Li Yong and Deshi were part of that cause. I told you of my limited connection. I'm concerned even more now. Both came to my club, sometimes separate, sometimes together. I'm really not involved in their cause, though. It's been going on for years – to stop the crime or at least slow it down. To rescue as many women as they can." Leelee had reason to worry. "I only provide you with information that was shared with me. They are both gone. Unless another source comes into my life, I have nothing more for you."

"Do you have any idea who else may be targeted?" Molly asked.

Leelee wondered why Johnny was so quiet. "I have great respect for you, Miss Penett. I liked your hands-on platform, but I only knew Deshi because he was my cousin. Deshi and Shui were… living together. I didn't tell you when we last met, Lieutenant, because I did not yet know that Shui was … dead." The three sat for a few minutes without a word. When Leelee spoke again, it was in a flood of words.

"They knew each other from China. They lived in the same village. Huangyao. They worked the same fields together. This village spans two rivers, giving Shui Li Yong her name. Eventually, they went their own ways, but found each other again here in the city." Leelee's eyes pleaded with Johnny to understand. "The Chinese community is small in so many ways, even though it seems vast to outsiders. Once someone from our country arrives, they have immediate contacts, immediate connections with our culture."

Leelee continued. "You see, Miss Penett, we believe that at the moment of death a spirit is taken by messengers to Ch'eng Huang for a sort of hearing, a trial before the sun can rise. Will the dead go to the Buddhist paradise to dwell with the Taoist immortals? Deshi and Shui will be together now eternally, in paradise. Because they were good. Because they helped stop evil."

"Here on earth and together forever and ever," Molly said, getting misty eyed in spite of herself. "That's my idea of true love."

Dames. "This is all great information, Leelee, but we still don't know who the smuggler is or the doctor called the Janitor," Johnny said.

"That's your job, Detective," Leelee said, standing. She held both hands up by her side. Empty hands. "I have no more information. I've provided you with much. Please do not come here again. It's too dangerous for me."

"We can have a detail stay with you wherever you go," Molly suggested, standing as well.

Leelee shook her head. "The smuggler is not getting into the harbor without paying someone. My guess is that both Deshi and Shui could identify the Janitor. That's why they're dead." She softened a little. "A detail would only bring attention. I will call if I hear anything else, but … good bye." The beautiful Leelee turned, and walked away, behind the brocade curtain that hung behind the stage.

Johnny and Molly watched their best informant vanish and wondered if their case was doomed.

CHAPTER 41

Leaving the club through the rear, they walked through the alleyway to the sidewalk. In other circumstances, Molly would wait for the gentleman to hail a cab, but something about Johnny always made her feel the need to assert herself. Holding up a hand, Molly said, "That really wasn't a whole lot of information. We didn't know that Deshi and Shui were childhood friends, or lovers. Who knows, maybe living together was a matter of convenience and not love at all." *I can't believe I just said that. He might misinterpret. But isn't that what we are, convenient lovers?* "She could have told you over the phone."

Johnny was confused, and gently pulled her arm down as a cab slowed, then sped off. "I can drive you home. Remember, we drove here together." *What's up with her?*

Molly's eyes were unreadable. "It's getting late and I have to prepare for a trial." She didn't, but she was tired of Johnny taking her for granted. If he walked her back to the office and things got stirred up, she would be upset. And if things didn't get stirred up, she would be furious. *Poor guy. He really can't win.*

Johnny was taken aback, but he just stared at her. "How was your weekend with good ole' Cousin Charly from California? What did you two wind up doing?"

I can keep this going for a while. "It went very well, thanks." Molly could stare just as hard. "The last time we saw Leelee, she mentioned *South Pacific,* and I liked what I heard. I was able to wrangle some tickets for center row, orchestra. Charly and I enjoyed it very much." Johnny just stood there, hands in his pockets. "It shed some light on our case. You know, a mixed marriage facing challenges. True love conquering all." Hoping Johnny would get a hint, she continued. "*You* know, Johnny, deep love. That's what it's all about. Regardless of what people say or do. Don't you agree?"

Johnny turned his head away, studying the street intently as she prattled on. "Then we went to the Rainbow Room to see Glen Gray and his Casa Loma Orchestra. We had a great time! Sunday we went sightseeing in the morning, then lounged the rest of the day, listening to jazz, drinking wine. Catching up, you know." *He's rattled*, she thought triumphantly. "What about you?"

Johnny had persuaded Grace Tilly to lighten up on the headlines in the manner in which she had grown accustomed. Several times. He had left her bed feeling cheap and used, but also a man again. "Nothing really. Watched a couple of ball games, went to dinner with a few flatfoots from the 5th trying to pick their brain."

Molly held her arm up again, and a taxi appeared out of nowhere. Opening the door to the taxi, Molly slipped in, holding the door with her hand so that Johnny got the message. He had a car. And he wasn't getting a kiss.

"You need to get more on this investigation. You need to get deep inside," Molly said, hoping he didn't see her flush at the poor choice of words. *I want you deep inside of me, dammit.*

If he noticed, he attributed the rising color in her cheeks to the warmth of the day. *She's criticizing my police work? Fuck that.* "Don't you think I know that? My recovery set us back. We'll get there."

She heard him, heard the hurt in his voice, but all she could think of was *Johnny deep inside, and him whispering "we'll get there."*

Closing the door a little too loudly, Molly sank back in the seat, eyes forward. "Turtle Bay Gardens."

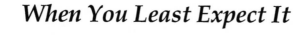

When You Least Expect It

CHAPTER 42

The Federal Court House lobby was buzzing with activity as usual. Johnny stopped to pick up the morning paper at the lobby newsstand as was his custom before dropping evidence to Molly's ADA involving another case. It had been so easy; open and shut. Those were the fun ones, not like the Chinatown murders. Catching the eye of one of his informants, Johnny gave a slight nod, acknowledging his presence. Willy, his snitch, answered with the requisite tilt of his head, meaning *I've got something you'll want to hear.*

Willy operated one of the busiest shoeshine stands in Manhattan. With all the lawyers and other suits in and out, he did well under his simple bold lettered sign that read:

WILLY'S SHOE SHINE
BEST SHINE EAST OF SPOKANE

Willy's rag poppin' shoeshine skills were epic, and his singing wasn't bad either. If those didn't draw customers, the sign did. He wished he had a nickel for every customer who said, "Why, you must be Willy, from Spokane!" As if this was the first time he'd heard it.

In a way, Willy did indeed hail from Spokane. Wrongly sentenced to 15 years-to-life for second degree murder at Spokane Federal Prison, Willy had been in the alley when the deed was done, easily identified. But the only thing Willy had shot that night was dice.

Then-Officer Johnny Vero knew Willy was a good God-fearing man despite the vices of women, whiskey, and gambling. After years of determination and learning gumshoe detective work, Johnny found the real killer, bringing him to justice and proving Willy's innocence. Johnny got his gold badge; Willy got his freedom. In the many years since his release, Willy had never failed him.

"Good morning, Lieutenant. You look like you can use a shine."

As Willy shined shoes for criminals, law abiding citizens, and judges, he listened. Closely. Men would chat together, waiting for one of his chairs to open up. They'd talk while they sat for the shine, oblivious to Willy's presence. If the accountants knew how much money Willy had accumulated over the years based on what they'd indiscreetly disclosed under his sign, they would have been shocked that he hadn't retired yet. Willy had done hard time, albeit only a little, thanks to Johnny, but he'd learned some tricks and used them well.

"Lieutenant, you're the best dressed flatfoot I ever shined a shoe for, in them fancy Florsheims, you know?" He gave a quick turn to be sure no one else was around or about to step up into the second seat.

"What do you have for me, Willy?"

Willy began applying polish. "I had two in the seats the other day, you know? One Chinaman and one colored. Uppity, if you ask me. If they were both Chinamen, they'd be talkin' that gibberish when they're together, but I heard ev'ry word, you know?"

"I'm all ears, Willy."

Willy grinned as he worked. "Speakin' of ears, yours looks like a boxer's cauliflower ear, you know? Did I ever tell you about the fight I was at back in 1927? Chicago, visiting my middle sister. Dempsey against Tunney. Dempsey lost, never regained the title. Stupid is as stupid does, you know? Dempsey knocks Tunney down." Willy couldn't contain himself at the vivid memory, waving his hands, throwing punches into the air. "The ref can't start counting Tunney down until Dempsey's in his corner, you know? By the time Dempsey realized he had to go to his corner, Tunney had been down 14 seconds, but the ref had only counted to nine when Tunney got back up!" Willy cackled. "If Dempsey had done right, he would have won by a knockout, you know? You were just a scrapper back then, Lieutenant, off in the Navy."

"So, what happened?" Johnny asked.

"Dempsey lost his title by a decision," Willy went back to work.

"That's too bad Willy."

"Yes sir. Too bad. I lost a lot of money on that fight, you know?"

"Willy," Johnny said patiently, "you started to tell me about the men."

"Oh, yes sir! Chinaman says he needs younger women. Virgins. I thought he was talkin' personal, you know, like he couldn't get it up 'lessn they's young. Colored guy says he can get 'em but it's going to cost. I figure any good hooker's gonna to cost, you know, so my ears aren't twitchin' yet. Then the Chinaman says something interesting: 'We've got to come to a *compromise*. I know you're paying to get into the harbor and for protection.'" Willy looked up at Johnny and saw he had his benefactor's undivided attention. "He says, 'I want you to pay *me* for protection and drop whoever you're paying now.' Says 'I have a lot of payoffs to do business in Chinatown. I have to pay for what we're shipping and need more money.'"

Willy started snapping the rag with his expert hand, never dropping a beat as he continued. "So the colored guy says, 'What do you mean? You're Mo China. You run Chinatown, motherfucker. I don't give a shit who you have to pay to do business in Chinatown. We have an agreement.'"

"All the time, I'm just doing my thing down here, Johnny, and they actin' like I'm invisible. It's a gift," Willy said. Johnny raised his eyebrows, agreeing, but wanting him to keep talking. Someone else could sit down any minute. "Colored man says he's not going to fuck with who's giving him protection and getting him into the harbor. Says more women and virgins gonna cost. And the Chinaman says; 'Griff, you know I have a meeting coming up with someone who knows my business and sent a message loud and clear saying I'm next. They're worse than me. My family's still in China and they'll find them. I had no idea who you were paying.'"

A man approached as if to take the second chair, but Johnny glared at him and laid down his newspaper. "Sorry. I'm saving it for someone. Went to the john." The man scowled, but left. "Go on, Willy. And hurry it up, will ya? You're about to polish my shoes clean through."

"Okay, okay. Colored guy says, '*That's* why your guy got hit? You're on your own. I'm not fucking with this guy and neither should you. Chinaman says he's not going to fuck with him. He's scared of what the guy wants. Asks the colored guy if he knows what he wants from him."

"Meantime, I'm rag poppin' and hummin' so they don't think I'm listening, you know? Colored guy says, 'I have no fucking clue. Who knows? Maybe I'll never see you again and all my business goes to him' and he started laughing, you know? Then he leans over and says real low, 'You want virgins and younger, pay the fuck up."

Griff. A name! "Did they mention any names – the powerful people there are afraid of?"

"No, sir! But Chinaman says he has a meeting set up with someone over on Mott Street as soon as he puts up bail for Chin-Chow somebody, you know?"

Johnny's heart sped up. "Did he say where on Mott or mention anyone by name?"

"No sir! The Chinaman got up and gave me a dollar for a 35-cent shine and whispers something to the colored guy but I couldn't make it out, you know? I asked the colored guy if he wanted a shine, but he just got up and walked away with the Chinaman. Rude, you know?"

"What did they look like, Willy? Did anything stand out? Anything at all you can tell me." Johnny was excited. Mo China was not only real, he'd been seen in public by his very own snitch. *I'd bet my life the other man's our smuggler.*

"Chinamen all look alike to me, you know, but the colored guy had a *big* scar running down his face across his neck. First thing, I noticed. He looked mean, you know?" Willy relaxed. "You're all done, Lieutenant. I can see myself in those Florsheims!"

Johnny wanted to get it right. "Willy, you're absolutely sure you heard the names Mo China and Griff?"

"Yes, sir! Wouldn't say if I didn't, you know?"

Johnny reached into his pocket for a ten dollar bill. "Here you go, Willy. You deserve it."

"No, sir. I owe *you*. You saved my life!" Willy always said the same thing.

"You worked for it just like I worked my job to help you. Take it."

"God bless you, Johnny, God bless you," Willy said in gratitude, making the sign of the cross. He kissed his fingers, then reached up to heaven before picking up the racing form to see who was running that day at Saratoga, the reason he would probably *never* retire.

Johnny walked out onto the street, thinking. He well knew who ran Mott Street and that entire area – the New York Italian mob. It was also out of his jurisdiction. *The mob, shit. Connections all the way back to Italy. Powerful connections.* Things were starting to make sense.

CHAPTER 43

Johnny sat in his office hashing over the files of information with Billy. *Did we miss something?*

"Johnny, you're just staring at those files like they're going to say something to you."

"They are, Billy." He'd been sitting on the news from Willy, savoring the moment he'd spring it on his partner.

"I'm going cross-eyed looking at this stuff. What are they telling you?"

Johnny smiled in anticipation. "We have one more bit of information to tie into our Chinatown murders. I grabbed a shine at Willy's and you'll never guess who was sitting in his chairs recently."

"Good ol' Willy. Knowing who comes and goes through that lobby, I can't imagine."

Johnny paused for effect, but could contain it no longer. "Mo China and the smuggler, in person. Can you fucking believe it?

Billy let out a war whoop. "Holy Mary, Mother of God. Are you sure it was them? Both of them out in the open?"

"Willy described the smuggler to T. It was the scar that cinched it."

"What else? Did they say anything?"

"Mo China was going to meet someone over on Mott Street who now has an interest in his business. Or rather, if Mo China wants to *stay* in business, he has to deal with this new partner. They even mentioned the note in victim number two's mouth saying Mo China's next. Mo is scared shitless."

This was all great news, but still Billy frowned. "How the fuck did they know about the note, when *we* didn't know until Fang said the ME had found it, and that the report got misplaced?"

Johnny had been so excited at the development, he'd overlooked that point. "Good one, Billy. Mmmm. I don't know." Johnny thought better on his feet, so he got up and walked around the room as he mused out loud. "It could be the leak in Mo China's organization we heard about. Just when things are getting tidy, you have to throw a wrench back into the mix!" More to himself than to Billy, he said, "How *did* word get to Mo China about that note? Goddamn it!" He stopped. "But we do know who runs all of the rackets in Manhattan."

Billy bit his lip in thought. "How is it that the guy 'who runs all the rackets here in Manhattan' is only *now* grabbing the Chinatown action?"

"How deep is the ocean?"

"Pretty fucking deep!"

Johnny grabbed his hat and umbrella in case of a spring shower. "Let's go. We're going to Molly's office to share the latest. I don't trust the phone. You get the car; I'll be out front in a minute."

CHAPTER 44

Molly's cold shoulder, and the fact that he'd given Grace Tilly exactly what she wanted to keep quiet for a while had Johnny's head in a spin. He'd taken a minute to prepare for the trip to Molly's office before they left, but now, his mind was reeling again as he and Billy stepped off the elevator.

"Go ahead, detectives, Miss Penett is expecting you," Louise cooed. "And how have *you* been, Lieutenant?"

Johnny just gave her a nod as they headed for Molly's office. After a terse "Come in" they shut the door again.

Molly didn't beat around the bush. "We need to get something on the table. The mayor's calling daily for updates."

"Hello to you, too, Molly!" Johnny quipped. "But we didn't come all this way to say hi." The men had a seat in the chairs provided. "This is getting more intertwined than we ever thought it would be. Starting out, we thought we had a single murder. Now we're up to three."

Molly blew out a breath and shook her head. "I apologize, you're right. We're all under pressure. Fresh off the Budapest Hotel murders, people are counting more carefully. *We* know this isn't the work of a serial killer, but the brass doesn't. They react to public pressure, to headlines. None of us likes it. I shouldn't have taken it out on you."

"You're a walk in the park compared to the ass-chewings we get from Captain Sullivan," Billy offered helpfully.

"I got reliable information from one of my informants only today," Johnny said, eager to please her. *Huh. Since when has that been a priority with a woman?* "Both Mo China and the smuggler were seen together talking about someone from Mott Street. Someone they're scared of. Scared they'll end up like victim number two. Any ideas who the Mott Street monster is?'

Molly's eyes were round. "Only one of the top Cosa Nostra dons in the United States. In Naples, he'd be called the *camorra*, the *camorristi*. That's who they were talking about?" Molly asked.

"I'd forgotten that your father and family are from there," said Johnny.

"Yes, he's one dangerous man. Alvise LaPoshio, but he manages to keep a low profile. He was behind that ship fire, the one from Finland the Navy brought over?" Johnny nodded. He'd forgotten the name connected with the incident years ago, because there'd never been any hard evidence. "His name means 'famous warrior." He's known as *Al Pazzo*, but no one calls him that to his face." Molly rolled her neck to relieve some of the built-up tension. *What I wouldn't give for a good massage right now. And the best masseur in town is sitting right across from me. Great hands. And we're back to business terms, it appears.* She blew out another breath. "He has a stable of expensive attorneys that have greased him out of any convictions we've tried."

Molly went on to describe a hardened criminal who had felt life was hard back in the old country. Death, on the other hand, was easy. Killing became a way of life for him, second nature. Helping the slick lawyers were a growing number of "coincidences:" Any witnesses to his crimes ended up dead.

"There was only one charge we ever got enough on to bring him to trial," Molly said. "Passing me in the hallway outside of the courtroom, he made it a point to stop me and say that he remembers my people back in Avellino. ' Such a nice *famiglia*.' Bastard. Like he could scare me off. LaPoshio killed his way to the top of the organization, even if it meant going after other gangsters. And if anyone came after him, they are no longer with us." Molly's face was grim. "He gets what he goes after. It doesn't surprise me at all to hear he's mixed up with our bodies in Chinatown."

"*Al Pazzo?* Translate please," Billy asked.

"*Crazy Al.*"

"Well, then, at least we know who the son-of-bitch is we're dealing with. *Al Pazzo* sent a message to Mo China telling him to bow down, or else."

"So a few more pieces to put in the puzzle box."

Billy snapped his fingers, remembering something. "Listen to *this*, Molly. Tell her, Johnny. About the slugs where you got shot."

The sound of that phrase was enough to make Molly's heart sink. The look of anguish that briefly danced across her face was not lost on Johnny. "The slugs were all too smashed to determine their caliber, which means they had to be dumdum bullets." When she frowned, he continued. "Dumdums are made to hit their target and sort of explode inside the body. When they hit the walls, they flattened. They're used by professional hit men, which means –"

"Which means you have a contract out on your head.! LaPoshio's work, most likely, although you've made more than your share of enemies over the years." Molly tried to hold it together for Billy's sake – and her own – but it was difficult. "I don't want you to take this lightly, Johnny. LaPoshio imports men from Italy and Sicily to make the hits, and then they're sent back. And if they're very low-level, make mistakes, or show they can't be trusted for some reason, they're killed, too. Poof. Gone, never to be found." Molly didn't frighten easily, but she was getting there.

"Real honor among thieves," said Billy.

"*No* honor, Billy. I'll put something together for the brass so maybe they'll call off the dogs for the time being. You'll have to deal with Captain Sullivan yourself, but his bark's worse than his bite, as you know. If you don't mind showing yourselves out, I have a call I must make. Oh, Johnny–"

Johnny stopped at the door. "Go ahead, Billy; I'll catch up."

Molly walked toward him with a look in her eyes he'd been missing. Mesmerized, Johnny leaned down to kiss her waiting lips. This time, there was no cool response. Holding his cheeks as she parted her lips and tickled his tongue with hers, she whispered, "Don't be a stranger. Be safe out there." Her hands slid down his chest, and lower, until she pushed him gently toward the door. "Don't keep Billy waiting."

New Thoughts

CHAPTER 45

Returning from his meeting with Captain Sullivan, Johnny found Billy flipping through a stack of files.

"What do you have?"

"I pulled the arrest sheets on Alvise LaPoshio, and the list is a block long: aggravated assault, armed robbery, extortion, burglary, attempted murder, bookmaking, loan sharking, and on and on and on *ad nauseum*. He did a short stint at Dannemora, but like Molly said, his attorneys got him off. Witnesses disappeared.. *No name, no one to blame.* So we know who and what we're dealing with. *Al Pazzo.* Oh, and listen to this. Guess why he didn't get deported?"

"His attorneys made him become a United States citizen?"

"Now we're cooking on all burners. They're pretty slick, Johnny. He must want it all: the Fafi gambling money, the prostitution, *and* the opium."

"He won't stop at anything until he succeeds. Even putting a contract to kill me." Johnny bolted upright. "Shit! That's it."

"What's it?" Billy asked.

"That last ad for the Janitor. That was for me."

"So, the Janitor's cleaning job is not to clean up their fuck-ups?" Billy asked.

"Could be both, Billy. It makes sense – the ad ran on a Sunday and within days, we were shot at. If you got lead pumped into you, too, he figured it would be collateral damage. Two birds with one stone. It could have been one of LaPoshio's hit men, tailing us until we were trapped in the tunnel."

Billy knew they were getting warmer, just as the city was getting warmer each day. "Johnny, too many threads aren't being sewn together. How does the Janitor know the who, what and where? The ad doesn't say any of that. He still has to get that info somewhere. And if LaPoshio is into everything, could he be behind Monica at the Nostalgia Café?"

"The devil's in the details, Billy. We have to figure out how to get LaPoshio – *our* devil – involved with something that has real bones. Something he can't escape. Send him up the river once and for all." Johnny had an idea. "Let's contact undercover vice, see if any of ours has infiltrated his inner circle. This guy is so damned greedy, I just may know of a way to trip him up."

"Spill."

"Well, his sheet says he was arrested and did time for a plea on a loan shark charge. The vig, the – the *interest* gives a high return in cash. To LaPoshio, cash is king. Let's see if we can get a briefcase loaded with counterfeit bills and get it to him. Nab him out in the open, on the street, anywhere we can handle his bodyguards. That would be two federal offenses: counterfeiting, money laundering. We wouldn't have him on the murders, but it should be enough to send him to the Big House."

"Alcatraz?" Billy whistled.

"We could only hope."

fred berri

Billy started taking note. "We'll have to start surveillance on him. I'll set it up."

"Good, Billy. I'll tell the captain and Molly; see what strings they can pull."

160

CHAPTER 46

Alvise LaPoshio was a nefarious individual who would not stop at anything to gain and keep control of the rackets in the city, including murder. And he accomplished all of this with the perfect disguise: he looked like a regular person, not the monster he was. Sitting in a restaurant or watching a movie at the theater, he gave the air of a doctor, lawyer, or politician. Charming, polite, impeccably dressed in custom tailored attire, his handsome strong facial features, the clef chin and soft hazel eyes – to say nothing of his sensual Italian accent – won over many women's hearts.

Billy's team were close to coming up with a schedule – but only close. Hours turned into days, then weeks, of surveillance. Johnny reviews the report:

Always accompanying Mr. LaPoshio are two or three henchmen identified as private eyes with clean records, licensed to carry pistols. The entourage never leaves during scheduled haircuts (one per month), or manicures (weekly). Days and time constantly change. A shoeshine guy comes to the coffee shop on Mott Street which is the front for his illegal businesses. Men come and go all day and into the night, for varying lengths of time. A few times a week, high class prostitutes are chauffeured to and from the fancy hotel he resides at. One of these women accompanies him to Broadway shows and five-star restaurants where he always has a table waiting. Of interest: he has a regular a table at the No-It-Awl Jazz Club.

"Mmm. I never expected that!" Johnny exclaimed. When he and Molly had been at the club, he must have been elsewhere; Molly would have recognized that face anywhere.

"I was wondering about that too. He just walks in and there's always a table for him and a guest," Billy added.

Johnny was impressed with the report, both the summary and individual shift reports. "This is good work." *Why would Leelee Gaye have a table for him?* "I see one of two places we can open the door with LaPoshio. But where can we get to him the easiest – the shoe shine guy's the same every time?"

Billy nodded.

"What about the hookers, are they the same each time?"

Billy held up a finger while he answered the phone, told Nancy he'd call back later, then consulted his notes. "No and yes. They vary according to hair color. Different hookers, but always the *same* blonde, the *same* redhead, and the *same* brunette. Once in a while there's a woman with black hair, but the jury's still out on her."

"In what way?"

The phone rang again, and again Billy answered, nodding a few times and grunting before hanging up. "Besides not knowing if the mystery woman's Chinese or not, she's the only woman who has been seen during the day, and never at night. And we haven't been able to get a good look at her."

"Are there sheets on the hookers? Any pictures?"

Billy's team had been thorough. "We're still waiting on the pictures to be developed; maybe we can identify them. I'll send them out to surrounding precincts."

Johnny had a thought. "Was our undercover team in on this detail?" He hadn't seen their names, but Pan, Chang, and Fang had been of immense help.

"No, they were working another assignment. That was Fang on the phone just now. They have a lead they're moving on and asked if we want to tag along."

"What, where, and when?" Johnny asked, tilting his head slightly.

"Something about a raid hoping to find Mo China."

"Tell him we want in."

"10-4."

CHAPTER 47

Johnny had always enjoyed the comfort of the leather couch in the sitting area of Molly's office. He had waited many times for her when she would run late for their meetings. Today, as he flipped through the latest issue of *Life*, he heard Molly's laughter.

Molly sashayed into her office with a colleague. They'd come from the downstairs courtroom for a murder case she was prosecuting. "Johnny, this is Federal Agent Roland Bollinger. And this is Lieutenant Johnny Vero. I was just telling Roland that our accused stabbed his girlfriend *and* his wife 105 times. And he's pleading self-defense."

"Ah! Vero, I've heard so much about you. Glad to meet you." Agent Bollinger extended his hand.

Pleasantries exchanged, everyone settled. "Agent Bollinger, Molly told me you have a contact inside Alvise LaPoshio's organization that might help us get to him. We were hoping one of our own undercovers was buried somewhere in his organization, but this may work out even better."

"Please, call me Roland...Johnny? That I do. We want LaPoshio as well. No offense, but believe me, our person will be much more effective and will be much better getting information from him. Our person is deep inside." He glanced at Molly, then back to Johnny. "Or should I say, by all accounts, it seems that LaPoshio is deep inside *her*."

"You've made your point," Molly blushed.

"Are you saying that *she* is one of his regulars? Is it the blonde, the red head, the brunette, or the Chinese woman?" Johnny asked.

"You've already done your surveillance! Your reputation precedes you. I'm not at liberty to say, but she *is* willing to do whatever it takes to get LaPoshio."

"Who is she? And why is she willing to risk her life and do … anything?"

"She's one of ours, Johnny. And yes, she does what she does to infiltrate his organization. We don't ask, and she doesn't tell what she does when she's alone with LaPoshio. Her assignment's called Operation Orchid."

"An undercover police or a citizen informant?" Johnny asked.

"One of ours, as I said. She's FBI and knows the consequences," Roland said solemnly. "She would *die* to stop the smuggling of women and opium into the United Sates. She is highly educated, sought after as an agent. She's been on assignments throughout the world, and it seems she is already involved with your case. This was just brought to my attention recently, as Molly and I have been discussing things. She had information from both your victim number one, Deshi Garner and victim three, the floater, Shui Li Yong. Both civilians, both aiding Orchid. What type of plan do you have in mind to reach LaPoshio?"

"LaPoshio's record is long but one thing that stands out is his loan shark business. He likes his cash, so we'd use perception and leverage. If we can get your agent to convince

LaPoshio she has a contact in need of laundering counterfeit money, his perception would naturally focus on the potential for revenue. Maybe, just maybe, he'd take over the task himself, for the maximum payout. Your agent provides the leverage. We nab him with the bills and the arrest goes to you, the Feds."

"I like it," Molly interjected. "Let's see what we can come up with in conjunction with Agent Bollinger."

Johnny was needing to trust more and more people, and he wasn't entirely at ease with this. "Understandable. Just remember, LaPoshio has a lot of people on his payroll, both in and out of the Blue Brotherhood.[5]"

"We're aware, Johnny. Our resources can be trusted, as you say, in and out of the Blue Brotherhood. There are only a few people, including *you* two now, who know we have a female agent on the inside. That's all the others know. Her identity is not known."

"Then how do you –"

"Let's leave it at that for now," Roland said abruptly. "So, tell me. Why are you being so generous? What's in it for you if we get the collar?"

"You get him on extortion, counterfeiting, and laundering which will get him to federal prison. Later, when we've fit all the pieces together, we get him on murder, take him to trial. When his time is up with the feds, he can start his life sentence with us." Johnny clapped his hands lightly. "Or the death penalty. Fair and equitable."

That seemed to satisfy him. "Alright. Once you come up with a more definite plan, I'll need to approve it. Then we'll

---

[5]   Blue Brotherhood; denotes the unwritten rule that purportedly exists among police officers not to report on a colleague's errors, misconducts, or crimes.

proceed." Again with the pleasantries, the handshakes, the platonic hug to Molly. "Please be in touch. Good meeting you, Johnny. Molly, I'll see my way out."

After he had closed the door, Johnny gave his opinion, whether asked or not. "He seems to be a straight arrow. Willing to work with us."

"I've known Roland a long time. We were in law school together," Molly said with a slight giggle. "He always wanted to be a G-Man."

"I'm glad you're on board with it, too, Molly." Her kiss the other day seemed to have thawed her. He'd take the plunge. "How about dinner or just a drink at the No-It-All? Look around, enjoy the company, kill two birds?"

Molly drew in a breath, but then let it out. "Sounds good, Johnny. But I'll have to take a rain check."

One minute she's grabbing me by the shorts, and the next she freezes me out. I don't need this shit. Johnny's eyes were dark as he turned to the door. "I'll work my end. I'm sure you and Agent Bollinger will work yours." He glared at her for a second. "Keep this in mind, Molly; we *both* have lives outside the courthouse and the law."

CHAPTER 48

A few days later, Molly's intercom buzzed. *Miss Penett, Lieutenant Vero is on line two.*

"Thank you, Louise….Hello, Johnny."

"I have some thoughts on our investigation and our meeting with Agent Bollinger."

Molly's stomach churned. *Does he or doesn't he. Did she, or didn't she. Would they ...* "Okay, let's set a time for you to come here, so we don't have to hash this over the phone." She checked her desk calendar, full of pencil marks. "I have free time in the morning. What about you?"

"I was thinking more in the line of dinner and drinks, say, at Leelee's club?"

He is persistent, I'll give him that. Maybe I can give in a little. And we do have lives outside the courthouse. Jazz is always a good idea. "Okay Johnny. How about tomorrow evening right from work?"

"Sounds great. I'll stop by to get you, and we'll grab a cab."

"Good," she said, not resisting the opportunity to get in a dig. "I'll have time to pick up my photos from Rexall's, the ones from Charly's visit. I'll bring them."

Johnny felt a little blood rush through him. Maybe her cold shoulder was thawing for real. *This should be interesting if she's willing to 'fess up about the mysterious Charly.* "I'm looking forward to seeing you *and* the photos. See you then."

I just bet you are.

Affection, doubt, or affirmation?

CHAPTER 49

Johnny's anxiety escalated throughout the night watching the seconds on the clock, as if it were a pot slow to boil. He kept hoping his thoughts would give him a rest, but no. It had been a while since he sat sipping Old Crow whiskey, his favorite, listening to classical music. The whiskey knew it had a job to do and always did it extremely well: *Muddle the mind. Alter the thoughts that were painfully clear.*

What if Molly's cousin is an old school friend? A man? Where do I fit in? Why would she string me along? Does she want a part-time lover or does she have real feeling for me?

Wow! What are my feelings for her? Am I starting to fall for her, really? Do I really want to fall in love? Get married again? My God! This is crazy. I'm not a kid.

Slumber arrived without notice. The bottle was almost empty, and when he slumped over, it fell to the floor, not even breaking as the turntable continued to spin throughout the night, the music over.

CHAPTER 50

Molly and Johnny made a handsome couple as they walked effortlessly through the crowded Federal Courthouse lobby. Giving a nod or tip of the hand as a salute, every bailiff and uniformed cop wanted to be sure they got points for greeting two of the city's top law enforcement agents as they passed by. Everyone was in a hurry to catch a train or bus, or hail one of the cabs that were lined up outside like little soldiers ready for battle.

"I usually wait until the last of the late workers leave," Molly said as Johnny opened the door to a cab. "It's usually quiet down by seven."

"It's almost that now. Driver, the No-It-Awl Jazz Club on 52nd Street."

"Yes sir."

The ride was quiet, for the most part, arousing the curiosity of the cabbie. *They look like they was made for one anudder,* he mused, *but you'd think they was brudder and sister, the way they're sittin.*

Once they entered the club, they were treated like royalty, strategically placed at a ringside table. Leelee herself scrutinized the reservation list each day to ensure that certain tables went to certain politicians, dignitaries, or others who were owed favors. High class hookers got a kick-back for bringing in clients. Celebrities got their perks, as did baseball players and, of course, law enforcement.

Drink orders were taken. The crowd was bustling. Patrons filled the room with indistinguishable chatter and cigarette smoke while a three-piece ensemble provided musical ambiance.

Taking a sip of her wine, Molly seemed to have just remembered something. "Oh, here! Let me show you the pictures from my cousin Charly." Gone was the all-business DA voice; replacing it was a pleasant lilt.

Johnny was a blank slate as he took the photos from Molly. He looked through them with pursed lips, feeling her scrutiny. "These are nice, but where's Charly? All I see is this lovely woman. Who is she? Did he take the pictures of you both? Didn't he want his picture taken?"

Molly smiled, but didn't answer the question. "You seem overly concerned about Charly, Johnny." She stood and took his hand. "Come on let's dance." As she led him out onto the dance floor, she said, "I know you're not a flatfoot on the floor – New Year's Eve, remember?" Molly wanted to distract him, to see how far this would go. It was simple ploy, one she recognized as being beneath her, but she needed to see what he was made of. What his heart was saying. The thought of asking him directly never entered her mind. In the courtroom, she was a tiger, in the bedroom as well. Here, in limbo-land? Not so much.

Molly felt comfortable in Johnny's arms, but perhaps he'd gotten too comfortable, too soon. It was a good thing if he were a little jealous. It brought the wind into her sail. It made her feel good to think that there might be deeper feelings for her than he was ready to show. Molly put her hand on the back of his neck and rubbed it softly as they smoothly moved in rhythm to the music, pulling his head just enough that she could whisper in his ear. "The woman in the photos *is* my cousin Charly. As a little girl she couldn't pronounce her name, which is Charlotte. She said Charly. It stuck." She looked up to gauge his reaction.

All of the tension in Johnny's body released and he kissed her upturned forehead.

"I'm glad you're relieved, Johnny," she said. "Although it was kind of cute seeing you a little jealous, I must admit. Thinking Charly was a man. And not my cousin at all."

"Whatever would make you think that?" he said, the mask back down, the tension back. *Am I that easy to read? And is that good, or bad, with this woman?*

"Oh, honestly," Molly fumed, walking briskly back to the table. Johnny followed, watching her hips sway.

Leelee was making her rounds, greeting the patrons at all the VIP tables with kisses and handshakes. She held a beautiful bouquet of exotic flowers. "Good evening, Lieutenant. Lovely to see you again, Miss Penett." Leaning in to give Molly a kiss on the cheek, she whispered, "The smuggler is known as Griff," before moving seamlessly on to the next table.

Molly turned to Johnny excitedly. "We have a name, Johnny! Leelee just whispered it. The smuggler is known as..." She hesitated, fearful someone might be listening.

"Well?"

Molly leaned toward him and made a big show of kissing him on the cheek. Anyone watching would think the couple was having a grand night out together. She kissed his ear and said, "Griff. She said he's known as Griff. But where's she getting her information now that her cousin and his friend are dead?"

"I'm wondering the same thing. But Leelee isn't the only one getting fed information. I already knew about Griff. I told you my snitch saw Mo China and him together."

"I certainly would've remembered a name! I don't think you mentioned it. But I can run it through the system to see if anything comes up. She's getting info from *someone* above ground." Molly's eyes were furtive as they glanced around the room. "Do you think she knows the female agent Bollinger spoke about. To get information from?"

"Good thought," said Johnny. "But she also knows Monica from the Nostalgic Café. Monica led us to Leelee in the first place, remember?"

"Yes. And we can't forget our boys in undercover, and whoever else you use as a snitch or to plant stuff."

Just Willy Shoeshine. Billy and I haven't been out on the streets in years, cultivating informants. Well, there's Grace. "We'll just have to wait and take anything we can get, sort it out later. It'll come together."

"And if it doesn't… c'est la vie."

"What?"

"Such is life. Charly says it a lot. I was talking to her about something that was weighing heavy on my mind" – *you* – "and that's what she said. 'C'est la vie.'" Molly shook it off. "C'mon Johnny, let's hit the dance floor again. You're not such a bad hoofer, you know."

Pressure

CHAPTER 51

"Hey, Lieutenant," called one of the squad detectives, "here's another help wanted ad asking for a janitor." Everyone had been told to look; not everyone knew why.

"Thanks, Gibbons." He took the paper into the office and found the ad. "Shit! Goddamn it!"

"What are you thinking, Johnny?" Billy knew it did not bode well.

"After the last ad, it was days before we were shot at. I believe I was the target, but who knows, maybe you are a target too. After all, you are involved in this case."

"There haven't been any reports of any bodies lying around."

"I guess that's always a good thing." The men were increasingly frustrated by the lack of information in the ads. "The ad runs. A few days later, a dead body appears. Or we get shot at."

"*Janitor wanted for upcoming cleaning job* is so vague. Is he going to clean up by disposing a body? Clean up some other bloody mess? Doctor someone with surgery?"

Johnny sat with his fingertips touching, bouncing his hands together as they brainstormed. "That's good Billy, the process of elimination. *Not* cleaning up a bloody mess. He *makes* the bloody mess and *we* have to clean it up. My gut says that a 'cleaning job' means murder. That's how he cleans up, by eliminating witnesses or potential problems who could put them in prison, or put them out of business."

Billy weighed this option. "Alright. Let's go with that. Now what?"

"If we can't get any information from our short list of informants, we don't have a choice. It's a wait and see situation."

"Particularly when potential snitches are winding up dead. That's making it a real short list. Let's hope the new ad isn't to finish what they started with you." Billy grumbled. "Or me."

CHAPTER 52

"Lieutenant Vero and Detective Sergeant Bradshaw are here, Agent Bollinger," the efficient receptionist spoke into the intercom.

Send them in.

The agent's office was more clinical than theirs, more formal. "Detectives. Thank you for coming. I want you to know that we're still working on getting a large sum of counterfeit bills to fill an attaché case as part of Operation Orchid's assignment."

"I can't imagine it's going to be easy getting that amount out of evidence without a trail of paper work a mile long," suggested Johnny. "I know what *we* have to go through to get evidence pulled to use locally. It's like pulling *teeth* sometimes."

"You're correct, Lieutenant." Johnny noticed that here at the FBI field office, Bollinger was much stuffier, even though it was only three floors above Molly's office where they'd first met. The first names were dropped in favor of titles. "There's so much red tape, it could choke a horse. And take weeks." The men sat down in rather uncomfortable chairs. "We're told you still have your surveillance on LaPoshio. You may want to back off a little. One of our agents spotted your team, not knowing it *was* your team. They thought the guys might be hit men until we did a little digging of our own. We don't want to blow our operation. We've invested over a year so far."

"10-4," agreed Johnny. "I'll call off the dogs momentarily and won't put them back on until after I get you're okay."

Hit men! The guys will be pumped. "We don't want to mess up your operation," Billy assured him.

"In the meantime, Agent Bollinger, we'd like any information you have for us."

"Agreed, Lieutenant. I'll have my agents put a package together that we can share without compromising our efforts thus far."

"Thank you. We'll show ourselves out."

As the partners made their way down various elevators and hallways, Johnny was quiet. As soon as they were outside the building, however, he said, "Billy, do *not* pull any surveillance off that detail, you follow? Clean it up, change them around. Mix in a few females to take away any suspicion. I don't want Bollinger's picking our team out of a crowd. How the fuck did that happen?" Johnny was incensed. "Our team better tighten up. Now we have two completely separate groups to fool."

"Two?"

"Some of LaPoshio's men have been private eyes. They know how and what to look for. Now the feds, too. You got that?"

"I do, Johnny. I do. I'll take care of it."

CHAPTER 53

Johnny's entrance interrupted the morning roll call with all the uniformed beat cops.

"Listen up!" barked the sergeant in charge. "Lieutenant Vero's got something to say."

From the back of the room a voice yelled, "Is the Captain selling Irish Sweepstakes raffle tickets again?" Everyone in the room snickered. The voice was unmistakable.

Stepping up to the podium, Johnny said, "My God, Stanislaw. Maybe you should've been a baseball player with that name. You could be called Stanislaw the Coleslaw, because you shred things to shit."

This time the room howled with laughter pointing to the man in the back, some striking a batter's pose.

"All right let's get to it! " The men settled down quickly. "I need your help on the Chinatown murders. We have three murders as you know. Two found on land, one pulled from the drink. We're pretty sure they're all related to a smuggler known as Griff. He's from South America and has to have connections to get into the harbor. He smuggles Chinese women, some of them just girls, for prostitution." A lot of the officers were fathers of young girls; he could feel the temperature of the room rise. "And he smuggles opium. The gangs run by Mo China aren't touching him, though, in fear of who we feel is behind him: Alvise LaPoshio."

Johnny could feel the sighs, and heard more than a few audible groans. They'd all heard of him, of course, by reputation anyway. "You may remember that during the war, he arranged to have a fire set on a ship the Navy brought over from Finland because Finland helped Germany. The Navy made it a transport ship, and it sank in the harbor right here. No one was able to prove LaPoshio was behind it, but the feds *and* us are extremely motivated to nail this guy on anything and everything. I need you to cozy up to your snitches and dig out what you can. I don't care how you get information as long as it sits well with IA. You know the drill. Detective Bradshaw's passing out a description of Griff – dark skin, distinctive scar. You can't miss him. There's also a classified want ad looking for a janitor for an upcoming cleaning job. That same ad is placed days before a body turns up. It's directly connected to our case, so if you hear something, say something. Dig deep men."

Johnny was about to keep the pep talk going when one of his detectives ran in. "Lieutenant, we just got a call. Another body in Chinatown."

"That's number four, goddammit! Get your asses out there and bring me back something."

Billy had finished passing out fliers with the precinct artist's guess as to what Griff looked like. "There's our body for the last ad. We need to find out how this fucking operation is working, and find it fast!"

183

CHAPTER 54

Within minutes, Johnny and Billy were en route. "What's the 10-20?"

"Orange and Anthony Street," Billy answered, grasping the steering wheel to brace for the inevitable.

"Shit!" Johnny exploded. "Columbus Park. Goddamn Five Points again. Step on it." He reached out the window to place the siren on top of the car. Usually they tried to keep a lower profile, but this wasn't the time.

Johnny barked instructions as Billy maneuvered through all the other police vehicles crowding the narrow streets. "Billy, just pull up on the sidewalk, I don't give a shit. Leave the beacon light on. Just look at this fucking crowd."

Billy put the car in park, stepped out of the car and shouted to the first uniformed sergeant he spotted while Johnny walked directly to the body. "Get a barrier up and push these people back."

Hopefully the crowd hadn't compromised any evidence. Dr. Michaels was already at work. "Doc, this is a busy year for you so far. What can you tell me?" Johnny asks.

"Busy for both of us. I haven't found much so far. I'd say the TOD is five, maybe six hours ago."

"So right before dawn, give, or take," Johnny said. "Billy, have the uniforms get whatever information they can get from the crowd. Maybe someone saw something. Maybe we should get Pan, Chang, and Fang here."

Billy smirked, "Sounds like a Charlie Chan movie. As a matter of fact, I saw Detective Fang working the crowd." He left to talk to the uniforms.

"See here?" explained the ME "Two slashes to major arteries. One on the left side of the neck, the carotid; one below the clavicle, the subclavian artery. He bled out in 2-3 minutes. The slasher knew what he was doing. And he's right handed."

"Are you sure?"

"Look here. The incision starts top to lower in a downward slash. The same with the second incision. A slasher using his right hand, facing the victim, would go for the victim's left side. He knew he didn't have to go far, just underneath his first slash. That cut alone would have done him in. He must have wanted to be sure. It's sort of overkill. Literally."

"I guess he wanted him dead-dead, not just dead," Johnny snickered.

"Same time of death, but different method as the others."

Billy jogged up with an update. "We've got a uniform and his partner who speak Chinese. They said they can handle some of the questioning."

Johnny stood in the warm April morning air, observing the surroundings, the shadows, the buildings, escape routes. *Maybe our slasher's the one who gave Griff his scar. Or did Griff get revenge for what was done to him here?*

185

Continuing his own examination of the body, Johnny asked the doctor if, in his opinion, the slasher might have been trained medically.

"He certainly could've been. Clean incisions exactly they'd do the most damage. He may have even used a scalpel, the wounds are so precise."

"Would a veterinarian know where to make these cuts?" Johnny probed.

Michaels was surprised. "Suuuure. The arteries run along the same framework, although there are variables for size and species. This was close up and personal, Johnny. Whoever did this isn't squeamish. Blood spurted everywhere as you can see from the spatter. He probably got quite a bit on his clothes. He's an animal himself, and one bad motherfucker from the looks of it." Michaels shook his head sadly. "This did not faze him one bit. But yes, he very well could have been a veterinarian or gone to medical school. If I get more during the autopsy, it'll be in my report. Will there be anything else, Lieutenant?" Dr. Michaels, veteran Medical Examiner, was not squeamish about blood, either, but his back was killing him.

"No, Doc. Thanks."

Michaels had two assistants with his today, a tall woman who might have been the same one Johnny had seen bundled up for number one victim, and an older man, perhaps a retiree volunteering his time. "Bag him and tag him and get him on ice as soon as he's through," Michaels instructed. "I'm heading back." The two went immediately to work.

There wasn't anything more to see at the moment. When Johnny spotted Detective Fang speaking with bystanders, he signaled for him to come join him. "How'd you get here so quickly, and what do you have, Detective?" Johnny didn't mean to sound like an interrogator, but he did have questions.

"I was working a snitch across the street and down the way a bit. We were in a deep discussion concerning a certain opium den where he thought I might see Mo China, when I saw all this going down, everyone hurrying this way." Jin squatted down by the body. "Look, Johnny." He turned the victim's left palm over. "See this tattoo on the inside of the wrist? It's a Tong gang tattoo. This symbol means he was head of the Chinatown faction. It means *long life*. No one's allowed to kill him." Jin stood up. "He got that in China. It's called Ci Shen; a stick dipped in ink, the point is tapped into the skin" Jin wasn't sure Johnny understood. "This man was sent here to be *a boss*. Like the Italian mob's 'made man.' No one is *allowed* to kill him, under great penalty."

"Well, I guess whoever killed him, either can't read Chinese or didn't give a shit who he was, where he came from, and or that no one was 'allowed' to kill him. Doc says this one was before dawn, too."

"At the moment of death our spirit is taken –"

"Yeah, yeah, it's taken to Ch'eng Huang for a hearing," Johnny snorted. "We *all* have superstitions and beliefs." Easter was just in days; although he didn't think it was a fairy tale, he knew people who did.

Jin remained respectful and undaunted. "Yes, Johnny. However, let me tell you that although these people were murdered, the superstition is strong. The Chinese believe that the moon is the abode for departed souls. They have to go to Ch'eng Huang for their hearing before going to the moon. This has to be done before dawn, before the sun rises. The timing is no accident." When Johnny didn't interrupt, he kept going. "Also, Deshi Garner's watch was not taken. Also

Chinese superstition. Giving a clock is bad luck, so the watch and the other things were left on him."

"Jesus Christ, Jin. I wish I'd known that all along."

Jin was chagrined. "I'm sorry, Lieutenant. It's just second nature to me. I didn't –"

Johnny got in Jin's face. "Every fucking piece of information is imperative, every single piece! I don't care if you believe in ghosts, I want to know. Are we clear?"

"Actually, Lieutenant, there is a belief that if you whistle, you will attract ghosts," Detective Fang answered more formally, and smiled nervously. "I hear you loud and clear. Seriously. And good luck with this one. I'll let you know if anything turns up on my end. I want to find my snitch again."

Fang was soon lost in the morning beehive, leaving Johnny alone with the body as he watched Michaels' assistants prepare the body for transport back to the lab. *The killer's either Chinese or knows enough to make us believe he's Chinese. Jesus Christ! It's a goddamn conundrum.*

CHAPTER 55

Billy came into the office with several file folders. "I pulled the records of Alvise LaPoshio's known associates. I don't know who's worse, the On Leong or Hip Sing Tongs. Most of these gang murders are never solved."

"True, but these latest aren't just gang related. Connections to all four victims tie them to Mo China, Griff, *and* LaPoshio. The ME's report matched his initial findings. Clean incisions, quick to bleed out, two to three minutes. There's a possibility that the slasher is the Janitor and that the Janitor is our veterinarian. No ID found on him but our undercovers say he' s known only by Bo Qin, sounds like a K, but with a Q. Don't know how anyone even *learns* that language. Bo Qin means 'senior respect,' exactly what Jin explained about the tattoo meaning."

"Someone couldn't give two shits about his prominence or what his tattoo symbolized or his given name and its meaning," Billy pointed out.

"My thoughts as well. Who has enough power and *chutzpah* to disrespect centuries of a foreign culture while understanding ancient culture and rituals themselves? Just flip your wig and take a guess."

"Alvise LaPoshio."

"No rhubarb from me there, Billy. He controls the unions and the longshoremen and one of them is putting a stronghold on the docks. If it wasn't for President Truman stepping in last year preventing their strike...." Johnny's voice trailed off.

Billy encouraged Johnny; "What? What were you going to say about the strike?"

If it had been a cartoon, a light bulb would've turned on over Johnny's head. He always got excited when the puzzle started coming together. "That's when our smuggler Griff started getting in, and now he's still getting in with the help of LaPoshio or his dock boss. Because of all the chaos going on with the union disputes and dock workers."

Billy smirked and waved him off. "That strike was on the West Coast."

"It may have been focused from California to Alaska, but every dock, in every sea port around the country was watching, listening, and scrambling to get better organized. Nobody wanted to draw attention to themselves with the Taft-Hartley Act[6] in place." Johnny held his hands out for the files. "So what did you pull on Laposhio's KAs?"

"Just as you started saying. In addition to his regular goons, hit squad, button men – *those* sons-of-bitches – some associates are union delegates AKA union enforcers with a heavy hand. Or rather, a heavy *bat*, and knives and guns, whatever the job requires. Some bosses visit the docks on a daily basis. It's starting to piece together, Johnny."

---

[6]   Taft-Hartley Act is a United States federal law that restricts the activities and power of labor unions.

"We have a ways to go to get the arrests we want and put these bastards behind bars for a very long time." The thought of Molly, in any capacity, brought a frown to his face. "Molly got us some information which is no information."

"What do you mean?" Billy asked.

"LaPoshio isn't wanted anywhere and has no criminal record in Italy that Molly could find. The only exception's that short stint upstate, that is in his file. That thing you read to me."

"Sure, the gambling operation with horses, numbers, crap games, loan sharking. Whatever he did to cut his teeth back in Italy was a steppingstone to here. Probably thought the streets would be paved with gold, like so many. His MO is the same, but he's expanded." Billy started flipping slowly through more files as he talked.

"Well, he was smart enough to build relationships. He came with recommendations from Italy that helped him get established toot sweet right here in our great city," Johnny said with distaste.

Billy nodded absentmindedly as he read. "Exactly. He came here with a key that opened doors for him. So his sponsor had to be someone big enough to have the connections to get LaPoshio here. Like Molly said – good attorneys that get him off with no convictions. Those don't grow on trees," Billy said.

"He definitely has connections outside his own realm. Witnesses turning up murdered before his trials? Could be we've got bigger fish to fry."

"Then dig we must! And we need a few more shovels. I'll bring the squad detectives up to date and to see if they came up with anything," Billy said, walking out of the office.

Johnny stared at the telephone. *Make the call.*

CHAPTER 56

"Hello, Grace. It's Johnny," he said.

"Johnny Boy! Are you calling for another get-together? A sleepover? Hope, hope?"

"C'mon, Grace. We hashed this out the last time."

Grace put on her best pouty voice. "I know, but you can't blame a dame for trying." Grace sighed. "*I* think you're sweet on our illustrious and beautiful DA. I also think you're on the square. You'll make a good ham n'egger, Johnny." Grace laughed quietly. Johnny could picture her at her desk, twirling the cord with one finger. "I don't have a beef with the idea of you settling down. I could never understand why Simone ditched you. For artwork? C'mon. France versus you and Angie? I think she was crazy." Grace sighed again, determined not to get emotional. "Well, as they say in France, c'est la vie."

"I just heard that the other day."

"What? Oh. The French. Life goes on. Lay your cards on the table. I'll show you mine if you show me yours." She chuckled. "And we've certainly seen each other's cards."

It was good to hear her laugh. "Grace, you really can be a sweetheart when –"

"Uh-uh. No. Do not go there," she hissed, suddenly weary of the sentimentality. "We had our thing. I hoped it would work out but it didn't. I know I fucked it up, stupid me. But like I said, I'm a scorpion taking a ride on the frog. There are a few guys I'd like to sting, but not you."

The words practically stuck in his throat. "Grace, I need your help."

Grace let him wait a few seconds. "I'm listening."

CHAPTER 57

It was a sight to behold: Mayor Philip Bernhard, the Police Commissioner, and Captain Sullivan, all on the steps of the Mayor's house, Gracie Manson, for a press conference. Surrounded by the usual New York City and New York State police details, they ate up the attention. The crowd contained the usual suspects, the regular reporters all shouting questions at once, hoping theirs would be the one chosen for an answer.

Captain Sullivan scanned the crowd. *Just as I thought.* Grace Tilly would have raised the level of attractiveness, had she been there, but why would she be? She was too savvy to waste her time on such trivialities like facts. She had the city in the palm of her hand already with her fallacious headlines.

"Mr. Mayor, are these murders the result of another serial killer loose in New York City like the Budapest Hotel killer?"

"Captain Sullivan, do you have a suspect?"

"How many more bodies will there be?"

"Where's the District Attorney on this?"

"The Daily Globe *reported that our city isn't safe. Is that true, Commissioner?*

"Commissioner, where do you stand on these murders?

"Why haven't there been any arrests?

"Why isn't anyone in custody?

"Mr. Mayor, will you be running again come election?

The mayor stepped forward authoritatively. "Settle down, settle down," he shouted, lifting his hands up and down repeatedly. "I want to begin with a statement that should answer your questions. For now, it is the only statement I will make and there will be no questions afterward...."

Breaking the Ice

CHAPTER 58

Like it or not, Johnny's conversation with his on-again, off-again lover had actually encouraged him to keep trying with Molly. *Why not? What do I have to lose? I need to know if it's me that's the problem, or Molly, or a little of both.* He dialed the number, then rolled his shoulders to ease the tension as the rings began. She picked up.

"Hello, Molly? It's Johnny."

"Yes, Lieutenant, how can I help you?"

When Molly addressed him formally, it usually meant that there were others around; it was understood. But with Molly's dispassionate demeanor as of late, he couldn't be sure.

"I have new information that will help us with the Chinatown murders and the attempted hit on me and Billy. When can I get to your office?" There was nothing new, they both knew all too well, but if anyone was listening, he wanted to cover his bases.

"That would be great, Lieutenant. Let me check my schedule and have Louise get back with you. Perhaps we can include Mr. Hawkins in that indictment. You remember him, don't you? Coleman Hawkins?"

Instantly, Johnny sensed an undeniable reaction, completely physical. Had Billy been there, he would have needed to slide his chair closer to the desk. Obviously she couldn't talk freely at the moment, but when Molly mentioned her favorite jazz man, Johnny knew exactly what she meant: a quiet evening at her place, dinner, wine, and if he had anything to do with it ... dessert.

"That should work out, Miss Penett. I'll expect to hear from you."

Click.

CHAPTER 59

Molly was delighted by Johnny's boyish nervousness. He was practically stammering as he told her how happy he was to be there. She smiled, refilled their glasses, hers with Chablis and Johnny's with his favorite bourbon. The needle on the Victrola slowly dropped to Molly's favorite, Coleman Hawkins playing his soulful saxophone. His music never failed to send a delicious tingle up and down her spine. "Oh, Coleman. How could anyone resist you?" she murmured.

Johnny took the glass, but set it down on the coffee table so that he could lean forward to kiss her. She kissed him back with more craving than she ever had before, and that was saying a lot. They sat back on the sofa, enjoying the moment. "We've come a long way, Johnny." Her voice was low and sultry, but she was relaxed with him.

Johnny lifted his bourbon toward the music before taking a drink. "Hawkins' sax reminds me of my music teacher. He had this thick German accent and he was always saying things like 'Preetend cello is beautiful woman you vant to karr-ess. You vant to become one mit her, be inside her, feeling her warmth and the sensation you get. You must feel da vibrrrations mit her.' It was quite an education!"

Johnny was trying to muster all the self-control he could, not wanting to move too quickly after the long drought where Molly was concerned, but she didn't have to do much of anything before desire made itself apparent. He thought of strategically placing a throw pillow in his lap. but glanced at her, catching her eyes directed to his erection. *She's smiling. That's my cue.* She tilted her neck back in invitation and he kissed it, moving up to her earlobe. Slowly and methodically, they undressed each other. Johnny unbuttoned her blouse and slipped her bra straps from her shoulders. One quick movement around her back, and her breasts were free. He admired them for a few seconds. Beautifully formed, mocha-tipped, they seemed to grow under his gaze.

Following his eyes, Molly raised one eyebrow. *I think I love this man.* Their kisses grew more compelling, his tongue in her mouth, her breasts pressed against his chest. Molly took his head in her hands, gently urging him downward until he could enjoy her delicious scent. Her moisture had already seeped through the lace, a sign of her readiness and passion. Johnny lifted her hips so he could pull her panties off with his teeth.

He had behaved boyishly earlier, but this was no boy, and this was no coy young girl. There was no innocence to slow them down, no lack of confidence. They knew exactly where and how to fan each other's flames to intensity. Skillfully, she wrapped her fingers around the head of his penis, focusing on the ring of sensitivity, rotating her fingers around and around, firmly but lovingly. Johnny slid his hand slowly down her belly to her inner thighs positioning his fingers on the spot he had come to know. Molly's hand fell limp as she was lost in her own pleasure. Her eyes rolled backward as she climaxed.

201

She was hungry for him to be inside of her, even as she reached the pinnacle of her orgasm. He entered slowly, agonizingly, penetrating her to relinquish the fire that only grew in both their loins. Arching her body like a cat stretching, she sighed again with resurging passion. Johnny drove himself into her hard, going as deep as he could and then some, as she climaxed again. *Not enough, not enough,* she cried inwardly, raising and lowering her buttocks so that he would press against her there...*there*...as she climaxed a third time. Johnny held back just enough to join Molly's rhythm, pumping in perfect sync. She placed one hand on his stomach so that she could feel his muscles tighten with each successive explosion that filled her.

Rolling over on their sides, nestled together for a few more kisses, they held each other as Johnny felt himself slide from inside her. She was already asleep, completely spent. Johnny got up to remove the needle, stuck in a continuous loop of crackling, hissing, and pops. *The record was over, but we're ... what?* He poured himself another bourbon and carried it to the shower with him. *I don't understand her. She runs as hot and cold as the shower.* Johnny set the glass on the little shelf inside the tub enclosure and turned on the water, steam enveloping him. *Grace was right. I'm starting to get real feelings for Molly. Is it lust, though, or love? And what about her feelings for me?*

Au Courant...
A French expression meaning
well-informed

CHAPTER 60

Molly walked into South Central and headed directly to Johnny's office. She was holding a file.

"Molly?" Johnny blurted. Two days and Sunday's Easter mass had not diminished her power over him. After the lengthy but joyful service, his first in so long, he'd made it a point to flag down the priest who had tipped him to the Old Brewery in January, but the man had no new information.

"Lieutenant."

Joining her, drawn to her like a magnet, Johnny looked around to see if anyone might be listening through the open door, or watching.

"What brings you to our house Molly?" Johnny whispered, pointing his finger back and forth. "Are we okay?"

Molly smiled. Brilliantly. "We're fine." She lowered her voice. "More than fine. But we agreed to be professional when we're in certain places, right, Lieutenant?" Her voice rose on the title with emphasis.

"Right, Miss Penett." Smiling himself, Johnny guided her to a chair, briefly sliding his hand along the small of her back.

Molly settled into the chair and cleared her throat. "I was able to get more information on Alvise LaPoshio and felt you should have it as soon as I received it. This file proves it. Not only did he have one very big sponsor to bring him to the United States, he had two."

"Okay, I'll bite." *I'd love to bite your nipples right now,* said his eyes, and she blushed. "Who are they?"

Molly squirmed a little in her chair. Professionalism had its merits, but she hadn't counted on the challenges. "They are cousins. James Enrizzi, better known as Jimmy the Rat, and his cousin, Ralph Mariozo. They organized the docks and the union laborers, putting in place who they wanted and where they wanted them. They're the force behind two of the most powerful unions in the country. They made a fortune importing and exporting stolen goods using the ships as their personal shipping companies. Stolen cars were shipped out of Miami to South America, Mexico, and who knows where?"

"So, these two grew the stronghold on the docks to their favor?" Johnny had paid attention, despite the overwhelming desire to touch her. "You said *two* unions and you said *were,*" Johnny said.

"Correct on both counts. Ralph branched out into trucking to get a hold on *that* union to transport stolen merchandise around the country and into Canada, including bootleg booze during Prohibition. Then loan sharking, gambling, and opium. They were in all of that together, building the strongest mob-run organizations in the country. Then the tides turned."

Johnny frowned, an unspoken question hanging in the air.

"They brought a third cousin into the mix. LaPoshio."

Johnny sat up, completely focused. "What? Alvise LaPoshio and these two are cousins?"

"It gets better. From prison, Ralph had Jimmy, killed because Jimmy turned state's evidence against him. They'd both been arrested for bookmaking, loan sharking, and

moving stolen merchandise across state lines. They beat the
bootlegging rap. Hence the nickname: Jimmy the Rat!"

"And Ralph…?"

"Ralph died in prison," Molly answered.

"Shank in the shower?" It happened frequently.

Molly shook her head. "He died in his cell. Nothing was
proven, but it was considered suspicious. Ralph and Jimmy
had brought LaPoshio here to eventually run things when
they retired. He was younger, he'd built a good reputation, so
to speak, and he was related. A third cousin, something like
that. They sponsored LaPoshio, so he arrived from Italy to
work for them." Molly tapped the file. "Keep in mind that
with their connections they could get him in easily. And they
counted on the fact that blood is thicker than water.
Supposedly."

Johnny could guess what was coming, but said nothing.
"LaPoshio is smart and ruthless, regardless of his charm. He
made his mark, worked hard, rose up the ranks. Within time,
he earned the spot the cousins had planned all along, third in
line to the throne. After Jimmy, and then Ralph, bought the
farm, LaPoshio had some others in his way taken out. That's
what put him where he is today… the crime boss."

Johnny was incredulous. "All in the space of, what, ten
years? Do you think LaPoshio was the one who got to Ralph
in prison?"

"Most likely," Molly nodded. "No honor among thieves,
related or not. The autopsy report was indecisive and cause of
death is officially 'undetermined.'"

That wasn't right. "What the hell does that even mean?
Who screwed up the autopsy? Did a doctor perform it?"
Johnny raising his voice in disbelief.

Molly shrugged. "Johnny, an undetermined cause of death simply means that the ME couldn't classify it any other way. ' Choice of five: accidental, suicide, homicide, natural, undetermined. The ME couldn't say for sure it was one of the others, so … undetermined."

"I know, I know. I worked a few cases like that myself. For example," he recited, moving his head back and forth in cadence to words well-memorized at the police academy, "if there's evidence of a possible homicide, it may still be ruled as undetermined because if the death cannot be proven to be the result of a violent act." He stopped and struck an academic pose. "Gunshot to the head. Is it homicide, suicide, or accident?" Johnny shook his head. More often than not, prison deaths were fairly clear. "But Ralph Mariozo? Undetermined? How is that possible?"

"In his case, it could have been a heart attack, or the pills he was taking *for* his heart. It could've been suicide. Or homicide." Molly squished up her face. "We don't know."

"I get it. Goddamn it, I get it. It would just be nice to have one more body to pin on *Al Pazzo*. What about Griff?"

"I ran his name through Interpol but got nothing."

Johnny blew out a long breath. "What about our vice guys? Pan and Chang said the smuggler was from Guyana? Captained a freighter with chemicals? Any leads there?"

"I was able to run bauxite and sugar cane through a shipping system. Nothing came up with the name Griff, either first or last."

Johnny stood and began to pace. He needed to get upwind of Molly's perfume. "Wouldn't there be a record of him with the shipping company that fired him?"

"My office ran a check on them, too. They'd gone out of business before the war. All the records were destroyed."

Molly answered, understanding his frustration. Her staff had spent many hours, only to come up so short. "Keep in mind, undercover gets their info from all over. You remember how you used to get info you needed. But we don't have some of it on paper. In black and white. So basically, we are still up shit's creek without a paddle."

"Well, so far, yeah, although, we *are* getting small pieces to add to the picture. Like LaPoshio being tied into this whole shebang, that's helpful."

Molly crossed her leg, revealing a sliver of skin where there was a slit in her skirt. Johnny ran his fingers through his hair and turned away so seamlessly, she wasn't even aware of the reason. "You're right Johnny. That *is* a strong piece. It could be the key to Griff's smuggling. How convenient is it that all of LaPoshio's connections to the docks and laborers are still in place, the ones that reach all the way back to Jimmy and Ralph. Only a few of their guys went to prison. Hopefully the mysterious Miss Orchid can discover who has the power at the docks to bring in a forty-foot boat without suspicion."

"That's your department, yours and Agent Bollinger. That federal stuff is above my pay grade," admitted Johnny. "Keep in mind; not only does that forty-footer have to dock, women and opium have to make it off without being noticed. With the exception of all these bodies that keep popping up, this is one smooth operation."

Molly looked at the watch and stood. "I'll see what else I can find on Ralph and Jimmy and I'll check back with Interpol. You know me, still grasping at straws … or whatever." She gave Johnny a little half smile as she headed out the door.

CHAPTER 61

"Ahoy, Lieutenant," Commander Fred Cunningham greeted the men. "I see you brought your deputy with you this time. If it isn't Billy the Kid Bradshaw. You know, Detective, it really is too bad you threw your arm out. You could have been a great pitcher. You were *this close* to the majors," he said, holding his forefinger and thumb close together. "Where did it happen, the minors for the Giants? Sit down, gents, sit down."

"Thanks for the throw back, no pun intended, Commander. I'm surprised you remember my short-lived career," Billy said. "Not too many do these days. And yes, I was that close."

"I follow the minors a lot. More of a home town feel, not as commercial as the majors."

"You know, shit happens." Billy tried not to dwell on what might have been. "Currently, it's shit like the rash of murders in Chinatown."

Johnny held up his hands in a time-out gesture. "Let's can the radio show, guys. Got a bit more pressing questions than 'This is Your Life.' Fred, we're stuck on how a forty-foot vessel, your estimate for the size needed, can get in and out of the harbor unscathed. We're up to four homicides now, all alluding to the ties of Alvise LaPoshio, our smuggler AKA Griff and a big shot in Chinatown known as Mo China. Any help will be graciously accepted."

"We all know who crime boss Alvise LaPoshio is," Cunningham said. "I'm of the mind that his time is short lived: Live by the sword, die by the sword. But in the meantime, let's jump on a thirty-six-foot life boat and take a spin around the harbor. It's only four feet short of what we spoke about." As they stood to depart, the commander asked, "You guys don't get seasick do you?"

"No, we're both Navy," Billy answered.

"Then you know the drill," he said, handing out life jackets.

Outside, the officer in charge asked where they would be heading.

"I want you to navigate the shore line from the south tip to Fort Tryon Park on the east side of the island, and from the tip on the west side up to Alphabet City. Relax gentlemen; this is going to take a while."

"Fort Tryon Park?" Billy inquired. "That far north?"

"Those 'in the know' say that there are tunnels from downtown leading God-only-knows-where," Cunningham replied, reverting to a friendlier style. "Isn't that right, Johnny?"

"We're aware of them. Our theory is that there'd be too big a risk to unload cargo and people somewhere and then trek all the way back down to Chinatown," Johnny said. "I think we can stop around Hell's Kitchen without touring the west side of the island. Whadda you say Billy?"

Billy agreed, "I second the motion."

"Alright then, Hell's Kitchen it is." Cunningham revised his orders to his crew.

The wind was brisk as the boat sped toward their destination, but it was a warm April afternoon.. Above the howl of the wind and the roar of the engine, Johnny asked how far a forty-footer could get into the shoreline without being docked.

"Depends," Cunningham shouted back. "The pilot, the boat, the tide, sand bars, rip current, wind, if the pilot's experienced with angling the boat. Lot of variables."

"What if the captain's experienced with piloting a freighter?"

Cunningham threw back his head and laughed. "Why didn't you say so? Easy as 1-2-3. Second nature." The boat slowed to avoid a large wake, and Cunningham could speak normally "Driving a boat is like driving a car. Things come to you automatically after a while. If your smuggler's an old freighter captain, this would be a cinch."

"We believe he is. Also that he's a dangerous and ruthless man who won't stop at anything standing in his way," Billy said.

"Our cutters will blow him out of the water, if we find him," Cunningham said, looking up to the task.

Johnny slapped his old friend on the back. "I've no doubt about that, but that wouldn't be good. He may have innocent women on board. Girls. We need to capture him alive. Wounded, sure, but alive."

"Aye, aye, Lieutenant," he saluted Johnny with a grin. "If that can be helped, we will abide."

They'd picked up speed again, so Johnny had to lean in closer to be heard. "So, what are your thoughts of our guy not docking at all, just getting close to shore and dropping his cargo?"

Fred shook his head vehemently. "Not likely. Conditions dictate how a cargo reaches the shore, particularly in waters with temperatures of 32 to 40 degrees. Hypothermia causes exhaustion or unconsciousness in less than fifteen minutes. If these women can't swim, they'd die, at least during winter months. You'd have had a lot more floaters on your hands!"

Billy leaned in on the other side of the commander so that he could hear, too. The commander continued, "I say he docks his forty-footer. We'll pull into every inconspicuous place he would be able to dock under darkness. There are only a few."

The men closed their eyes against the wind and appreciated the sun on their faces. Johnny thought, *If only this was a pleasure boat and we were on our way to a picnic.*

Billy called over to Johnny. "What about LaPoshio controlling the docks? Couldn't he get the boat in anywhere Griff wanted?"

Johnny stretched as he gave it some thought. "Sounds reasonable. But what if he's forced to get into the harbor without LaPoshio's help? We need to know every possible angle."

CHAPTER 62

Johnny had been across the room when the phone rang, and someone picked up in the squad room before he reached it. "Hey, Lieutenant," a distant voice called. "There's a Detective Fang for you on line three."

"Got it! Vero."

"It's Fang. I have information that may be useful, Lieutenant."

Johnny couldn't resist giving a little dig. "Well, well, well. I thought you'd dropped off the face of the earth."

"Lieutenant, you know undercover work. I know you've been there."

Johnny grunted in agreement. "Two years and I begged to be pulled out. Undercover was getting to me. I was raising a daughter by myself, the hours were insane. Sleeping was just an escape from the day before. When I got the transfer to homicide, I've slept like a baby ever since. Tell me you've got something, Jin."

"We may have a leak in the Medical Examiner's office."

"I'm all ears, minus a piece," Johnny said.

Fang laughed softly. "At least you have a sense of humor about it." Then, all business. "It's about Mo China and the note found in Hèng Lìwùshì's mouth. We know that it was found during the autopsy, not at the scene. It must have been designed that way, so that Mo China would find out through a reliable source that it is a real threat. Now it seems that the note is missing from evidence and found its way right to Mo China as proof he might be next. If someone at the ME's office is helping him, he would know it hadn't been planted after the fact just to scare him."

"There are a lot of people who work there," Johnny said angrily. "Dozens!"

"We've been trying to narrow it down but I wanted to keep you up to date. When there's more, you'll be the first to know, I promise. You helped get me in undercover and I am thankful. I want these murders to be solved, too." Abruptly, Fang said, "I have to go." *Click.*

Everyone in the ME's office would have to be interrogated, but before he could think it through further, the phone rang again.

"Lieutenant Vero, how may I help you?"

"Johnny, its Grace. I have that information you asked me about..."

CHAPTER 63

Johnny knew he had to keep Captain Sullivan in the loop but no way was he going to give up all the information he had until the right moment. The Captain preferred to throw it in the face of the mayor and the PC when everything was tied together with a bow, a Christmas present ready to be put under the tree.

Johnny handed a summary to Sullivan. "Captain, here's a brief update on the Chinatown murders."

"Let's have a look, Lieutenant," mumbling as he read:

Four dead bodies are tied into illegal prostitution and opium being smuggled into NYC Harbor. A crime boss, Alvise LaPoshio has ties to entire operation, entry into the harbor, and the distribution of the contraband. Chinatown gangs are involved with boss, Mo China. Three of the victims were connected to a resistance to stop the smuggler. NYPD and FBI both following leads.

Sullivan made a show of throwing the report into his trash basket. "What the fuck am I supposed to do with that? Jesus, Mary, and Joseph, Vero. Do you think the brass is going to say 'What great detective work' to that shit? Grace Tilly could have written this, from what I read in her column. Now the feds are involved! I hate that they'll get the gold for this when it goes down."

Johnny was undeterred. "Not entirely, Captain. We'll eventually get Alvise LaPoshio. The feds get him now, but only him. Mo China, the smuggler, the dock bosses, the Janitor – they all belong to us. After LaPoshio's released from federal prison, we get him on murder. We'll get the recognition ,Captain, don't you worry. I called in some markers."

Sullivan's face was red. "Your *markers* better pay off." He blew out a deep breath, the color in his face returning to normal. "Somehow, Vero, you always come out on top. Your old man must be looking down on you. You better ask him to give you more direction or something, though. I can only cover for you for so long." When Johnny said nothing, Sullivan exploded again. "Now get out! Go solve something!"

CHAPTER 64

After a few scheduling conflicts, Johnny was able to meet Grace for breakfast at the Crosstown Diner.

As he walked in, Grace waved her hand, calling, "Hey, Johnny, over here."

"Thanks for meeting me, Grace." Johnny slid into the booth facing her. After an awkward silence, they both started to speak at the same time, stopped, and smiled. The awkward silence returned. "Ladies first, Grace."

"You were always thoughtful like that, Johnny, letting me go first. You know… wanting me to finish first." She gave him a little wink; he responded by crossing his arms over his overcoat. "Anyway, the ad for the janitor is being placed by a woman, maybe forty or forty-five years old."

"Chinese?"

"No, but always the same woman. It cost me, you know, to get that information. But I don't want anything in return." Grace's eyes dropped. "I guess in some ways I owe you."

This was a good lead. "Thanks, Grace," Johnny said. "How does she pay? Does she leave a name or address?"

"Always cash. She just walks in, fills out the information card. And she tips the clerk before leaving. The newspaper doesn't care about details as long as ads are sold," she said.

"However, I *was* told that the woman's well-dressed. Hat, gloves, the whole nine yards." She smiled. "I hope this helps you, Johnny."

It was his turn to smile. "It does. A lot. Someone real's attached to those ads. Now I just have to find the face that goes with it. Any chance of getting one of those forms she handled, you know, for finger prints?"

Underneath the table, Grace's bare foot slipped beneath the cuff of his trousers and slowly moved upward, then downward again, back and forth as she spoke. "Maybe. But that might cost you more than a cup of coffee. You know, *quid pro quo*. I'm a scorpion that bites, remember?"

"I guess I'll have to stay open to that possibility, Grace." Both fell silent as the waitress brought their coffee.

Grace removed her foot and seemed to be fumbling around for her shoe. "Isn't this the diner your friend Audrey worked at before her accident?"

"Yes," Johnny said. Memories. "Death is tragic, no matter the age, but she was much too young."

Grace sipped her coffee. "I'm sorry about that." She looked up at him. "I know you were seeing her, Marlene, and me at the same time. Regardless how I felt about that, I feel for her. For her short life and her family's loss. Your loss as well. 'What might have been.' I'll let you know if any other information becomes available." She leaned in to give him a kiss along with a close-up view of her ample cleavage, as she slid out her booth. "Don't get up. Thanks for the coffee. I'll let you know about that form so we can work out your payment. I'm always here if you need to call me."

"Grace...."

Grace silenced his words with her finger. She picked up her purse, walked out the door, and was gone.

CHAPTER 65

The elevator up to Agent Bollinger's office was crowded, not that Johnny and Molly minded. They had successfully maneuvered into a corner, where Johnny could feel Molly's breasts pressing into his back with complete discretion. Detectives Bradshaw, Fang, Chang, and Pan were also aboard.

Agent Bollinger had set up for the group in a larger conference room. He opened the discussion with a little speech of welcome. "Thank you all for coming. I believe we have all met, with the exception of…"

Interrupting, Detective Ru Chang and Detective Jimmy Pan introduced themselves.

Bollinger continued, standing at one end of the room, facing those seated around the massive table. Someone near the door turned off the lights. "Let's get started. As you see on the screen, we have surveillance pictures. We've also got tape recordings we can listen to – Alvise LaPoshio and some of his cohorts. We'll begin with photos. We've been trying to nail LaPoshio for quite a while. This first photo was taken outside LaPoshio's coffee shop with his cousins, Ralph Mariozo and Jimmy Enrizzi. We all know what happened to these two, Ralph and Jimmy." Larger than life, the photo was projected onto a large white screen. Bollinger used a wooden pointer to identify the men. "So much for family love." The slide carousel jumped to the next selection, operated in the rear of the room by another agent. "The next photo is that of the union boss, Carmine Catalina, AKA Fat Cat." You can see by the size of this guy why he got that nickname." Bollinger enjoyed having an audience. "Not only does his name begin with CAT, he has to walk into elevators sideways!"

The group politely chuckled, although Billy issued a little groan.

"The next one is of an unidentified woman coming out of the hotel with LaPoshio. They're about to get into a limousine. In every picture we take, she has her coat collar up or she's holding her hand up high, covering her face, waving to someone. The two goons are LaPoshio's guys. They frequently block a full view of her face. This last one is of LaPoshio outside his coffee shop. Just before getting into his big ass Cadillac with his bodyguards, look at the colored guy he's talking to. Look at his face and that scar across his neck."

Another click of the carousel, and the screen went blank. "We need to focus on the colored guy with the scar, and Carmine Catalina."

"What about the woman?" Detective Pan asked. "Our surveillance noted hookers of different hair colors, and one who may or may not be Chinese, who only showed up during the day. This one could be she."

"We're not really concerned with her now, Detective," Agent Bollinger, answered. "Before we listen to the tape recordings, does anyone recognize anyone in the photos?"

Detective Pan said, "The colored guy is from South America. From Guyana. He would not be considered colored there. We do believe he is our smuggler."

Molly chimed in, "We believe he is known as Griff."

"Since we know that LaPoshio's cousins are out of the picture and we have some idea who the Griff guy is, we need to focus on Catalina," suggested Johnny. "But has there been any other surveillance on the woman?"

Bollinger did not disguise his annoyance. "As I said the last time, she's not our focus right now, Lieutenant. She's either a well-hidden secret with ties to the Chinatown faction which LaPoshio is bullying his way into, or maybe she's a high-priced call girl. That's our best guess. You could see how nicely dressed she was, and he has many women going and coming. But again, she is not our focus. As far as Carmine 'Fat Cat' Catalina goes, he is the guy with the say-so at the docks. He could get the smuggler into the harbor undetected. I'm asking for your undercover operation to help dig up more." It sounded like more than a request.

Detective Chang had weighed all of the information quietly. "This Griff guy appears and disappears like a lightning bolt. We have a pretty good idea that whoever that woman is, she's not part of any faction. No one feeding us information mentioned her. Neither victim one nor three, who were working with us as civilian snitches, ever mentioned another woman."

"So, let's put her to rest right now, if we all agree that the woman is nothing more than one of *Al Pazzo*'s prostitutes and concentrate on the others," Molly said, trying to move things along.

Bollinger wasn't prepared to close the door completely. "We really are not sure," he interjected. "We just can't assume. That's why we need your cooperation. Combining our teams would keep us from overstepping, or duplicating our efforts in a wasteful manner."

Detective Pan said, "The goons with the woman. I'm pretty sure I recognize them. They may have records of petty crimes, maybe misdemeanors."

"It would be hard to get a license to carry a gun if they do," Billy said.

Molly pulled out a pen and notepad from her purse. "Maybe not. LaPoshio has a lot of connections and who knows who's on the take. Names?"

"We'd have to verify, but I'm almost certain they're both ex-prize fighters. Joey Tremont and Bobby Hoffman, both from the Bronx. They used the names of the streets they lived on. I don't know their real names," continued Pan.

"Got it. I'll run sheets on them too."

Bollinger took charge again. "Let's listen to some of the tape recordings we have from bugs we planted in the coffee shop. The quality is iffy on some of them, very scratchy. The first tape is LaPoshio giving Catalina instructions about paying off dock workers to dock Griff's boat. Here we go...."

CHAPTER 66

Being summoned to the DA's office, Johnny left Billy behind to motivate the squad. *We need to solve these murders so Molly and I can get into a normal kind of routine,* he thought. But it had been so long. What *was* a normal routine?

Johnny tapped on the door, which he had found ajar, and stepped in without waiting. "So, Molly, what's the big hoopla about this time? Anything concrete we can sink our teeth into?" Johnny rubbed his hands together. "The serial killer case last year took us to France. So what? Are we flying to Guyana next?" He sank into a chair. "Jeez, the Budapest came along faster than this one."

Molly leaned back in her chair, enjoying the view. "Well, our serial killer used his intelligence to try and fool us with Biblical codification. This time there's no systematic code to go by, is there? Just plain fucking greed, power, who will have control. My office is just as frustrated with this as you are, believe me. Be thankful you don't have the brass calling you every other day." Molly rested her elbows on the desk and leaned on her hands with a pouty look, fluttering her eyelashes seductively. "So, I suggest that you and your squad hit the streets and fucking pound your snitches." She laughed and sat up, all business once again. "Maybe a few arrests will shake the trees."

Johnny was pensive. "Yes, I'm frustrated with the case. But more than that – I don't want police business to get in the way of our relationship. I value what we've got, where we've reached in our … journey. I don't want to jeopardize it."

Molly was surprised, even touched. "I'm happy to hear you say that, Johnny. A woman wonders. I...I feel the same way." She stood up behind her desk. "So let's establish this right here and now. Any police business that pits us together – regardless of any accompanying yelling, cursing, or giving you orders as the DA – is just that: business. I can deal with our relationship on two different levels, and I hope you can too."

Johnny nodded. "I can too. Thank you. It's nice to get things out in the open, so neither of us needs to wonder."

Molly walked around the desk and leaned her back against it in front of his chair. "Well, as your DA, I'm telling you to work harder on the outside relationship aspect," she said, their eyes locked in a shared understanding.

That took him off guard. "I will, Molly."

Molly sighed, back to the task at hand. "Alright, let's review what I have on the people we saw at Bollinger's office," she said, returning to her desk. "First up is Carmine 'Fat Cat' Catalina. Italian from Italy, same area as Ralph Mariozo, 'Jimmy the Rat' Enrizzi, and of course, the man of the hour, LaPoshio. Not a relation this time, but a *paisano*, a goombah, a friend." She looked up at him. "I'll have to teach you Italian, Johnny." Back to the file. "He came here years ago, with the promise that he'd be put in charge of the dock workers union; there's nothing from Interpol on him. Quiet life according to our surveillance, divorced with one daughter. His ex- and the daughter live up in Washington Heights. And we have nothing more on Mariozo or Enrizzi."

Molly was just getting started. "I was able to run backgrounds on the two goons Detective Pan pointed out. It was easier because they still hold boxing licenses. Tough guys from the Bronx in the Fordham area. Both are Italian, which makes sense. Very few outsiders – Irish, Germans, Jews – come into LaPoshio's fold. They took the names of their streets for their professional names, like Pan said. Joseph Vani – probably shortened from something else when his family came over, same as mine – lived on Tremont Avenue, hence Joey Tremont. The other bodyguard is Bobby Hoffman, formerly Roberto Caserta from Hoffman Street. Both used their real names on their gun licenses. Both have clean records. Oh, and Bobby is also known as 'Bobby Shoes' in the world of boxing."

"Oh, yeah!" Johnny exclaimed. "I remember him. Of course, Bobby Shoes. He was flamboyant, wore a pair of colored shoes every time he fought. Pretty good, too. Southpaw. I followed his fights – it's interesting that he and Joey never fought each other. I bet they trained at the same gym."

"They both bounced around. Boxers are easily exploited. These two have worked for other mobsters too. But apparently once they connected, wherever they moved, they moved together."

"It's like working with a partner, like me and Billy these few years. You learn each other's moves, get into each other's heads."

"According to our surveillance neither Tremont nor Hoffman has family nearby. They pretty much stay with

LaPoshio everywhere he goes, including to his hotel. They share a small room right across the hall."

"That's odd, don't you think? Why do they keep a room there?"

"No, they live there full-time, courtesy of LaPoshio. Every once in a while they'll get hookers. All part of the job. LaPoshio doesn't want them far away. End of story. So, these two are nothing to write home about. It's the ole' Fat Cat and whoever he's paying off for the docks we need to look into. The mystery woman is secondary at this point, don't you agree?"

"Yeah. Where do we go from here?"

Molly looked at her watch. *Everyone should have left by now.* Getting up to lock the door, Molly said, "I know where *I* would like to go. Do you know where *you* want to go, Johnny?" She draped herself playfully across his lap. "Now, don't lay any of that Jewish mother guilt on me. I know, I know, 'My mother isn't Jewish!' Now follow me to that couch and start undressing me. We've got to work on that secondary relationship you agreed to."

Johnny's head was spinning, trying to put two and two together but always coming up with a different number. *This woman's driving me nuts!* But in decidedly a good way, he had to admit. Molly, sprawled on the couch in a most non-District Attorney position, layback in wild anticipation of the lust that was about to consume her.

CHAPTER 67

Yet another phone call to interrupt the day. "Homicide, Detective Vero."

"It's Jin." His voice was low, and he spoke rapidly. "We have a strong lead on the opium den I told you about. We're going to pull a raid at midnight tonight. Do you want in? We got a tip that Mo China may be there, but there's no guarantee. I want you to understand that. It might be a big zero."

Johnny didn't need time to decide. "Count us in. Me and Billy will be there. Just tell me where to meet you. All the tea in China won't keep us from this."

"I get it, Lieutenant."

Johnny was the type to make sure all the T's were crossed and all the I's dotted. "No offense Jin, but you've got all your back-up in place? You don't need anything from me?"

"No, we're good. Here's the address. Are you ready?"

CHAPTER 68

Billy turned the unmarked car onto Mosco Street. Any address within the notorious Five Points section was likely to be socially and morally offensive. Very little of a legal nature transpired there. The Old Brewery building was close by. Between his own history and this case, Johnny knew the area well. Quietly, they left the relative safety of their vehicle to meet Detective Fang and his entourage of armed officers.

Being vigilant and keeping one hand on their firearms, they approached a particular passageway known as Murderer's Alley, the agreed-upon rendezvous point. Even at midnight, the bees were buzzing on Mosco Street. Shops were still open with shopkeepers sitting near the doorways. What, exactly, everyone was doing at the witching hour was indiscernible, but they were doing plenty of something.

Approaching the target building, Detective Fang signaled to move forward following his men. All were dressed in civilian clothes so as not to arouse suspicion. The entrance to the building was ground level, with a steep staircase leading to floors above. Fang held up one hand showing five fingers. A single finger on the other hand pointed up. They had a climb, then, all the way to the fifth floor. All are

With Fang was on point, the climb was fast. With every flight of stairs, the air became heavier with the delicious odor of mystic temple incense, heralding their destination – the opium den. When they reached the fifth floor, weapons drawn, badges pinned, all seven police officers moved quickly, expecting to bust down a door.

To their surprise, there was no door. Open 24 hours, every day, people came and went continuously. A door was deemed unnecessary, so confident were those who ran it and frequented it. An elderly Chinese man stood at the ready to take each patron's order and payment before escorting him (or her) to a vacant bed or carpet. Approaching the man in silence, Fang put his finger to his lips and whispered, "Mo China, Zài nail?"

Sheepishly, the man pointed. Paid mostly in opium, he no longer had the strength or desire for conflict.

Although not as posh as the opium dens one might find in San Francisco, this one obviously catered to a clientele with means. The women lounging in a drug-induced daze were dressed in silk robes or in their Sunday best, as if on the way to a bar-be-que after church. As the men snaked their way to find their target, they couldn't help but notice that a few women lay naked, oblivious. These were there for a more nefarious purpose. Absorbed in their personal pipe dreams, they didn't even register the presence of several men dressed in suits and ties, waiting for their turns. The perfumed aroma emanating from the opium masked the stench of cheap, stale, illegal sex.

As soon as they were all inside, they saw through a darkened glass partition, a flashing red light. Evidently the wizened doorman had flipped a warning switch that went on outside Mo China's private room. Such a system would, should just this circumstance arise, give him extra time to escape. For now, the police ignored the drugs and prostitution. All they wanted was Mo China.

Hearts pounding, minds racing, knowing that a split second could change life forever, Fang kicked in the door and the men charged the room.

A small doorway in the back led to an escape route. Mo China's bodyguard opened fire to protect Mo China as he made his getaway. The well-trained officers took cover, turning over couches and tables, whatever was near, before firing back, but the bodyguard and his meal ticket had fled the room.

Flashlight beams followed the exit. Fang, still in the lead, could make out a hallway, an open window, and a fire escape. Suddenly, Mo China's bodyguard stepped out of a shadow in the alleyway below and fired, hitting Fang. He went down, but continued to fire a few rounds before collapsing completely.

Swaying from the weight of the officers stepping onto it, the rickety metal steps undoubtedly saved them from more injuries. Fang, they would attend to when they could. The men rushed down to street level, dodging the bodyguard's fire; Mo China was nowhere to be seen. Seeing the numbers, the bodyguard revealed himself as he began running down the street in a serpentine motion, aimlessly shooting behind him,

Billy, always meticulous when it came to shooting, allowed himself a second to carefully take aim, calmly pulling the trigger on his police issued .38 snub nose special as he caught the pattern of the escaping thug. An expert, he fired not where the perpetrator was, but where he was headed. A single bullet hit him in the head, killing him instantly.

Early in Billy's career he had fired his weapon once, only to have the perp surrender without harm. Standing in the cold, dark alley, he knew this was going to be different. Mo China had slipped through their fingers, unscathed. And Billy the Kid Bradshaw had just killed a man. He wondered how long it would be before the DA, Captain Sullivan, the Commissioner, and Internal Affairs would reach the scene.

The Lieutenant

CHAPTER 69

Johnny and Billy knelt by the bodyguard. Fang applied pressure to his left arm and grimaced in pain. "Fang, I'm in charge here now. Mo China got away... this time." He instructed one of the undercover officers to check the shooter for a pulse. He did so, and shook his head. Johnny called to the others in a low voice in case others might be listening from open windows. "Okay, everyone listen up. He's dead, but we're not. Billy, are you okay?"

"I'm good. Don't worry about me."

"Everyone over here now!" Johnny said in a fierce whisper. "It's a good thing this alley was empty without onlookers, but this was a clean shoot. Jin, this was your party, call it in." He looked around at the men, still breathing hard from the adrenaline rush. "You all know the routine. Kick his gun close to his body. Billy, you don't say a word except to request a GO-15 and ask for the PBA lawyer when IA, the DA, and the brass arrive. Everyone start making entries in your memo books *now* without talking to each other. We all saw how it happened. The perp was firing at us, trying to kill any one of us. And he shot a cop."

Stepping closer to the body, avoiding the puddle of oozing blood from his head, Johnny whistled softly and held something up in the moonlight. "Well, looky here. Two guns. One in his waistband, one next to him on the ground. So, he had plenty of ammo. Be sure to include that you saw two guns. Jin, have one of your men get crime scene tape from their car and set up a perimeter. Rapidly, men! Finish your notes, then start look for shell casings." Johnny quickly wiped the gun before returning it to the body, distracted by Billy's look of dread.

Billy could see the silhouette of a suited man walking toward them from the street. "Ah shit! Jesus Christ! IA's here already?" Billy had hoped for a little longer to gather himself.

Johnny poked him in the chest. "Just *remember*. You know the routine. It was a clean shot. You saved us. There are six of us behind you, Billy. We got your back."

The Disquiet

CHAPTER 70

Johnny was clearly agitated. "Billy's shooting shouldn't go to the Grand Jury. It was clean, no question about it," he said to Molly.

"I know, but it's procedure," Molly said, concerned. "The court is reluctant to criminalize police behavior, and the report from Internal Affairs said he was justified, fit for duty, had not been drinking. His weapon checked out. All the detectives' reports back up his account." Her eyes were probing. "Johnny, *your* print came back on one of the guns." She checked the report on her desk. "Let's see. The report indicates it was on the weapon found in the perpetrator's waistband." She looked up, genuinely worried. "How do you think it got there, Johnny? The Grand Jury may ask about it or it may not. Just be prepared if you're called."

"It probably was when I…"

"Stop. Don't tell me!" Molly exclaimed, holding up her hands. "I don't want to know. The Grand Jury can only call the witnesses. The judge favors wide discretion for officers to use whatever force is deemed necessary to protect themselves and the public. It'll be okay. Billy still has to have a psych evaluation and be cleared." She flapped a hand in his direction. "You know the drill."

Johnny could pout with the best of them, especially when it concerned his partner. "He's on mandatory desk duty until his 'mental stability' is cleared, whatever the fuck that means. I need him, Molly! I need him on the street with me, free of this bullshit!"

"At least he's not out on administration leave. *Use* him on the desk to free up your time to investigate. As soon as the Grand Jury convenes and his psych report is in, I'll push for him to get back on the street." Molly softened. "No criminal charges, no indictment brought. Isn't that good news? Now Detective, what do you say we call it a day, go to dinner and who knows, maybe a nightcap at my place?"

CHAPTER 71

"Johnny, I need to talk to you. Like *now*. Privately." Billy and Johnny were getting refills on their coffee after the morning briefing, but other detectives milled around.

Johnny frowned. "You never ask to talk. You usually just blurt stuff out, or keep it all in. Let's go," Johnny agreed, leading Billy back to the office. He pulled the door shut behind them.

The men stood there for a second. "I'm all ears Billy, well almost," he smiled, reaching up to pull on the mangled remnants of the tunnel attack. What's going on? Molly says you've got nothing to worry about."

Billy squirmed uncomfortably. "Johnny, remember I told you that Nancy wanted me to put in for my time and join her in the manufacturing business?" He stood straighter. "I'm seriously considering it."

Johnny exploded, causing a few of the officers on the other side of the door to look in that direction, grateful their own asses weren't getting chewed this time. "Wait a fucking minute, Billy. You love being a cop, you told me so yourself. Not that you needed to. This is your career, man! I can't even imagine how you feel about shooting that scumbag you shot, but just remember that. He *was* a scumbag. You took him off the streets and because of that, you may have saved countless innocent women's lives, civilians' lives, maybe even some of your brothers in blue."

Johnny was getting worked up and he began to pace. "He worked for Mo China! That whole mess, them, LaPoshio, the Janitor – they're evil. If they have to all get clipped, so be it. One down, the rest to go. They're bottom feeders, Billy." Johnny got up in Billy's face, and his voice dropped. "Don't go soft on me, Billy. Or on yourself. You told me, Billy. *You* told me: 'What am I going to do all day, sit behind a desk in a factory?' *You* said that. Don't you remember?"

"I know, I know, it's just that –"

Johnny interrupted harshly. "What do you know, Billy? What?! Do you know that if you do this now, you'll probably be divorced in a couple of years because you'll be miserable? You'll blame Nancy. I give it a year before no matter how much more money you've made, the two of you will be arguing every day." Johnny remembered those days. "You'll drift apart. And finally, you'll go your separate ways."

Billy nodded sadly. "I understand what you're saying Johnny. What's haunting me isn't the shooting, it's the Grand Jury. It's staying behind a desk all day. I'm too young for that." He pounded a fist into the other hand. "*I'm too good a cop for that, Johnny!*"

Johnny put an arm around his shoulder. "Molly assured me that her office is doing all they can. You're not as far away as you think, for your twenty years. Don't blow it, Billy. You earned your pension and benefits. I've never been in your shoes, and honestly, I hope I never am. But if it makes you feel any better, I wish I would've clipped him myself." Johnny rubbed his chin back and forth. "We're all going to bat for you with the Grand Jury. And I believe Molly – you've got nothing to worry about. All the witnesses are ours. It was a clean shoot. And Molly, the mayor, the PC – all of them advocate for necessary use of force." He glanced at his watch. "For now, though, I need you to keep things running smooth here and be our gumshoe at the desk." He looked at his partner, his friend. He'd killed a man. "Do you want to take some time off?"

"*Shit* no! Billy exclaimed. "That would for sure send me into a straitjacket."

Johnny slapped him on the arm. "See, you just answered your own doubts. The Grand Jury is only a few days from now." He paused. "My errand can wait; let's grab an early lunch."

CHAPTER 72

Johnny rolled his neck from side to side as he answered the phone. "Vero."

"Hi, Johnny, its Grace,"

Johnny groaned inwardly but he kept his voice casual. "Grace! To what do I owe the pleasure?"

"You owe me *my* pleasure – remember you asked a favor of me? I have that favor for you now. Which means that I want to collect my fee, Scorpion that I am."

Johnny fumed. "That's extortion, Gra – "

"Call it what you want. I call it *quid pro quo.*"

There was an awkward silence, with only the sound of breathing at either end of the line.

"Lieutenant, are you still there?" Grace asked suspiciously.

"Yesss, I'm here," he hissed. "I can't discuss this over the phone. Meet me at the Crosstown Diner in the morning."

Grace was jubilant. "What I have ,Johnny, is what you need. We spoke about all this before and if I recall, it was at the Crosstown Diner, too. See you in the morning, Johnny." *Click.*

Son of a bitch! I need what she has, to help break this case. I can feel it. She knows what she has is crucial. Molly's face flashed before his eyes, which he closed, shutting the vision out. *It's just paying an informant. We do it all the time. Pay cash to the snitch, sure. Except it's not cash she wants. Goddamn, you Grace!*

CHAPTER 73

Johnny was so *tense,* standing there in her bedroom. "C'mon, Johnny, loosen up," Grace cooed. "Make yourself comfortable. I know I'm going to. It's not like this is our first time." The sound of his fly being unzipped punctuated the quiet of the room as she moved to her knees in front of him. *With Molly, there would be jazz playing. With Molly ...* Grace's tongue was experienced, soft, and warm, encouraging him to grow, to harden. He couldn't deny that it felt great.

Suddenly, she pulled away so that he wouldn't cum just yet. She had other plans. Slowly she began to undress him. *I can't seem to move or is it – I don't want to. It's like an invisible thread connects me to her and I can't break it. I'm no different than Orchid, bedding the enemy for my own purposes.*

Pushing Johnny down on the bed, Grace took off her clothes, fully aware that Johnny's eyes were anywhere but on her nudity. Fully in charge, Grace took his hand and placed it between her legs. "Feel my energy, lover," she whispered. Johnny had always admired how lovely Grace was with her short brown bob. He closed his eyes. *She's not as beautiful as Molly.*

Grace released his hand and turned her back as she mounted him from the rear, guiding him into her with her thighs, beginning a slow rotation of her hips as she lowered slowly onto his full length. With her buttocks facing him, his hands instinctively reached to hold her stomach and thighs. She arched her back as she eased out, then back in in perfect rhythm. It was like a symphony. He couldn't believe he'd never felt this sensation before, not with any of the women he'd been with, not even Molly. This was *heaven*.

Johnny pushed her off and rolled her over in one frantic motion, to enter her from the front, pumping wildly, sending the bed into a series of squeaks and creaks. Grace's breath was short between words that were almost gasped in their intensity. "Yes … yes … right *there*. Don't stop! Oh my God!" Her hands moved to her breasts, rotating and squeezing her nipples to heighten her own pleasure. "*That's* it, Johnny. OHHhhh..."

Grace's commentary was simple, but it excited him profoundly as he gave way to his climax.

Released, he lay on her without moving. She stroked his back with her short, polished nails. "Oh Johnny, you feel so good inside." She sighed. "You are by far the best lover I've ever had. And I've had a few."

He raised his head. "Grace...."

"I know. You earned it. Just give me a moment to treasure this." She kept stroking his back, and could feel him beginning to grow inside her again. But a deal was a deal. She pushed him away and stood up. "I keep reminding you, I'm a Scorpion. I may have to steal you away from Molly, you know."

"Grace, I –"

Laughing, she sauntered down the hallway. "Hold that thought, I have to pee and then I'll get what you came for. Haha. Get it? *Came* for?"

The bathroom door closed, and Johnny rolled over onto his back, feeling like a complete heel. Used. A user. *Whatever she's got had better be worth it.*

Good News is Always Good

CHAPTER 74

Over the past few days, some things had fallen into place, and more quickly than any progress thus far. Johnny had received the information he'd requested from the police lab, but he hadn't had time to give it more than a cursory glance before heading back to the Grand Jury. Several index cards handled by the person placing the ad for 'janitor wanted' had been processed. *Grace really came through. Wait until I tell Molly. Well, some of it.*

After two days of testimony, the Grand Jury was expected to bring in a verdict that afternoon. He couldn't fathom why he hadn't been questioned as the very first witness, day one, since his fingerprints were on the perp's second gun. He felt a bit smug about this, but kept his face blank as he stepped from the elevator. Waiting in the hallway outside the courtroom were Molly, Billy, Nancy, and Captain Sullivan. Billy was pacing a little.

"How're you holding up Billy?" Johnny asked.

"I told him everything should be good," Molly answered for him. She noticed Johnny's restrained expression. "You look like the cat that ate the canary. What do you have?"

Just then a bell rang and the light above the Grand Jury door was illuminated. Billy stopped pacing,

All eyes were glued to the door, which opened swiftly. The court clerk stepped out and handed the decision paper to Molly as everyone gathered around her.

Her hands were shaking a little, despite her confidence, but she couldn't open it fast enough. "NO BILL!" she exclaimed. "The Grand Jury does not have sufficient cause for finding a TRUE BILL," she squealed a little. "In other words, NOT GUILTY!

Billy embraced Nancy with a sigh of relief as everyone congratulated him and gave him thumps on the back.

Molly beamed. "Billy, go. You and Nancy enjoy the rest of the day. You're all right with that, aren't you?" she asked Sullivan.

"Yes, of course," replied Sullivan. Had they found otherwise, it would have been a black eye on his bureau's face. This was his victory, as well as Billy's.

As Sullivan walked with the Bradshaws to the elevator, Molly grabbed Johnny by the sleeve. "What do you have for me? I know that smirk. And I may just have to find a way to remove it," she said with a smile. Leaning in conspiratorially, she said quietly, "You may have dodged a bullet with the Grand Jury, Johnny Vero – and you know why – but you won't dodge mine." More loudly, as passersby noticed the handsome detective and the beautiful District Attorney talking shop, "Let's discuss this further in my office, shall we?"

CHAPTER 75

"Okay, Johnny," Molly began, office door closed and locked as she leaned in to give him a kiss. "Now that I've removed that simper from your face, tell me what it's all about."

Johnny was glad he could finally tell her. "I got the original index card forms that were filled out for the Janitor's ads."

"Holy shit!" Molly exclaimed "That's great! How did you get them?"

Johnny had hoped to avoid a lot of questions, and stammered a bit.

Molly kissed away the words. "Oh, never mind. Part of being a detective is not revealing your snitches." Molly rubbed her hands on his chest. "But I'll bet I can guess where. And who."

"Molly, you know I can't play that game."

Dropping her hands, she returned to her desk and sat down. "Well? Are you going to tell me or we will be playing *my* game?"

"The prints came back. Thankfully the woman spotted taking out the ads has an arrest record. But I still haven't put it all together as to the 'why.'"

"Who is it? Whose fucking prints are on those forms?" Molly demanded, slamming her hand on her desk.

"I love it when you talk dirty," he said, handing Molly the incriminating arrest record. Name, photo, prints.

"Oh my God!" Molly shrieked with excitement. "I'll get a judge to issue an arrest warrant immediately."

CHAPTER 76

An afternoon off would have been nice, but Nancy had to get back to work, so what was the fun of that? Besides, things were moving, finally. Now that Billy had cleared both the Grand Jury and psychiatric hurdles, he and Johnny headed to the Nostalgia Café where they knew they'd find the subject of their arrest warrant seated at the bar.

Monica was surprised to see them. Her eyes locked with Johnny's. "Well, boys, to what do I owe the pleasure?" Monica asked nervously.

Johnny didn't want to make a scene, but he was willing. "Monica, put your hands behind your back. You're under arrest for conspiracy and collusion to murder," he stated matter-of-factly.

Monica was confused. "What're you talking about? You *owe* me. You and Billy used my girls and I turned my back."

"Better get yourself an attorney," Billy said, dangling his cuffs in front of her face. "That was a different lifetime. One thing has nothing to do with the other."

Johnny shook his head at Billy, who put the cuffs back into his pocket. "We found your fingerprints all over the forms used to place ads for the criminal known as the Janitor. Ads that resulted in multiple murders."

Monica was furious. "You owe me and that *wasn't* a different lifetime, *Detective*. You don't know who you're dealing with here, and I don't mean me. This is deeper than you think," she hissed, writhing as if to break free. "Stop looking at the trees, Johnny. There's a whole forest standing there. Let me go and I'll tell you ev –"

"Oh, you'll tell us, all right," Billy sneered. "You've crossed the line, Monica. We're talking *murder*. And maybe some other charges to piggy back on that."

"What charges?" Monica asked. She looked around the room. It was early, so there were few patrons. The bartender had seen it all before, and kept himself busy at the other end of the bar.

"Aiding and Abetting, old friend. Smuggling, murder, prostitution, drug dealing, and human trafficking," Johnny said.

Monica began to cry, hardly able to speak through the tears and runny nose. "I had to Johnny, I can explain, I need your help. Please help me. *They'll kill me!*" Furtively, she looked around the room again. She seemed genuinely frightened.

"As a courtesy, I won't cuff you yet. And I'm sure we can work something out with the DA to help you reduce your charges," soothed Johnny. "But know this, Monica: If you bullshit me, I'll pin your ass to the wall with no mercy. No mercy."

Despite her sobs, Monica flashed a weak grin for old time's sake. "You know Johnny. That sounds kind of exciting."

"Monica, you are what they call 'incorrigible,'" Billy said, leading the woman outside the bar into the hotel lobby that led to the street. "But you better get serious quickly. Screw up, and we can have two uniformed officers curbside in minutes to transport you to South Central, where you'll be booked on all charges." He looked at her expression. "And don't even say anything about *screwing*, just keep moving."

"Can't we just go to my room to talk?"

"Not a good idea, Monica. Is there any other place we can go?"

"I can use the office behind the bar," Monica said nervously, suddenly realizing her predicament. "I can't have anyone seeing us talking, either."

"Lead the way," said Johnny.

Monica nodded slighted to the bartender as they passed, getting his tacit permission to keep heading to the office. Billy whispered to Johnny, "I hope you know what you're doing. I *need* this job."

There were some cheap folding chairs in a rough semi-circle; the three sat down. Monica breathed deeply before starting. "Look, I never wanted to get involved with all of this. I just wanted to live a simple life with my girls, keeping us happy and fed. I minded my own business. You know how I feel about things, Johnny. Prostitution and gambling should be legal. I don't like operating behind closed doors."

Johnny was losing patience. "I don't have time to go fishing today. Just like you, we gotta do what we gotta do."

"Okay, okay. I'm fucked either way. By you – a girl can dream – or by them, not so much. I am so fucked!" Monica wailed, the tears running again in torrents down her face. "I am so fucked! Oh God." She took a deep breath. "Here goes…"

CHAPTER 77

Molly made a special trip to South Central so that she could hear firsthand what the street arrests were saying. Detectives Jin Fang, Jimmy Pan, and Ru Chang had brought in three individuals, and they had no qualms about striking deals. They were ready to go to prison, rather than be deported back to China to face the direr consequences of their disgrace.

Molly couldn't believe it when she stepped into an interrogation room. The three men were cuffed together spouting Chinese gibberish back and forth. "Goddamn it! Separate these men now and put them in separate rooms. Take turns questioning them!" Molly showed her disgust. "Yes, it will take longer, and no, I do *not* care."

The detectives scrambled quickly.

"What the hell is going on here?" Johnny asked. All he could hear was six raised voices talking loudly in Chinese. When Molly threw up her hands in disgust, he smirked, "Welcome to my world, Miss Penett."

"Jesus Christ!" Molly mumbled. "You'd think they'd know to keep them separate."

Detective Fang, his arm still in a sling from the gunshot wound, was embarrassed at the corporate error. "The good news, Miss Penett, is that all three say the same thing. Our smuggler gets into the harbor via a payoff to someone known only to them as Fat Cat. The payoff goes to someone on Mott Street. Mo China wanted the smuggler to pay him, but someone Hēishèhuì zhōng zuì yǒu quánshì de rén..."

Molly rolled her eyes. "Really, Detective?"

Fang gave a little bow. "So sorry, Miss Penett. ' Most powerful person, like tiger, in criminal underground who is in charge gets the payment.' We know who that is on Mott Street," Fang translated.

"Alvise LaPoshio," Molly whispered. "Book 'em, Detective. I'll speak to the judge. No bail!" As the detectives led the suspects out, Molly grabbed Johnny's arm and glared. "Explain to me what kind of fucking deal you made with Monica before consulting me!"

Johnny had hoped she would understand the value of Monica's information. "I know you're upset –"

Molly was incensed. "Upset! *Upset?* You can't even imagine how upset I am. Now I have to go before the judge, get the warrant quashed and probably reissued later. Judges come down hard for this kind of shit, and I don't blame them." Molly's beautiful features were twisted with anger. "This had better not ruin my chances in politics down the road, I'll tell you that."

Johnny was momentarily dumbfounded. That's *certainly something new,* he thought. His surprise was difficult to disguise.

Molly planted her hands on her hips. "Don't tell me you don't want to move on to Captain or Chief or Commissioner!"

Johnny shook his head. "Actually, no I don't. I was thinking about spending... more time..." he hesitated, trying to read her, mouthing the words "... with you."

She gasped. He was so sincere. It was mesmerizing, exciting. She felt warm all over, fighting an almost overwhelming urge to kiss him right there in front of God and everyone at South Central Headquarters. For once, she was tongue-tied.

Johnny leaned in, concerned. Her face was pale, and she seemed to be trying to talk, but nothing was coming out. She just stood there gaping, like a beautiful exotic fish. "Are you, okay?" he whispered.

Molly shook herself a little and sighed. She had to get hold of herself. "It's already 6 p.m." she said, grabbing his hand and closing his fingers around something small and hard. A key.

"What's this?" Johnny asked.

"What does it look like, Einstein? It's a key to my place," Molly said, back to herself. "I was waiting for the right time to give it to you. You should bring a change of clothes to leave there. You can't be wearing the same thing the next day." She gathered her things. "Take your time; I'll be there waiting with Coleman Hawkins, and a brand new bottle of Old Crow."

As she vanished down the hallway, Johnny's head was spinning. *What is this? What are we? infatuation, admiration, lust? Could it be love?*

A Discommode

CHAPTER 78

After getting the detectives on track with the three thugs, and a long day in the courtroom, Molly couldn't wait to get home, take a hot bath, and wait for Johnny to get there. At least she hoped he'd be over, using his key for the first time. Just about to push the button for her floor on the elevator, a hand grabbed the door before it closed, and the person attached to it stepped in with a bit of a flourish.

"Good evening, Madame. May I push a floor button for you?" The man was not much taller than she was, smartly dressed wearing a suit and tie; he had a well-groomed Van Dyke beard. While he waited for an answer, he pushed the button to close the elevator doors, but the elevator was not moving.

Molly snapped her purse open and reached for her handgun along with her gold DA badge. As she brought the hammer back, the tell-tale click got the man's attention. "Are you new to the building?"

Nervously, the stranger said, "No, I'm visiting."

"Visiting whom?"

Flustered and ill-prepared for a confrontation, he blurted, "Miss Blazhè."

"I know everyone in this building, sir. There is no one here with that name."

The color drained from the man's face. "Isn't this 1801 Red Hook Terrace?"

"No, it is not!"

The man laughed awkwardly. "Oh, no! I'm at the wrong address. Forgive me," pushing the door to exit quickly.

Leaning back against the elevator wall, Molly sighed with relief, releasing the cocked hammer on her revolver. *Was that a legitimate mistake or an intimidation from Alvise LaPoshio?*

In minutes, she was safely inside her apartment, but her heart was still pounding. She dialed the phone. "Johnny, how soon can you get here?"

CHAPTER 79

Molly always gave an impassioned speech of how the city's heroes conquer the demons that keep citizens free. During her campaign, and later as the elected DA, the speeches furthered her connection to the NYPD. On the podium, she never failed to dazzle her audiences, bringing them to their feet with loud applause and cheers. She carried the same magnetism into the courtroom. And the bedroom.

Watching her undress that evening, Johnny recalled Molly telling him that she hadn't been very sexually active since graduating from law school. *Could've fooled me,* he thought. *Or is it beginner's luck? Maybe it was all pent up inside her and she's finally letting it loose. Or the alcohol ? Delaying the inevitable with slow dancing to that soulful music? The superiority of my kisses? Whatever it is, here we are again – naked!*

His next sensation was not by sight, but touch, as he felt her moist warmth swallow him deep inside her as she guided him with her hand. Molly couldn't seem to get enough of him. She was on top, like a western Bronc Buster with special skill taming wild horses. Placing her hands on the side arm of the couch to help her push back onto him, she sighed deeply, breathing heavy and fast. When she spoke, at first Johnny thought he had heard wrong.

"Slap me, slap my ass!" When he didn't, she repeated it, more loudly. "Johnny! Slap my ass, slap my ass!"

Slap, slap, like the crack of a bullwhip. "Again! Harder!" she commanded.

Is she drunk? he thought, not really caring. *SLAP! SLAP! SLAP! Whatever the lady wants ...*

Molly's nipples hardened. Johnny took it as a sign to capture them with his lips. With a deep throaty moan, Molly cried out, "Yes, YES, there it is! Don't. Stop! Don't ..."

Johnny couldn't hold out any longer. The sounds, Molly's cries, her perfume, her magnificently sculpted curves brought it all together as he impaled her molten core with his orgasm. A double whammy: the excitement of watching her climax, followed by his own.

Molly rolled off to his side and sat up. Johnny was still prone, and when he reached up to stroke a breast, she caught his hand and squeezed it. Hard. Her eyes were as well. "Grace Tilly played you, Johnny. Don't ever do that again to get information or you will *never* see me again. I could have gotten those forms from the newspaper for you." She looked across the room as if at faraway horizon. "How long?"

"How long? How long what?" Johnny was stunned.

She turned back to him. "How long before you can go again."

Questions Need Answers

CHAPTER 80

Days later, Johnny was still befuddled. *How did Molly find out about Grace? And the entire wonderful love making without saying those three little words. Is it love or lust? I can only hope it never stops!*

Billy interrupted his thoughts. "Johnny, I've listened to the tapes we got from Agent Bollinger on Fat Cat Catalina."

"And...?"

"I couldn't make out anything worthwhile. He talks to someone about getting a larger payment for 'such a big boat.'"

Johnny shook his head. "Well, hell Billy, that's *something!* Could you make out who he was talking to?"

"No. The tapes weren't very clear. There was another man, and a third voice I couldn't make out at all. Could be a man, could be a woman."

Johnny chewed on his pencil. "Not to change the subject, but I'm really happy you and Nancy came to an agreement staying on until retirement before you join her in the business."

"Yeah, me too. Her in-laws were okay with it too, which made it easier for her. Say, what's the latest with Monica?"

Johnny explained that Molly had practically put his head on the chopping block for striking the deal, but she did meet with Monica. "The Aiding and Abetting stuck for sure, so she'll eventually go to prison. And I made it clear to Molly that it was my decision alone to hold off arresting Monica, so we could get as much information from her as possible. So, back me up on that, if she asks. You were ag'in it the whole time. All me."

"No problem there! I heard she was on the war path. How is she now?"

"Better. Monica spilled the beans about her involvement with LaPoshio. She had to make a deal with the Devil himself to avoid getting dumped in the river. She placed the ads thinking the 'clean-ups' were moving women out of the city to other locations – in other words, getting rid of her competition. It felt like a no-brainer – it helped her business, *and* meant she could keep breathing. She's agreed to cooperate and let us know when he tells her to place another ad."

According to Molly, that was it. She didn't know anything about other possible meanings, or who'd get killed or when.

"So, it's only the Janitor and LaPoshio who know who's going to get hit," Billy guessed.

Johnny nodded. "Of course Monica doesn't deal directly with LaPoshio. She only deals with Fat Cat Catalina; Molly put twenty-four-hour surveillance on her. She can't go to the bathroom without us knowing it."

Billy whistled through his teeth. "I hope nobody famous gets caught with his pants down. Maybe the other voice on the tapes with Catalina is Monica's?"

"Could be. I have a feeling we'll know sooner rather than later."

CHAPTER 81

Detective Fang could not have been a better choice for undercover. His bio was overlooked for far too long, in Johnny's opinion. Now he was earning what he deserved,, having cultivated well-established, proud, and bold CIs. In Johnny's experience, sometimes informants took their pay gladly but had the attitude that the police were working for *them*. Not Willy, obviously, but he heard from other guys. Johnny didn't mind. *Let them think whatever the hell they want as long as the tips are accurate.*

Fang had brought him something similar already, but it was better when Monica backed his latest with even more details.

Monica explained over the phone that Carmine Catalina had come for one of Monica's girls. "As usual, when he was done – and it never takes him long," she said with disdain, "he came to my booth and bought me a drink. This time someone came to meet him, though, so I excused myself and sat at the bar."

"Who?"

Monica made a little humming noise. "I've never seen him before. He was tall, dark-skinned, good looking, even with a butt-ugly scar across his face. They were drinking heavily, so I moved to a closer bar stool when I thought they wouldn't notice. They started talking about bringing in a shipment and needing a drop point."

Johnny drew in a quick breath. "Did they indicate where it might be? ... Monica? Are you still there?"

He couldn't tell for sure, but Monica may have started crying. "Johnny, I'm scared. I'm getting in too deep."

Johnny liked Monica, but he had little patience for whiners. "You're too late for that, Monica. We have a deal. Go on."

Monica sighed. "Tomorrow night, Friday. Around midnight between the two bridges. That's all I heard. Honest, Johnny."

From years of experience, Johnny recognized the truth. "Okay Monica. It'll be over soon."

Click.

I'll be a son-of-a-bitch! Two sightings. Two tips. Proof that ole' Griff is alive and well. Dialing Commander Cunningham's number, Johnny thought, *What could get better than this?*

CHAPTER 82

It had felt like Friday would never end. Johnny and Billy joined Detectives Fang, Pan, and Chang with Cunningham's crew to gear up at the Coast Guard station for a scheduled take-down of, hopefully, the smuggler Griff and who-knows-who-else onboard.

All day, not a word had been spoken about the operation other than on a need-to-know basis. They had invested too much to let word leak back the enemy. *Loose lips sink ships* was as true for them as it had been during the war.

Everything was in place. Commander Cunningham had his one-hundred-foot Inland Buoy Tender Patrol Boat fully equipped with .50 caliber machine guns, searchlights, siren, and flashing red Coast Guard lights. This boat had the capacity for a crew of twenty-six.

"You're loaded for bear, Fred!" Johnny exclaimed at the arsenal. "Don't you think this is a lot of fire power for what we are going after?"

"I don't know what Griff has on board or what he's capable of doing. Do you? I like to be prepared," Cunningham answered matter-of-factly.

The cool night air hit them in the face as they traveled to their destination. Positioning themselves strategically, they were at the ready for any situation that might arise. Approaching the designated location, Cunningham ordered the engine cut. All lights were shut off. The bleak night became eerie, the scent of salt emanating from brackish water. The only sound was water lapping the sides of the boat as it rocked slightly with the current. It was a quiet night, low wind. Nature was cooperating so far.

The low whining noise of an engine grew louder, and then much, much quieter.

"Show time," Cunningham whispered fiercely. He knew all too well the sound of an engine idling. The speed would be just enough to bring the vessel to the shoreline slowly and methodically. It was a ghost boat, purring like a kitten.

Cunningham was impressed in spite of himself. "This is one hell of a sea dog pilot," he said, before giving the word for all quiet. He waited for the kill, like a lion ready to leap on its prey, as the vessel drew nearer and nearer land.

"Ahoy!" shouted someone from the smuggler's boat.

"Ahoy!" echoed a reply from the shore, with three quick flashes of light to indicate the exact location for docking.

"Here's the line." Something hit the water.

Cunningham was surprised. *Griff should have cut his engine. He's playing it close to the bone.* "Let's move!" he shouted.

The engine roared into action, and the sky lit up with the simple flick of a switch. Huge search lights scoured the shore line and the enemy boat. Sirens blasted, and red lights flashed to create chaos.

Cunningham projected his voice through a megaphone. "This is the United States Coast Guard, cut your engine. I repeat, this is the United States –"

fred berri

Griff's engine roared as well, maneuvering away from his position. Machine gun fire exploded through the air. Bullets whizzed at the Coast Guard boat like angry bees whose hive was rattled. The aftermath smell of propellants overpowered the tangy saltiness of the air. Griff's boat streaked past at full throttle, a shooter or shooters firing aimlessly from machine guns. Bullets ricocheted off the thick steel of Cunningham's boat.

Hold your fire! Hold your fire!" Cunningham commanded his crew with the radio. In the bright beams of the searchlights, the men could make out the outlines of multiple people splashing and hear their pitiful, frantic cries: "*Bàng bàng wò – bàng bàng wò – bàng bàng wò – bàng bàng wò – bàng bàng wò!*"

Fang yelled, "They're calling for help! They can't swim!"

The team had prepared for just this contingency. If they didn't follow Griff immediately, he would get away. But time was now the greater enemy. It would take only minutes before *Shuìxiàn Zùnwàng;* the Chinese Eminent Kings of the Water Immortals would claim the floundering innocents trying desperately to keep afloat. The men hesitated, but only for a split-second. Johnny threw a life-saver into the water toward the drowning group, whispering, "*This son-of-a-bitch must have been born on St. Patty's Day.*"

Answers Are Hard to Find

CHAPTER 83

"Things are not going well, Lieutenant – Commander – Miss Penett. As a matter of fact, this has become a fucking disaster. Excuse my French, "Agent Bollinger said, nodding in Molly's direction. He did not mince words as he opened their meeting. The other detectives and Captain Sullivan rounded out the gathering in the FBI's conference room again.

"I've heard it before, Agent Bollinger, and I've said it myself. Please proceed," Molly retorted. Manners was one thing; patronizing her was quite another.

Bollinger held up a folder. "This report indicates that eight women, all Chinese, were pulled from the water. One drowned at the scene, the others were taken to Gouveneur Hospital on Water Street to stabilize their condition. None had identification. We have two in custody. Two! Out of eight! Five escaped from the fucking hospital. How, goddamn it! How!" Bollinger was indignant, but he lowered his voice a decibel. "We agreed to be in this together," he said, pacing beside the group seated at the table. "Why wasn't I informed about this? We could have had FBI boats at the ready to avoid exactly what transpired."

Bollinger instructed the group as if they were children. "We could have put boats along the perimeter, creating a circle so he couldn't away. Now that he is apprised of our abilities, he'll change his previous arrangements. Jesus Christ! You had him right there in your hands. We could have gotten him! This is not good," he muttered. "Not good at all."

"Try to understand the situation," Captain Sullivan intervened. "We had barely any time between getting the information, and putting something together. It was either move fast, or miss the opportunity. We certainly didn't have time for any federal red tape bullshit. We did what we had to do, when we had to do it."

Johnny was gratified by Sullivan's words. He knew the captain held a dismal view of the Bureau, and he was holding his temper down surprisingly well. "We agreed to work together when we can and share information that will be helpful to all of us. So yeah, maybe we should have told you. But this all went down Friday night around midnight. If we told you when *we* found out, about *4 p.m.* on Friday, could you have done anything in that span of time?"

Johnny and Billy shared a quick glance at one another. Sullivan had found out the day before the operation was scheduled, when they told him. He was covering for them, and for himself. He hadn't wanted any FBI fuck-ups on his watch. Sullivan glared at Johnny, who read him loud and clear: *We should have included them.* Twenty-twenty hindsight.

"I'm just at my wit's end with this guy. Now he's escaped, as did Mo China during *that* little debacle. I want to bring these pieces of shit to justice!" Bollinger looked tired. "At this point, dead or alive."

Molly didn't need much of an opening to speak up. "We have at least two women in custody that did *not* escape. Our detectives also have three thugs in custody who are willing to cooperate if they can stay here in the United States. They fear retribution and possible death if returned to China."

"It depends on what they bring to the table, Miss Penett. If it's scraps and leftovers, they'll be on the first flight to China. However, if they can give you what we need, I believe it could be arranged for them to serve their time here. What are they saying? And the women? Are they able to give substantial information on these bastards?" Bollinger took a seat at the head of the table.

Detective Fang spoke up. "The two women have spoken of safe houses they were supposed to find when they got on shore. They were given addresses and a map. It would've been easy for them to mingle with people on the streets without attracting attention."

"That's a good lead; where are the safe houses?" asked Bollinger.

Sullivan snapped, "We don't know. Whatever these women were carrying was lost in the water and confusion."

Bollinger put his head in his hands, as if in pain. When he lifted his head, he was not smiling. "Your police department stumbled into an ongoing investigation we've had into Alvise LaPoshio for a long time now. The *only* reason we're now in bed together are the dead bodies that keep showing up on your streets. We need full cooperation going forward. Do I make myself clear, everyone? You have a short window of time in which to get real information from the five in custody. If you can't comply, we're taking over the operation completely. Now get out, everyone out!" The pain was real.

CHAPTER 84

Upon leaving the meeting with Bollinger, Johnny and Billy headed off to find some answers, and find them fast. The No-It-Awl Jazz Club was at the top of their list.

As they approached the front door, however, it was evident that their day was not going to get better. The door was padlocked, and a sign boldly announced: **CLOSED FOR RENOVATIONS. RE-OPEN SOON. WATCH FOR DATE.**

"What the hell is going on?" Billy asked rhetorically. "Let's check the alley door." There was a padlock on this door as well.

"Let's shoot over to the Nostalgia Café. Maybe Monica's there with something new," Johnny suggested.

Entering the lounge through the hotel entrance, they were greeted by the bartender, "Hello, detectives. If you're looking for Monica, she's not here."

Billy fumed. "Well, where is she?"

"Don't really know," he said as he wiped a glass. "She said she had to take care of business out of town and left Lilly in charge."

"Get Lilly down here NOW!" Johnny exploded. *Could this day get any worse?*

Lilly arrived within minutes looking her usual beautiful, sophisticated self. Both detectives had experienced her somewhat bountiful charms in the past, and they knew what to offer her for her time. Billy took the lead.

"I'm not laying down any money on this bar for your whiskey until you give us some answers," Billy said.

"Pitch the first ball, Detective," she said, referring to his "Billy the Kid" baseball days.

"Where the fuck is Monica?"

"Simple," she said, tossing a head full of blonde curls. "I don't know. She told me to keep things in order until she returns, said she'd compensate me beyond my regular commissions. That's it. Some suits came in and sat with her in her booth for about an hour. The next thing I know, poof, she's gone. So here I am, running the show! Now, Detectives, what's your pleasure? I live to serve," she said, giving a little bow.

Billy threw down a sawbuck and called the bartender over. "Feed the lady." The bartender promptly set down a glass of Lilly's favorite.

Johnny waited for her to take a drink. His face was grim. "Lilly, in your best interests, and the interests of the Nostalgia Café and all the girls, you need to come up with concrete information as to Monica's where-a-bouts. Like, *now*." *I'll be damned if I ever get another ass-chewing from that twit Bollinger.*

"And if I can't?" Lilly asked.

"Be prepared for a lot of busts. A lot of rides for you and your girls to South Central."

Raising her glass again, Lilly smiled. "Cheers."

Johnny leaned in, ever-so-slightly. "What do you know about the No-It-Awl Jazz Club closing?"

"First I heard of it, Johnny. What does that have to do with me or Monica or *anything*?" Lilly asked.

"It seems everyone everywhere has some tie-in with the women being smuggled into Chinatown and used as prostitutes. Your competition. The club just closed. I don't put a lot of stock in coincidence."

Lilly shrugged, wishing the men were there for another reason. "Wish I could help, *Lieutenant*. I only hear things; I don't *know* things. But if it helps keep you and vice off my back, so to speak, I'll listen more intently." She put her drink down to free both hands to cup her ample breasts and push them up. "I'll use my *prowess* to get information."

Gotta give her points for trying. "That will be a start, Lilly," Johnny said, patting her on the back.

From down the hallway into the hotel lobby, a clock chimed the hour. "I have a client waiting, gentlemen. Can we continue this another time? I'll call if I get information, I promise," Lilly said, sliding off the bar stool.

"Make sure you do," Billy said gruffly. "Remember, we know where you live and what you do."

Lilly put a soft hand on Billy's cheek. "You certainly do. Although *I* certainly don't know what you're alluding to. My friends and I offer companionship and conversation. Sometimes, our clients buy us dinner and drinks. You shouldn't judge them, Detective. There's a lot of lonely men out there. You've been there, remember? I sure do."

Exiting the Budapest, Billy said, "That Lilly's got balls, Johnny. She called our bluff until we pushed her into the corner."

"Now that she realizes she may wind up *in* jail and *out* of business, I think she'll come up with legit information."

281

Billy was unconvinced. "I don't know. I hope it's not just her usual bullshit, wasting our time."

Johnny shrugged. "I'm not going to give her long. She delivers soon or I put the squeeze on her like Bollinger's putting on us. A day or two, tops."

"Then what?" Billy asked.

"We start making busts. We may have to get bogus warrants to get into their rooms while they have clients and arrest the Johns, too."

"If that's not a motivator, I don't know what would be." Billy punched Johnny on the arm and laughed. "You might want to give Sullivan a heads-up before we bust down any doors, though. I hear his missus is down in Florida visiting the relatives!"

CHAPTER 85

Not 24 hours later, Agent Bollinger set up another meeting for all those involved in the case to be held. As before, they sat around the conference room table, but the mood was definitely lighter. Molly, Johnny, Billy, Fang, Pan, Chang, Captain Sullivan, and Commander Cunningham – all present and accounted for, *sir*.

Bollinger was stern and business-like, but in a considerably better mood than at the last meeting. "We were able to extract a lot of information from the three thugs and the two Chinese women who survived. We have resources the NYPD doesn't have. All five will be taken care of. The three gentlemen, if you want to call them that, will be going to different federal prisons until time to testify. Eventually. That could take a week or two. The women will be in one of our secure safe houses. They've agreed to testify as well."

Johnny had pressing matters to attend to. "Agent Bollinger, you did not bring us all here for that information alone."

The agent had been looking forward to this all day. "No, Lieutenant. You were able to put together a portion of the smuggler's route which was pretty accurate. Our informants have helped us with more detail. The routes are quite extensive. Take a look at the map on the screen," he said. Someone turned the light off and flipped on the projector on the table.

Bollinger stood by the screen pointing to specific places with his finger. "These women are literally being kidnapped, because they think they're coming to America for a better life. They make many sacrifices to save enough money to get 'passage.' From China, they're taken and loaded onto a ship sailing from Burma. South to this indiscriminate island, Agaléga, off the coast of Africa. Coolies[7] are common there, they come and go unnoticed, the population is so small." He stopped to shake his head. "This is one hell of an operation. From there another ship sails around the southern tip of Africa, the Cape of Good Hope –"

"There's not much hope for these women," Molly muttered.

"No, Miss Penett, there is not. But to continue – the smugglers sail into the South Atlantic Sea north to Guyana. This is where Griff gets them, at his home ports. From there they travel to Panama, to British Honduras, to Cuba, to Miami, to New York."

"Jesus Christ!" exclaimed Molly. "These poor women are put through hell before they ever get here. I hope the two in custody will be well cared for."

"We're working on it, Miss Penett. Your concern is what happens now. The FBI is working on the operation in the other parts of the world. Obviously, this is not a simple one-man-band. But getting our hands on Griff will put quite a clog in the system."

---

[7]   A disparaging and offensive term for an unskilled laborer, especially formerly in China

As the magnitude of what they were up against began to dawn, amazement was evident on each face. This was much bigger than they'd bargained for. And after months of lethargic clues and leads, momentum had picked up suddenly.

Bollinger continued. "With all the stop-and-go, switching ships, all the countries involved, we don't know how many women start, who may be sold along the way, or how many die. However, what we do now know is that the other voice on the tapes with Carmine Catalina is the dock boss, Angelo Zimarino, AKA, Angie the Fish. These guys love nicknames – there's a fish with a name similar to Zimarino, the Zamurito fish. Since he's the dock boss… Angie the Fish."

He explained that the men would get nicknames in Italy, and continue to use them as criminals, so as not to bring suspicion on their families. "The nicknames also serve as protection if they get caught up in a mob war or police bust," Molly interjected.

Bollinger smiled, his first for the day. For the benefit of the agents running the projector and lights, he said, "The DA's family is from Italy and is familiar with their habits, as well as having prosecuted many of them."

"So, what's next on the agenda? Do you have any specific plans? Are your agents working anything we should be avoiding?" Johnny asked.

"Yes. I've broken it down to three sectors." The carousel advanced, projecting a neat outline on the screen:

1) NYPD Detectives continue to work the Chinatown murders and their CIs.

2) Commander Cunningham works the docks, port, and all waterways.

285

3) FBI will work Alvise LaPoshio and his side of things.

"This way we cover all angles without stepping on each other toes. Are we all on the same page with this?"

Reluctant nods kept everyone in check until Bollinger made sure he acknowledged a "Yes" from everyone present.

CHAPTER 86

South Central had not seen a day like this in years. It was filled with chaos, and filled with people. With Sullivan's approval, Johnny had put the word out concerning every lead they'd gotten from the CIs: crash down doors, make the busts. It looked like the haul not only shook the bushes, but also the trees. Both lobby and squad room were filled with pimps, hookers, drug dealers, even the girls from the Nostalgia Café. It was standing room only.

Captain Sullivan stepped from his office in disbelief, shouting over the indistinct but loud chatter.

"Goddamn it, Vero, get in here now!"

"I know, I know. We're working on it, Captain," Johnny said with a look of fatigue.

"Jesus, Mary, and Joseph, Vero. We'll be processing these people for a week."

Captain Sullivan took his seat behind his desk again. Johnny pointed to the sea of arrestees outside the office. "Captain, the answers we need are not walking through that door. We have to go out there and find them. The ones we have in custody gave us some good, solid information, but it's minimal. We need more."

"Well, we'll just have work through it," Sullivan mumbled begrudgingly.

"If the group here doesn't give us what we need, we'll keep getting new ones, repeats, until we see the light of day and get what we need," Johnny said. "This has to stop."

"All right, all right, now get out!" Sullivan yelled. As Johnny left he heard the captain add, to himself, "I hope this *is* my last year. I'm getting too old for this shit."

CHAPTER 87

Johnny had tasked a particular squad detective with searching the newspaper's classifieds daily. "Lieutenant, here's another ad for a janitor," he called to Johnny.

"No shit! Give it to Billy. Billy, get your ass back in here," Johnny calls out, knowing he was in the squad room.

Billy tossed the newspaper down and took a big sip of coffee.

"He wasn't lying. Another ad for the Janitor!"

"No shit!"

"That's what I said. I wonder who the fuck they're targeting now?" Johnny said, scrutinizing the ad as if new information would reveal itself. He had a thought. "You know what, Billy? We need an extra gun when we're out and about. I don't trust this bastard whoever he … or she ... is. *Wait a minute!* How was this ad placed? Monica's nowhere to be found!"

"Maybe Grace can find out?" Billy asked.

"I'll ask her right now," he said, reaching for the telephone. "Grace, its Johnny. I need you to check on something. There's a new ad for the Janitor, but Monica, the woman who *was* placing the ads is AWOL. I need to know who and when the new ad was placed." He blurted it out quickly, without giving Grace a chance to interact, question, or offer some new ultimatum. *Molly would be pleased.* He hoped.

"Hold on Detective, I'll call the front desk," Grace said.

Johnny nervously chewed on a pencil that had seen better days. A sound at the other end.

"Hello?"

"I'm here, Grace. What do you have?"

"You're correct. It was a different person."

"So who? Is there a way to track it down?" Johnny could feel another lead slipping through his fingers.

"Listen, Johnny. We take ads in advance. This one was placed weeks ago to run in this edition. Classifieds just put it on ice as requested. It's a common practice." Her voice dropped an octave. "When can we see each other?"

Johnny sat up to stretch his shoulders, which were suddenly very tense. "You know Grace, I just don't know."

"At least I sense the door might still be open?"

Johnny wasn't getting into it with her. Not again. Not now. "Grace, I have to go. We'll talk soon. Goodbye." Johnny rubbed his forehead, deflated.

"So?" Billy asked.

"It wasn't placed by Monica, apparently. But it was w week ago or more, when it was placed. Ahead of time. Scheduled to run today. Grace said it's a common thing people do."

"*Bupkis* once again."

"I hate to say it, Billy, but it's a case of wait and see. A cat and mouse game. I hate it. 'Who's going to show up dead next?'"

Billy slumped in his chair. "It could be you or me ... or Molly! for that matter. LaPoshio threatened before, why not make good on those threats now?"

"I remember. I'll call her now," Johnny said as he started to dial. "We need to know about Angelo Zimarino, AKA Angie the Fish too. Pull his sheets."

"I'm one step ahead of you, boss man. He's clean as the proverbial whistle. Nothing, not even a parking ticket."

Johnny made a *humph* noise as he listened to the rings. "Sounds too good to be true, don't you think? He's involved as deep as it gets. How does LaPoshio find these guys with such clean records?"

"Maybe he snaps his fingers and makes the records disappear."

"If he price is right, 'most anything's for sale," he said. "Heeeeey, Molly. It's Johnny."

CHAPTER 88

Lilly nonchalantly strutted into South Central. Every head turned to follow each calculated sway of her hips, a movie in slow motion that might have upset the censors. No one stopped her as she made her way to the Lieutenant's office, not even Billy, who was swapping war stories with a new man.

"Lilly, what a surprise!" Johnny jumped to his feet and closed the door behind her, noticing that some of the lads out in the squad room were practically drooling. He made a lecherous face at them before the door slammed shut.

"A surprise for me, too," Lilly said. "I came to cooperate so you'll stop hassling my girls and clients."

"Why would I do that, Lilly? Sit down please. I told you until we get the information we need, I'm going out in full force. For your information, your girls were last on my list. But that's not what brought you here, is it?"

"No. I got a post card from Monica. I wanted to show you that I was telling the truth when I said I didn't know where she was. Here," she offered it to Johnny.

"Well, what do you know? It's from her homeland, Monaco. She told me once she's from there and that's why she took the name Monica. What do you have to say, Monica?

Hold down the fort. You will not regret it. A L will take care of you. The night has a thousand eyes. Be home soon...M. Well, it's stamped from Monaco. She split right after that meeting she had with Fat Cat Carmine you told me about. How do I know –?"

"It's her handwriting; I know it well," Lilly interrupted. "She keeps a ledger of sorts."

"A ledger?"

"Shit! I should *not* have said that. Before you ask, I don't know where it is. I have the one she wanted me to keep current while she's gone, but that's not hers. And it's not just for record keeping, Johnny. All the clients and notes on each one are there, what they like, you know. Let me tell you, it's quite a list and their names are *not* all John."

Johnny smiled. "This got you some points on the board, at least for now. If you come across that ledger, you just might score a home run. The ledger might just take out of the game completely, and I'm the one who can make it happen." Johnny stood. "If there's nothing more, I'll see you out."

"Thanks, but it's better for me to leave on my own. I have a car waiting. But ... I'll remember that."

I think I just hit the jackpot, Johnny thought. Better than an Irish Sweepstakes ticket from Sullivan. LaPoshio's men were clients, probably other bad guys in the city, too. Ain't she sweet! He groaned. *That goddamn ledger better not still have my and Billy's names on it.*

"Bradshaw! Get in here and close the door," Johnny yelled.

CHAPTER 89

Molly poured Johnny a bourbon and Chablis for herself. "I guess the ad for the Janitor is what... a waiting game? You could be the target, or me, or Billy, or Agent Bollinger."

"Believe me, I've gone through the mental list already. All *we* know is that the Janitor, Alvise LaPoshio, and maybe a select few involved in his operation are the only ones who *really* know. When you think of all the people involved with this, how deep this operation is ..." Johnny's trailed off as he took a sip of Old Crow. *You can spend more money for bourbon,* he thought, *but nothing's better than this.*

"I finally got the brass to realize what we're up against. They're easing off a bit...for now," Molly said. It had taken incredible self-restrain not to give them a piece of her mind, but at least they were persuaded.

"Molly, I got a tip as to where Monica is, but I have to use your office for help."

"Tell me."

"Monica went missing the same time the No-It-Awl was closed for renovations. So we don't know where Leelee Gaye is either. There's just a sign on the door. Do you know anything about it?"

Molly frowned. "Nothing on Monica, but I believe Leelee went to visit family in Hawaii, while the club is being renovated. Where did I hear that? Bollinger? I don't remember."

"Oh!" Johnny mused. He hadn't thought of that possibility. "Monica appears to be in Monaco, in the southern tip of France. Remember our old friend from the Budapest Hotel murders? Inspector Laurènt?"

"Of course, how could I forget?" Molly put a mock-scowl on her face. "You are not going to France to get Monica! Tracking down a serial killer is one thing. You needing Monica to come back and run a *whorehouse* so she can place ads for LaPoshio is quite another." Molly could tell it was important to Johnny, though. "She can't stay away forever. We can get in touch with Inspector Laurènt and have his men put her on ice until we get an extradition order."

"I'll go along with that. How soon do you think you can get the ball rolling?"

"As soon as this conversation is over, I want us to spend the entire weekend on just you and me, but I'll call France on Monday. They're ahead of us by six hours, so 8 in the morning should be about right."

"I can be there, if you want," Johnny said. *Did she say we were spending the entire weekend together? That would be a first.* "Is there any word on the counterfeit money set up for LaPoshio?"

Molly was growing impatient to have Johnny all to herself, but knew in her head that there would probably always be a little police business mixed in with whatever personal time they had. She knew in her body, however, that enough was enough.

"Johnny, you know how difficult it is to get the feds to give up evidence from previous arrests. It's in the works. That's all I know right now." Gazing at Johnny, she surrendered that thought and went to another. *Grace Tilly. Is that over? He was always a lady's man long before we ever met – even before he got married and after Simone left. Never during his marriage though. I believe him when he says that. But look at him! Every woman's dream. I'm flattered that he chooses me over the others. Most of the time.* She'd put her own surveillance on Grace when he'd reacted so strangely. She wasn't the DA for nothing.

Taking a sip of his whiskey, Johnny felt, rather than saw, her withdraw a little. "Molly, are you okay? "

They locked eyes with a sudden connection, simultaneously kissing with a ferocious thirst that each knew was about to be satisfied. Neither had taken it for granted that their evening would start this way, but both had nurtured hopes. Within moments, Johnny's shirt was unbuttoned, revealing his rippled muscles. Molly threw off most of her clothes and stood there before him in her bra and panties. All of the disrobing was done accompanied by vigorous kissing, tongues darting in and out, their breathing getting faster.

All those hours I spent at the university library studying, Molly thought, *I could have been doing* this. *But Johnny was definitely worth the wait.*

Using one hand, Johnny skillfully unhooked Molly's bra, taking a deep breath as her beautiful breasts took on a life of their own. It was as if he'd never seen them before, so entranced was he by their shape and scent and feel. Still kissing him, Molly unbuckled his pants slowly, pulling them down together with his shorts so that he could step out of them, kick them aside. She was perspiring in the heat of their embrace, and she rubbed the palm of her hand under her breasts, using the moisture there as a lubricant, reaching for him.

Johnny's hand slipped into her panties making her lady muscles twitch. Seeing the pleasure on her face was like the music of his cello. Her moans of passion increased as her thighs began to quake. *There it is – one down and another soon to arrive.*

Picking her up, he entered her as her legs clamped around his waist, pulling him in even deeper. Each thrust became a rhythmic tempo. Quivering with excitement she whispered, "Oh please don't stop!" He obeyed – she came – and her face was again radiant. In some fragment of her mind, Molly imagined beautiful flowers and music. *This is what it feels like to be married to the man you love.*

But Molly was not given to fantasy. Floating with euphoria, her mind switched back to reality, and she plummeted back to earth.

CHAPTER 90

Monday morning, at 8 o'clock on the dot, Johnny arrived at Molly's office. "Good morning, Lieutenant," Louise greeted him "I don't see you on Miss Penett's calendar. Wait right here – "

"Last minute thing, Louise. She's expecting me," he said, continuing around the corner and into Molly's office.

Molly was holding the receiver and beckoned to him to shut the door. She put her hand over the mouthpiece and whispered, "I told Louise not to interrupt for a while since I'd be calling Europe ... I guess we could have just walked in together after the weekend, but –"

Johnny shook his head. "'Discretion is the better part of valor,'" he quoted.

Molly heard a faint voice in her ear, "Ah! Inspector Laurènt. *Bonjour!* This is Molly Penett, New York City District Attorney. We need your help again, I'm afraid."

Surprises and Bodies

CHAPTER 91

Later that day, Louise buzzed Molly. "Miss Penett, Agent Bollinger is on the line for you."

"Hello, Roland, this is Molly." They had agreed that during meetings they should keep it formal, but when it was just the two of them, they could relax the usual protocols.

"I hope you're sitting down."

Molly began to nervously twirl the phone cord on her hand, mentally bracing herself. "It can't be good news, then," she sighed. "Tell it like it is."

"The warden from North Eastern Penitentiary in Lewisburg just called. The three Chinese thugs we're holding to testify against Mo China and LaPoshio are dead."

Molly squeezed the receiver so tightly she could feel the pulse in her hand. Her mouth was too dry to speak.

"Molly, Molly … are you still there?"

Molly cleared her throat. "How?"

"There was a fire in the cell block right before dawn. Eleven dead," Bollinger said grimly. "We were working on sending them to separate facilities and then this. I'm sorry, Molly. There was nothing that could be done."

There were many layers to Molly's disappointment. If all of the suspects, murderers, and smugglers were arrested and put away, her chance at moving up to Attorney General would double. On top of the Budapest Hotel case last year, it would be a huge feather in her hat. She also knew that Johnny would take this hard. But none of that was Bollinger's business. "Do you think the fire was LaPoshio or Mo China? You know there was another ad for the Janitor just last week."

"Anything's possible with those two. Their arms are far-reaching. The testimony of those three would have helped put them away for a long time," he said. "This doesn't look good for me either, Molly. I'm so sorry." *Click.*

There was nothing to do but tell him. Molly dialed South Central and asked for his extension almost in a daze.

"Lieutenant Vero, how can I help you?"

"It's Molly. I hope you're sitting down."

CHAPTER 92

There had been a flurry of activity, but now, as April drew to a close, time threatened to drag. How long had it been since any real new information on the case? Johnny rubbed his eyes, weary from going back over the reports. *Now we have seven bodies, not including the other eight from the prison fire, or the women from Griff's boat who drowned.* His phone rang. "Lieutenant Vero, how –"

"Johnny, it's Molly again." She sounded miserable. "The hits just keep on coming, no pun intended. We have another body." She hesitated. "I don't know if you're ready for this one, Joh –"

"Jesus Christ!" he cut her off. "When will this nightmare end?" He could feel a tension headache coming on. "Go ahead, I'm sitting."

"I never expected this one," she said quietly. "Inspector Laurènt called back."

"And?"

"They tracked Monica to the Hòtel de Ville after questioning Marcel, the bartender at Lè Chesterield."

"I remember him. The hotel bar Billy and I stayed there when we were tracking Jean-Paul Vincent."

"They found her, Johnny, but they were too late. She's dead."

Johnny felt sick to his stomach. "Good God, Molly! That's number eight. In fucking *France.* Did he give you any details?"

"Some. Their medical examiner placed the time of death as before dawn. She was naked on the bed with her throat slashed. And she had had sex. Police assume it was with the killer, but there were no signs of a struggle, so probably consensual."

Johnny mumbled something about the dawn, and superstitions.

"What are you taking about, Johnny?"

"All eight victims were killed before dawn – we don't know for sure about the floater, but I'd bet my life on it. It's something Fang told me about the Chinese culture. The moon is the abode for departed souls. At the moment of death, the spirit is taken by messengers to Ch'eng Huang to conduct a hearing, to qualify for paradise. It's all supposed to go down before the sun rises."

"Monica wasn't Chinese. That makes no sense at all – it has to be LaPoshio's work. He's got all the contacts in Italy. Close enough to France, for sure."

Johnny tried to keep mental images of Monica from clouding his thoughts. She wasn't the fabled hooker with the heart of gold, but she hadn't deserved this. "It could make perfect sense to the killer! It makes me wonder if he is Chinese or is just immersed in the culture, taking on their superstitions."

Molly jotted a few things down as she continued. "So, our killer has a conscience and honors those he kills? I need to run that one by Dr. Misak."

"What about evidence? Do they have her belongings? She must've been living there at least a few weeks. She may've been turning tricks, too." Johnny didn't want to mention the ledger specifically, but it could provide important information. *Possibly incriminating information.*

"Laurènt said he'd share anything significant once they've finished their investigation."

Johnny did not look forward to breaking the news to Billy. He'd chosen a doozy of a day to take off. "Monica got caught in a quagmire. Whatever else she was, she was an innocent bystander in this mess."

Molly disagreed. "Oh, come on Johnny. She broke the law and got away with it for years. She could have chosen another way of life. I don't buy it. And there were ways around getting involved with LaPoshio. You live by the sword, you die by the sword. She was anything but innocent."

"I just can't buy into it one hundred percent, Molly. That's all I'm saying. To get her throat slashed? Had to be LaPoshio's doing."

Molly sighed. "We've got to get something concrete. We need to find who the Janitor is, and who's placing the ads instead of Monica."

Johnny held the receiver between his ear and shoulder as he began gathering some things together on his desk. "I'm going to let Lilly know. I don't want her throat slashed, too. Talk to you later, Molly."

Billy popped his head in. "I just couldn't stay away," he began, lighthearted, about to have his good mood vanish. "Jesus, Johnny, what's the matter? You look like you've seen a ghost."

Johnny stood up and gestured for him to be seated. "Couple of things, Billy –"

CHAPTER 93

Across the city, a radio call interrupted the commander's coffee break. "Commander Cunningham – over."

"Commander, we have a floater – over."

"You know the protocol. Mark the coordinates of the pick-up. Check weather, tide, wind, and current for accuracy. Transport to the closest pier. I'll call the ME and police – over."

"Aye aye, Commander. Hold on! Amend that last. Two floaters bound together. We couldn't tell at first, as the bodies were floating in a mass of debris-- over."

"Are you positive – over."

The ship's captain confirmed the details and informed him that they were headed for Chelsea Pier.

"Roger that," said the commander, not wasting a second calling the Medical Examiner and Lieutenant Vero.

CHAPTER 94

Johnny, Billy, Molly, and the ME arrived at Chelsea Pier within seconds of one another. Lying on the dock's edge were the bodies of two very large men bound together. Debris still clung to them. Dr. Michaels bent to examine them, but Johnny wanted to take a look first. He tapped Michaels to move aside.

The bodies were fresh enough to be recognizable. "Holy shit!" Johnny exclaimed. "Carmine 'Fat Cat' Catalina and 'Angie the Fish' Zimmerino. Good God! Two more fucking bodies for our collection. Ten, goddamn it! Ten fucking bodies!" He looked out at the water as if searching for clues as Michaels resumed his inspection.

"Both throats have been slit and their tongues are missing."

Billy stepped closer to take a better look. "That's a clear message. Maybe they talked about LaPoshio's ties to the smuggler."

Molly shivered, although the day was warm. "They smell awful."

"Good observation, Miss Penett. Lieutenant, these two may have come off a garbage scow with all that debris that's clinging to them," Michaels said. Both Johnny and Billy were taking notes.

Billy snorted. "How fitting. A garbage scow from their own docks for dirt bags like them. Garbage to garbage! That's what you call irony."

The smell was getting to Molly, and she began walking away, her voice trailing. "You know where to send the report, Doc. I'm heading back to my office. Johnny, when you finish here we need to get to find a better strategy. Come to my office ASAP."

"Billy, find Fang, Pan, and Chang. All of you get to Molly's office. I don't give a shit what they're doing," Johnny barked. "If they're getting *laid*, pull 'em off whoever they're with and drag 'em out."

CHAPTER 95

Leelee Gay was back in town and the No-It-Awl Jazz Club held a grand reopening to show off the new sophistication and ambiance. Up-and-coming artists had their paintings hanging on elegantly papered walls in hopes of being discovered. As Johnny and Molly were seated at their reserved front table, they took in the happy but indistinguishable chatter, the clamor of silverware, drinks being poured at tables nearby, the smell of fresh paint still detectable under the aromas of food platters being served – it was a feast for the senses.

The ten-piece jazz ensemble played softly as if providing accompaniment to the seemingly choreographed routine of waiters, hostesses, and patrons. A Grand Opening was always popular, and the room had filled quickly, including several entertainment critics. They'd observe and taste, rushing home to type up their reviews by deadline to make the morning papers.

Straight across the room from Johnny and Molly was none other than Alvise LaPoshio with a table filled with guests. "Well, what do you know? That's a happy coincidence, isn't it?"

"The two goons are the bodyguards you ran sheets on, the ones Bollinger showed us. Joey Tremont and Bobby Hoffman. The lady – in a manner of speaking – there beside LaPoshio is Lilly, from the Nostalgia Café. I assume the other two broads are Lilly's girls." One was a blonde, the other a redhead, the women from the FBI surveillance photos.

"I didn't recognize the men, all dressed up. What's this all about, I wonder. Any ideas?"

"The call I got telling us to be here was cryptic, from 'Operation Orchid,' so I assumed it was going to be something to help us get this son-of-a-bitch..."

He was interrupted by the emcee, actually a member of the ensemble. "Good evening, ladies and gentlemen. This is the evening that you've all been waiting for and the reason why we're here. The No-It-Awl Jazz Club proudly presents Miss Leelee Gaye."

Leelee's voice was better than ever, her costumes exquisite, the band superb. If the ninety-minute show didn't pull five star reviews from every critic present, every patron there would be surprised. At the final note, everyone rose to their feet for a standing ovation.

Applauding and whistling with everyone else, Johnny watched out of the corner of his eye as two waiters with briefcases set them down at LaPoshio's table. Quickly, each case was handcuffed to one of the bodyguards. LaPoshio and the men exited into the kitchen. *And out into the alley,* Johnny thought. "Goddamn it, Molly! Did you see that?"

"See what?" The crowd was still standing, applauding.

Johnny grabbed for his gun and leaned his face to her ear. "LaPoshio and his goons walked out with two briefcases handcuffed to their wrists."

fred berri

"I can't hear you," she frowned, still focused on Leelee. He was about to follow the men out when two waiters approached, one discreetly showing the FBI badge from beneath his apron while the other whispered, "Let it go, Lieutenant. Let it go." They took their place beside Johnny and Molly, clapping along with the crowd as Leelee continued to take her well-deserved bows.

Johnny stood dumbfounded. Molly had no idea what had just taken place. It appeared that no one else had noticed, either. Even the guests at LaPoshio's table seemed unruffled by the departure. *Their plan went off without a hitch, whatever it was,* he thought. Johnny couldn't wait to grab Molly and head out. He had nowhere to go at the moment, however, not with two feds at his side. Eventually, the men vanished into the crowd and Johnny grabbed Molly's arm so harshly that it startled her.

"Johnny, what's going on?"

"We're leaving. I'll tell you on the way." Hurriedly, they wound through the tables and went outside.

"Where are we going?"

"To your place," he said, hailing a taxi, then describing everything he had seen.

"Are you kidding me? Holy shit!" Molly hissed as they settled into the cab's back seat. Johnny reached over the seat to the cabbie with the amount he knew he'd owe – they'd made this trip plenty of times. "This is – is – is, I don't know what. It's out of control, that's what it is!" Molly kept her voice low because of the cabbie, but she was agitated. "LaPoshio runs the union on the docks. He's top boss for the crime syndicate in the City." Her hands were flailing for effect. "And think of the power he had to have had to set fire to a Navy-manned ship!"

310

"That was never proven," Johnny said, the weight of the world on his shoulders.

"I never told you everything about that. LaPoshio was going to be deported – too many suspicions and charges he kept beating. Even though he was a citizen, the government had had enough. When that ship sunk, it was message to the government. *Daring* them to kick him out. Poof! His deportation charges were dropped and he's still here. So you tell me. *I* believe it was him."

"So maybe they dropped the ball then, but this is now. *We* have deal with him. The briefcases had to be the counterfeit money Bollinger arranged for him to get, but why jeopardize Leelee and her club? That was taking some kind of chance, right out in the open."

"Sometimes hiding in plain sight is the way to go."

Johnny suddenly thought of something Monica had said. "We've been focused on the trees, Molly, and there's a whole forest out there."

Making Complicated Simple

CHAPTER 96

There was something about the elevator. Maybe it was that unique feeling when they were finally alone for the first time. As soon as the doors closed behind them, they were like teenagers. They began kissing sweetly, then more urgently. Molly's lips tilted against his as she unbuttoned her blouse to press her breasts against his chest. Taking full advantage of the undeniable invitation, Johnny backed her against the handrail at the rear and swirled his tongue in her mouth; her tongue fluttered against his in concert. Their hands were in constant motion running over each other's body, unbuttoning whatever they could get away with if anyone should spot them in the hallway outside of Molly's apartment.

What took place at Leelee's club had been out of his control, thanks to the feds. Being with Molly wasn't – or was it? As if in answer to his thoughts, Molly unzipped his pants, thrusting her hand in to grab hold as he swelled under her attention. He was about to punch the "lock" button on the elevator and have her right then and there when the car stopped. Molly giggled at the sight of them both, grateful the hallway was otherwise deserted. Holding his pants with one hand and reaching for the key with the other, Johnny fumbled to get to the door open. Molly dropped to her knees silently and took him in her mouth, bobbing like she was dunking for apples at a backyard picnic. He managed to get the door open; she walked backward on her knees a few feet until he lifted her up, kicking the door shut behind him. Awkwardly, they stumbled to the bedroom undressing along the way, stopping every few feet for another passionate embrace.

For some reason, Johnny wanted everything to be perfect that night. He held her tightly, with an air of proprietorship. Molly could feel his sincerity and felt a calm wash over her. Once he slipped inside her, Molly whispered, "You feel so good."

CHAPTER 97

The next morning, enjoying coffee, Molly ignored the clothes scattered everywhere. She could still smell his scent on her skin. *There was a time the mess would drive me crazy*, she thought, amazed. *He's changed so much.*

Johnny set down his steaming cup. "I don't know where this is going."

Alarmed, Molly grabbed his hand with hers. "I thought we were doing fine!"

Johnny smiled, kissing her hand. "We are. We *are*. I was thinking of the case, sorry. I'm talking about all the dead bodies and the smuggler. There are too many holes. This case is all over the place."

Molly didn't mind shop talk, knowing that she could look forward to the other later. "Don't you think that's just what LaPoshio and Griff want? They're not stupid. This has been well-planned down from the ads to everything else. We think we know how deep the water is and then we find out we're still in the shallows."

"With the exception of the unknown – how many more bodies will turn up before this is over? I ...*we* need to plug some holes before this ship sinks right beside that Navy transporter."

Molly agreed. "At this point, it looks like Bollinger got LaPoshio the counterfeit money as you suggested. First he nails him and we get Griff, Mo China and the Janitor. Until it's our turn to get LaPoshio for the –" The phone rang, interrupting.

"Hello? Amollia Penett's residence."

"Molly, its Billy. I sure hope Johnny is there."

Molly made a "yikes, we're busted" look at Johnny as she handed him the phone receiver and mouthed Billy's name.

Taking the phone, he slapped Molly on the buttocks with a shrug. He didn't mind his partner knowing. In fact, it felt right. "Billy, this better be good. It's Sunday and –"

"I know, I know. I just got a call from Fang. Thinks he found the leak that gave Mo China the heads up about the note in Hèng Lìwùshì's mouth. He's had surveillance on him and says he's got enough for an arrest warrant."

"Good. He deserves a big collar. He's been a real asset to this case."

"It's going down tonight. Said to meet him at the ME's office at eight."

"The ME's office?" questioned Johnny. Molly was confused as well.

"That's what he said," Billy said. "I even wrote it down."

Modus Vivendi

CHAPTER 98

Johnny and Billy arrived at the Medical Examiner's office as planned, not knowing what to expect. There had been some suspicion of a leak there before, but as time marched on and nothing had surfaced, they had hoped for the best. Detective Fang gave all the information he had to those that were there: Johnny, Billy, Detectives Chang and Pan. With guns drawn, they entered the corridor leading them to the point of destination – the autopsy room. Both light and sounds were emanating from the closed door as each detective wondered what was about to be played out.

Slowly, Fang inched the door open, then swung it wide as everyone followed. Taken by surprise, the startled doctor in the room almost fell, tripping over his feet as he instinctively stepped back. He pulled down his surgical mask in anger, revealing a neat Van Dyke beard. "What the hell is going on here? I'm conducting an autopsy. Who are you? What do you want? Identify yourselves." Recovering quickly, the man now exuded the confidence of a man who knows he is where he should be, all five-feet-six of him.

"We're New York City detectives," said Fang. "Now, slowly, lie down and place your hands on your head."

"I will do no such thing. My name is Dr. Dean Paul and I'm going to finish my autopsy. You must be in the wrong place," he said stepping back to table and reaching under the sheet that still covered a portion of the body. He pulled out a revolver, whipping around to face them, prepared to kill every last one of them.

The next few seconds were a blur of noise, shots echoing through the sterile tiled room as the detectives took whatever meager cover they could find as they returned fire. A cry of pain. The sound of a dropped gun.

"You shot me! You shot me, you stupid bastards!" Dr. Paul exclaimed, holding his shoulder.

"You'll live. You're lucky it's only a flesh wound. And you're under arrest, "Fang said.

"For what? I need a doctor. I've been shot," the man wailed in disbelief. "I'm bleeding!"

Fang shut him up. "You *are* a doctor! You're under arrest for giving out confidential police information that led to criminal activity and murder."

The man was still sputtering with indignation. "Are you insane? I'm a great doctor." Pride kept his mouth moving even as somewhere in his brain, a voice told him to clam up. "A doctor two times over, in fact, because I'm also a veterinarian. I could slice and dice you on or off of this table in minutes."

Johnny cackled with glee. "It's him! It's you! Not only did you leak information to Mo China, you're the fucking Janitor!" he exclaimed. "You get paid from LaPoshio. Cuff him, boys. I don't give a shit if he bleeds to death. Hand me one of those bandages over there. I'll wrap it until we get him to the hospital."

"Ahhh! You're hurting me," the man cried. "Let go! I don't want this man near me. Get away!"

"Make those cuffs as tight as you can behind his back, Jin."

"Sure thing, Lieutenant."

Incredibly, the so-called Dr. Paul continued to rant. "You don't know who or what you're dealing with. I'll have your badges and your souls. I'm dying here! Get these cuffs off."

"Let's get him over to Mercy General," Johnny ordered, then got into Paul's face. "You're lucky I don't stick my finger in the wound. That would give you reason to scream. Get him out of here!"

CHAPTER 99

It took 24 hours to process Dr. Dean Paul and have him arraigned due to his wound. Word got out, of course, and the courtroom was packed, mostly with reporters. After Grace Tilly received an anonymous tip by phone, she'd made sure to secure a front row seat.

Molly had appointed a prosecutor from her office, but wild horses could not have kept her from the arraignment. She had arranged to have Paul appear before this particular judge, knowing what a tyrant he was when it came to crimes against law enforcement.

Standing before Judge Gabriel Tillman next to Molly was Daniel Callahan, her prosecutor. Across the aisle stood the defendant, Dr. Dean Paul and his attorney John Greco. After the usual formalities and protocols, the charges were read: attempted murder on five New York City police detective, unlawful disclosure of confidential police information that furthered criminal activity including multiple murders.

Judge Tillman asked by rote, "How does the defendant plead?"

"Not guilty. I was abused and shot. I demand –"

Greco cut him off. "Please excuse my client, Your Honor. We will be filing an official complaint regarding his mistreatment by law enforcement. We would like to request that reasonable bail be set, Your Honor, and that Dr. Paul be released on his own recognizance. A defendant is innocent until proven guilty, Your Honor, and Dr. Paul is employed by the city's Medical Examiner's office. He is a reputable physician with no prior arrests."

Judge Tillman closed his eyes and sighed heavily. "All right, let's do this. Miss Penett, what does the State have to say?"

"The State requests that no bail be set, Your Honor. Dr. Paul is a dangerous man. He attempted to kill five detectives and –"

"I get the picture, Miss Penett. Defendant is remanded until trial. Is there anything else, Miss Penett?"

"No, Your Honor. Thank you."

"Oh, by the way, Mr. Greco, I will see to it that I am the presiding judge when your client comes to trial."

John Greco knew Judge Tillman's despotic reputation for harsh sentences. He was also aware that the judge knew Greco's services were retained by Alvise Laposhio. He would have his work cut out for him.

Leaving the courtroom Molly caught up with Fang. "Good work, Detective. One down and two to go," she said, giving him a wink.

Trust What Someone Says?

CHAPTER 100

Captain Sullivan was in a very good mood. Strings had been pulled to expedite Dr. Dean Paul's preliminary hearing with almost embarrassing speed. The Grand Jury came back with an indictment of multiple murders, attempted murder on police officers, and assault. Next would be pre-trial motions with Molly and jury selection. He might live until he could retire, after all. "I hear your Janitor is singing like a canary."

"Starting out. He says he knows the names of everyone involved, the hits, places where bodies are buried up in Yonkers. He also claims there are others within multiple ME offices that are involved. He even admitted it was him that shot at me and Billy. He *started* to tell of the murders he committed and the attempted ones that were missed., and then he stopped. Now he says he's willing to spill it all, but only if he gets immunity."

"That's not happening, Lieutenant, you know that, right?"

"Yes, sir, but that's not going to stop us from telling him we'll make a deal. Let the DA and the feds break the news they can't help him when the time comes. By then we should have what we need. What Molly *is* willing to do is not put him in gen pop. That would be a death sentence for someone like him. That is, if the judge doesn't give him a *real* death sentence." Johnny leaned back in his chair, allowing himself a little down time.

"What are you doing about his claim regarding the Medical Examiner's office?"

Johnny shrugged. "We have to look into everything, but it will probably turn out to be a dead end."

Sullivan nodded in agreement. "Good luck, Lieutenant. Cover all the bases. I don't want to hear that you left out Christopher Michaels himself. I know you two go way back, but no one is immune to suspect, no one. And say! That Detective Fang is one hell of a cop. How would feel about him coming to South Central?"

Johnny grinned. "That would be great, but I don't think the 5th will let him go, Captain. I'm hoping now that Laurènt found Monica, and we have the Janitor on ice, there won't be any more bodies turning up. We just need to get Griff and Mo China. The feds are working the Alvise LaPoshio angle. He's got the funny money in his possession, so they're creating a sting to catch him with it in hand. Then it'll be the penitentiary for ole' *Al Pazzo*."

From outside the open door, Johnny heard his name. "Hey, Lieutenant, there's a Detective Fang on line three."

"Well, speak of the devil," said Sullivan. "Use my phone."

Johnny picked up the receiver from the captain's desk. "Vero."

"Johnny, Dr. Paul gave us information on another shipment with Griff. He's due to come in tomorrow around noon when the harbor is busy loading passengers on cruise ships and all the sightseeing boats to Liberty Island. It's going to be a challenge." Jin paused. "I gotta tell you, that Janitor is one tough son-of-a-bitch. It wasn't easy to … encourage him?

327

But he's started naming names. We'll bring them in to interrogate. Oh, and I've already notified Commander Cunningham. Can you and Billy be at his station by 10?"

"We'll be there!"

CHAPTER 101

Johnny was up at dawn, anticipation for a repeat chance to nail Griff gnawing at his gut. He had to convince Molly he couldn't sleep in with her, that he needed to go to his place to feed the cat. Johnny didn't have a cat and never would – it was his way of saying he needed to check in on his own place once in a while, be in his private space. She understood. It was a big day. "Go get 'em, tiger," she kissed him sleepily goodbye, turned over, and tried not to think of the danger he'd be facing soon.

At 10 a.m. sharp, the group of detectives boarded the same Inland Buoy Tender at the Coast Guard station. They had been so sure of the outcome of the midnight operation, they weren't making the same mistake again. Anything was possible.

"You know the drill, life jackets on," Cunningham directed as he handed each one a rifle, riot shotgun, or sub machine gun in addition to their usual side arms.

"Cast off!" ordered Cummingham. He turned to the men. "This can become very complicated, but we need to keep things simple. My men have their instructions and know what to do. I know you've all put in a lot of blood, sweat, and tears to get this guy, but this is my vessel and we do things my way. If there's not a clear shot, don't take it! It's crowded out there. We can't jeopardize civilian lives."

"I have undercover along the shoreline at the anticipated arrival location and am maintaining radio contact with them," Johnny assured him.

"Good. It's common for the Coast Guard to troll the harbor on such a busy day. It'll look like we're on a regular routine check. Since we've already seen Griff, I'm sure he's changed boats. What we need to look for is something that blends in, but is also out of the norm, if that makes sense."

"Clear as mud," Billy joked.

Within minutes of getting out into the water, Cunningham spotted a large yacht through his binoculars, pointing to it for the helmsman's benefit. She was anchored about twenty-five yards off shore, just far enough from the shipping lane. "Detectives, my men can search that vessel without permission or search warrant. You cannot. Just stay for the ready," he explained as they came alongside the yacht.

"Ahoy, United States Coast Guard. We're coming aboard." The announcement was loud. No response. Johnny and Billy threw fenders over the side as the engine was cut. Cunningham's men lifted their weapons to their sides and climbed onto the other deck. It was eerily quiet on the yacht, and each man felt the well-trained inner warning. *Step slowly.*

"This is the United States Coast Guard. Make yourself known," shouted Cunningham, approaching the cabin door.

Silence. And then, a faint whimper. The cabin door opened slowly, as if it hadn't been closed tightly. Every weapon was pointed, every trigger finger was at the ready. A guardsman pushed the door with the barrel of his riot shotgun.

A young woman of perhaps 17 stood there. "Nì shi Mò zhōngguó?" she said in a hushed tone.

Cunningham stepped out of the group to shout at his vessel. "Fang, Pan, Chang, get over here!"

Johnny came with them. Stepping in the cabin he counted twelve women sitting on the floor.

Again the girl asked timidly, "Nì shi Mò zhōngguó?"

"What is she saying?" Cunningham snarled.

"She asked if one of us is Mo China," Fang said.

"Search every inch of this boat," Cunningham commanded.

Jin spoke softly to the girl."Mò zhōngguó huìjiàn nǐ ma?"

"Shì, Dài wǒmen qù gōngzuò. Cóng zhōngguó kāishǐ xīn de shēnghuó."

Fang nodded, then turned to Johnny. "She said Mo China was to meet them and take them to a house then find them work. A new life away from China. That's all."

The commander took charge. "Radio Mercy General, no, Mother Cabrini Hospital's closer. Tell them we're bringing 12 women to be checked, fed and issued warm clothes."

"Aye aye, Commander."

Johnny's disappointment struggled with compassion on his face. Some of these women were Angie's age, some younger. "One of these jaunts better bring us to Mo China and Griff."

Fang understood. "It will, Lieutenant, it will."

"You three speak to them, but be nice," Johnny addressed Fang, Chang, and Pan. "Do you have any women that speak Chinese that they'd relate to? That'd be good. All they see now is a bunch of men with guns. They've gotta be scared shitless."

331

CHAPTER 102

Johnny sat at his desk, his thoughts consumed with the nagging vision of Monica's ledger, out there, but where? He was primarily concerned that it not wind up in the hands of Alvise LaPoshio. That would get Lilly killed, more than likely. *Too many bodies already. I've got to persuade Lilly that I will be able to help her keep her operation going. If I befriend her, gain her trust, maybe...*

Billy came to an interesting point in the report on his desk. "So I understand the good Dr. Paul is getting more comfortable speaking with Molly."

Molly had been fairly successful convincing the man that she would work with him, at least to get the death penalty off the table. "He's spouting out murders he committed left and right. She hasn't mentioned that night in the elevator with her, and he hasn't either," Johnny said, thankful for something else to focus on. He kept seeing a vision of Monica, sprawled on a bed, her throat slashed. "Seems he has fiancée who works in the ME's office, as bad as he is from the sound of it. He'll flip on her for a deal, no doubt. He knows his number is up - we have him dead to rights with attempted murder on us and the killings he's confessing too."

"Fiancée?" Billy was intrigued. It always surprised him when a dirt bag had a romantic interest. Almost always, it was not a case of opposites attracting.

"We're getting a warrant on probable for her. Paul says he saw her kill three people – the John Doe in Columbus Park, Angie the Fish and Fat Cat Carmine." Johnny pulled out his notepad. "Her name is Carol Lynne, a mortuary technician. She assists with some procedures but mostly check-ins, storage of bodies, release of remains, that kind of thing. She creates death certificates and burial permits. But according to Paul she can also wield a scalpel with speed and accuracy. Said she'd assisted him on the occasional autopsy to cover up their own murders."

"We may never have found her without getting the Janitor." The idea of someone like her killing right under their noses was chilling.

"We may never find the bodies. Paul said they were buried in Yonkers, but their disposal site turns out to be Van Courtland Park," Johnny added.

"Are you fucking kidding me? Do you know how big that area is? It's over 1,000 acres, at least."

"At least. This Carol Lynne dame lives on the border of the Bronx and Yonkers. Inherited a house from her mother, apparently. She and the Janitor have been living there together. Thing is, the house is on the Yonkers side but right across the street is Van Courtland Park. Lynne grew up knowing those woods and swamp pretty well, but Paul assumed the park was in Yonkers, too. No Chinatown bodies there, but plenty of others."

Billy was tired of being inside. "Do you want to give it a shot? Pick Paul up, see if he can point out some burial spots? I wouldn't mind getting a few unsolved murders under our belt."

"Maybe, but we don't want to spend much time on cold cases when we got our own to close. Carol Lynne hasn't been back to the ME's since we got Paul, but she probably isn't just sitting at home twiddling her thumbs. I just hope she hasn't skipped town." Answering the look on Billy's face, Johnny nodded. "There's alerts at the airport, bus terminals, and train stations. Yonkers PD has a BOLO for her too."

Billy picked up his phone. "Let's go catch another dirt bag."

CHAPTER 103

Billy turned off the corner of Aqueduct Avenue onto Parkway North approaching the love nest of Carol Lynne and Dr. Dean Paul. Two Yonkers police cars and four officers awaited their arrival. After brief introductions, the Sergeant gave the go-ahead signal. Guns drawn, three officers approached the door while the Sergeant, Johnny, and Billy waited at strategic points.

"No answer, Sarge," shouted one of the uniformed officers.

"Let me see your warrant," asked the Sergeant. Johnny took it to him for a once-over. "Looks good, Detective." He gave the order to kick in the door.

The home was pristine, not a thing out of place, at least on the ground floor. After clearing it, they cautiously made their way upstairs where they found a different state of affairs. A bedroom had been hastily vacated. Clothes were strewn about, drawers were partially open, the closet was almost empty. A suitcase with a few things in it rested on a chair. In an ashtray on the bedside table, a single cigarette butt had been left to burn itself out. Johnny placed his hand under it. "Cold," he said. The whiskey glass beside it was almost empty, no ice. He picked it up and took a whiff. *Old Crow. Dame's got taste, anyway.*

Two Yonkers officers came in to report that the house was clear, including the basement and attic.

"She hightailed it out of here, Johnny." Billy was disgusted.

The sergeant was accommodating. "Detectives, I'm heading back to the station, but my officers will stay outside as long as you want to look around. I'll make arrangements to have surveillance put on the house, just in case."

"Thanks, Sergeant. We shouldn't be long."

Billy let out a howl of glee from another room. "Johnny, come look what I found ... holy shit!"

Wedged behind a bureau, Billy had discovered a doctor's black leather carrying case. "Well, will you look at that," whistled Johnny. It was filled with scalpels, knives, scissors, bone cutters, needles, thread, and bandages. Underneath the medical equipment they found a .22, two passports, and $3,000 in cash. Each passport had Carol Lynne's photo but with different names. *Navonni. Gerde.*

"This is coming with us, Billy. I wonder what passport she took." Johnny frowned. "These pictures match her employee file from the ME's office. The Port Authority, bus stations, airlines, and train stations all have her picture. But I wouldn't be surprised if she left this here for us to find just to throw us off. She may be sitting across the street, for all we know. We need to get a team up here and scour this place."

"This bag gives a whole different meaning to having a house call by a doctor," Billy said as he put everything back. "This broad may be shrewd. Gas lighting us."

Johnny shook his head. "Whatever her little scheme, we'll get her."

CHAPTER 104

The Medical Examiner's office was buzzing like a bee's nest that's been poked so many times it finally hits the ground. And just as a colony of bees protects the hive, the staff determined to protect the office's reputation. They'd worked side by side with murderers. To most, it was a horrible thought. It was the others, who had known all along – they must be found.

Word was out that South Central detectives had arrived to start interrogations. No one was immune to questioning; over the PA system, Dr. Christopher Michaels was called to the second floor conference room where questioning was being held. Other names followed.

Michaels looked very tired. "Johnny, I'm as shocked as you that anyone on my team has been involved with the Chinatown murders. Dr. Paul has been nothing but an asset to this office. He's one hell of a doctor."

"He's a veterinarian!" Johnny exclaimed.

Michaels shook his head. "He was, and still is, but he also holds a medical license in osteopathic medicine as well as animal forensic pathology. I know him as a gentle caring man. During his job interview, one particular comment struck a chord with me."

"What was that, Doc?"

"He said he didn't like euthanizing animals, and looked forward to not having to do it anymore."

"What a lying piece of shit!" Billy muttered.

"I am shocked about all of this, frankly. And Carol Lynne too! Her credentials were also immaculate. A caring woman who showed the utmost respect for both the living and the dead." Michaels looked as if he still couldn't grasp that he had rubbed shoulders every day with monsters. "She projected a quality of … spirituality. They made such a wonderful couple," he murmured miserably. "What can I do to help? I want this office cleared of any wrongdoing or involvement."

Johnny was grateful, but still wary. "I want a report on every file, case, and person those two ever worked on, no matter how small the involvement," Johnny said. "If Lynne so much as wrote a name on a file label, I want to know what color ink she used."

Michaels' shoulders slumped, but he was up to the task. "I'll have it to you by morning."

Johnny shook hands with his childhood friend. "I know you're clean on this, but … do you have *any* suspicions, any whatsoever of anyone else now that it's all coming to the surface?"

"My God!" Michaels was horrified that there might be someone else. "No … no one!"

"Send in the next person on your way out," Johnny said. It was going to be a long day.

CHAPTER 105

The next morning, Johnny answered his phone. A heavy Eastern European accent spoke loudly at the other end. "Detective Vero, this is Sergeant Libinski, New York Port Authority Police. We have a suspect from your APB in custody. Carrying two passports, one from the US, name of Carol Lynne. One from Italy, name of Carolina Nunni. We pinched her purchasing a one-way ticket to Abruzzi, Italy at New York International Airport. We have her in a holding cell."

Johnny was elated. "Nice work, Sergeant. She may be armed and she is definitely dangerous. We have her on multiple murders."

"We didn't find any weapons, Lieutenant."

"We're on our way."

As soon as he could clear it with the captain and have uniforms assigned, South Central's finest was on their way, sirens blasting and red bubble lights flashing as three police cars headed to the airport in Queens.

Billy's 1949 Ford Tudor sedan had reached the 98 miles per hour capacity on the speedometer, and still his foot pushed the pedal. "Johnny, this is one case that will go down in history!"

Johnny, Billy, and the four uniformed officers parked and exited their cars, trotting to the holding cells with Libinski. Inside, however, there seemed to be a tremendous commotion ahead. Numerous police officers blocked the cell entry.

Pushing their way to the front, Johnny shouted. "Let us through. NYPD."

"What the fuck happened!" he yelled. Lying on the floor of the cell was a naked dead woman in a puddle of still-oozing blood.

"Jesus, Mary, and Joseph!" exclaimed Libinski. "That's Officer Donna Hathaway. She processed your perp. She reported that she found no weapons."

"She didn't search everywhere, apparently," Johnny snarled.

Libinski barked orders in every direction. "What are you all standing here for? Get the fucking airport exits sealed. She can't be hard to find in Hathaway's uniform." As his men scattered, he turned to Johnny. "I'm sorry Detective. Hathaway is ... was ... on the job less than a year." He stared at the body.

"A thousand sorrys to her family won't be enough, Sergeant." After the adrenaline rush on the way, Johnny could feel himself crash. "With a cop's uniform and keys, our perp's long gone. Let's go," he said, walking slowly back to the car.

On a hunch, Johnny radioed South Central Dispatch and requested a call to Yonkers PD.

In answer to Billy's raised eyebrows, he shrugged. "That bitch might go back for the bag. Hit the lights and siren, will 'ya!"

Four Yonkers black-and-whites met them at Carol Lynne's house. They rushed in, but once again, to their chagrin, the house was empty.

One of the Yonkers officers called from the kitchen. "Lieutenant, come look!"

An opening in the wall was carefully devised to open by a buzzer. No one could have noticed it when it was closed, but smeared blood on the wall provided a dead give-a-way to the buzzer's location.

She got here so goddamn fast. "Rip the house apart. She may be hiding," Johnny commanded.

Billy had another idea. "She must have had clothes and another get-a-way bag stashed," he said. "My money's on the park. I'll call it in to the Bronx. The Riverdale precinct has access to horse-mounted units."

"This is now a Yonkers PD crime scene," Johnny barked, instructing the other officers to call it in to their detective. *Where was the fucking surveillance? Jesus Christ! This has got to end soon!*

Some Old-fashioned Recipes Never Change!

CHAPTER 106

Johnny opened the bathroom door open to an assault of heavy steam. Molly loved hot showers. Dealing with hardened criminals always left her with a need to scrub, as if just being in the room with dirt bags made her dirty, too.

When he opened the curtain, her back was to him, shampooing her hair. "Johnny?"

"Were you expecting someone else?"

She giggled. "I thought it might be my cousin Charly."

Johnny's thoughts raced for a moment. *She showers with her cousin?* "Is she in town?"

"Are you coming in?" she reached her hand out, feeling for him as he stepped over the rim of the tub. Molly pulled him in closer. *Such a safe and happy feeling. He's here, not chasing criminals, not being shot out, not with anyone else. Here with me.* She kissed him underneath the shower as the water washed the shampoo out and over them both. Opening her eyes, she admired his magnificent build, the equal to any of the younger lifeguards at Jones Beach, with their smooth tanned skin. Those boys were the desire of any woman who saw them, including her cousin Charly. *Boys. Who needs a boy, when I've got a man like this?*

The hot water dissolved the soap along with the day's residue of stress and strain into the drain below. Johnny returned her kiss and she demanded more. Molly's tongue searched for his; she began to suck his bottom lip. Gripping her wet, naked body tighter, Johnny delighted in Molly's every salacious move. Her hand reached down, stroking him firmly. Touching him made it clear what she wanted, but it also got her wet, prepared. She wanted him to listen to his erect phallus, not to his mind, to plunge into her right then and there, with no delay. She raised her leg to brace one foot on the tub's edge, encouraging him to lift her as she guiding him a little at a time, pushing down on him until he was all the way inside. She grabbed his cheeks moving against him in a pumping motion to find their rhythm. A low moan: "Oh, God! You feel amazing, so hard."

"You get me that way," he murmured, as she relaxed, giving way to her moment of ecstasy. As Johnny continued thrusting, Molly could feel him explode, pulsating with each orgasmic release while the water cascaded over them. His erection fading, he slipped from Molly's warmth and set her down. They stood there in the afterglow, their hands exploring still, sweetly, intimately.

This could be the last time we ever touch, Molly thought, as she always did. "Don't change what you do to me, Johnny," she murmured. "Don't change." Under the shower, he could not tell that she was crying with joy.

CHAPTER 107

The aroma of fresh coffee and the smell of toasted cinnamon bread were calling to Johnny. *Did I hear Molly?* Johnny opened his eyes.

"Hey, sleepy-head, I have good news!" Molly called from the kitchen. "Breakfast is ready. Oh, there you are." Johnny wore only his boxers; a morning erection was still apparent. *Time for that later.* "Bollinger called – he has LaPoshio's bodyguards! Joey Tremont and Bobby Hoffman have agreed to turn. They say they'll set him up to take the fall with the counterfeit money in return for full immunity."

Johnny kissed her before sitting at the table, untying the sash of her robe as he went. "Bollinger's agreeable to that?"

Molly rolled her eyes with a smile, tying the sash back. "He said he can arrange it since he has control of the case, and since they both have clean records. And he didn't forget our deal. After LaPoshio serves his term, we get him."

"Heh, heh, heh," Johnny laughed quietly. "We may be retired by that time. He could get up to 20 years. Besides, there'll be someone to take his place. The mob's not going to let millions of dollars pass them by."

Molly brought over the plate of cinnamon bread and poured his coffee. "So what! We did what we said we'd do.

Maybe he'll die in prison." Molly's mood was light. "We'll get Griff and Mo China. We already have Dr. Dean Paul."

He hated to bring her down, but he didn't share her enthusiasm. Still too many loose ends for his tastes. "There's one more missing: Dr. Paul's fiancée. Carol Lynne has a lot of blood on her hands." *Does Lynn still love Paul? Did she ever? Did he?* It was puzzling to him. Murderers, making love after?

Molly was undeterred. "She'll turn up, Johnny. Who knows? Maybe if she had the chance she'd try to rescue him, and we could nab her."

"Or find him so she can slit his throat for turning on her."

"Well, that's a happy thought," Molly chided. "She's a smart one, but eventually she'll resurface. They always do. In the meantime, I'll keep leaning on Dr. Paul. I'm working him. He's..." She stopped abruptly.

Johnny knew the look on her face. "He's what?"

Molly brushed some hair from her eyes and winked. "I do believe he thinks he can sway me with his flirtations."

Johnny nodded. "That's what killers do. They win you, try to get you to empathize with them, make you vulnerable. Remember our favorite serial killer?" Jean-Paul Vincent had done everything in his power to win them over.

"I will never forget that case," she said, nibbling on a piece of bread thoughtfully. "I'm going to ask Dr. Amiric Misak to be on the other side of the two-way mirror when I interrogate him next. Maybe he can decipher any hidden agendas."

Johnny didn't like the idea of a cold-blooded murderer hitting on his woman. "Why not, we need all the help we can get. But if Paul so much as –"

"There's always a uniformed officer close by, Johnny. Don't worry. He also has one hand cuffed to the table." She put down the piece of bread and slowly licked her lips, fully aware that he was studying her. "And speaking of handcuffs ..."

CHAPTER 108

"Whoever loves money never has enough," Agent Bollinger said pompously, but laughing.

"Wise King Solomon," Molly quipped.

"Maybe so, but old habits never die. LaPoshio is one greedy son-of-a-bitch. He'll never have enough money, women, or wine."

The feds had struck a deal with bodyguards Tremont and Hoffman. Bollinger called in the same group to bring them up to speed. "We have the counterfeit dough in place and they're going to set LaPoshio up with all the cabbage in hand. Two briefcases, the ones you saw at Leelee's club, Lieutenant. His men carried them out, they'll get them back into his hands in due time. That's when we'll move in. Which is why I brought you all here today." After chewing them out for the failed boat raid, he didn't want them to think that they were keeping them out of any loops, either. "There will be $25,000 in each case. This has got to go down as planned, people. I signed for that money. It may be counterfeit, it can't wind up lost. I'm still responsible for it. As soon as we cuff him –"

"There'll be another just like him to take his place. His chair won't even get cold," Johnny interrupted. "Those bodyguards will be dead within a week."

"We've got that covered, Lieutenant. They'll be in hiding, with a good cover thousands of miles away. If they decide to return, it's on them. At that point, we've fulfilled our agreement with the both of them. In this scenario, we're the victors and we get the spoils – namely, Alvise LaPoshio."

"What's our part?" Billy asked.

"Good question, Detective," Bollinger said quietly. "You have none. Well, at this juncture, anyway. Remember our deal: You can have LaPoshio *after* he serves his term. You get everyone else. With what I'm hearing about the Janitor giving all the details, *he'll* never get out of prison, but you'll get LaPoshio in due time. If your guy spills more about the bodies buried in Van Courtland Park, and if they've been transported across state lines, then that's ours, too. We can work on that together and share the glory." Bollinger laughed. "I'm not greedy! Oh, by the way, I followed up with Inspector Laurènt regarding your dead hooker."

This was news to Johnny. He listened to Bollinger with increasing agitation. "Because she is – was – an American murdered in a foreign country, we're working on the details together. I'll be sharing what we feel is LaPoshio's involvement with him. The woman –"

"Monica," said Johnny. "Her name was Monica."

Bollinger clearly did not care. "*Monica's* sister lives in Montpellier, France and will claim her body. As soon as Laurènt is finished with his investigation, he will send her belongings to her sister." He let out a breath. "I think that about wraps it up. Any questions?

I've got to get the sister's name and address, Johnny thought. *That fucking ledger!*

A Chicken's Modus Operandi---
They Always Come Home to Roost!

CHAPTER 109

Johnny and Billy were summoned to Captain Sullivan's office where they found Molly waiting.

"This doesn't look good, Johnny," Billy said as they took a seat.

"You worry too much."

Molly greeted them formally. "A Port Authority car was found in a swampy part of Van Courtland Park. Lynne must have thought that the water still ran there, hoping it would sink. Instead it got stuck in the swampy muck and has been torched." The detectives let out a simultaneous groan. "The Fire Marshal and Riverdale PD believe teenagers discovered it and lit it up." She sighed. "We may never have found it, if not for the explosion and smoke, but any evidence is also gone. Obviously no sign of Carol Lynne either."

"Too bad she wasn't in the car when it happened," Billy muttered.

"We all feel that way, Detective," Molly said.

"There's an APB out for her," Sullivan assured her. "You need to lean on the Janitor. If anyone knows her MO, he does. I spoke with the captain over at Yonkers, and he'll place men inside the house around the clock."

"A day late and a dollar short, if you ask me," Johnny mumbled. "We need to talk about Monica's sister," he said, looking at Molly. "There may be something in Monica's belongings that Inspector Laurènt wouldn't realize was significant. Maybe she's written things, codes, names that we may recognize. Laurènt may discount something we should see, and give it to the sister."

Sullivan agreed. "Miss Penett, see if you can work your magic. Maybe we can get *everything* that was found at the scene before the sister gets her hands on it. Vero's idea is a good one. If there's nothing of importance, I can see to it personally that it's returned to her."

Johnny was relieved. *Now that I asked openly, and Sullivan's on board, no one should question my motives.*

On their way out, Billy leaned into Johnny and whispered, "Good one, Johnny. Fast thinking. I want a peek at that ledger, too."

"Lieutenant, can you wait a moment?" Molly asked.

"Go ahead, Billy. I'll catch up with you later. Would like to step into my office, Miss Penett?" He closed the door and locked it.

Molly's face was so close, Johnny could smell her perfume.

"Detective, I think I'm starting to fall for you," she whispered, kissing her finger before placing it on his lips.

In answer, he caught her finger and put it in his mouth, sucking it before she pulled it out and cleared her throat. "I actually have something else to tell you." They sat down. "You'll love this, Johnny. Dr. Paul gave up Griff. There's a schedule, something that takes place on a certain day every three months. Do you want to know what day that is?" she asked coyly.

"What do *you* think?"

"You're planning to be at my place tonight?"

"Where else would I be?"

"See you there soon. I'll tell you the rest then." Molly blew him a kiss from the door as she unlocked it. He rose as well, standing in the doorway, watching her saunter out, knowing she could feel his eyes on her.

CHAPTER 110

"Molly's information from Paul was accurate. Just like Pavlov's dog, salivating at sounds associated with food, Griff salivates on the same day, every three months, knowing that his delivery of women and opium will bring in a big payoff," Johnny told Billy. "He stepped things up when it was evident we were getting close – maybe to throw us off a larger drop-off, who knows? We have no way of knowing if Griff was on those boats. But he's still got his original target date circled on the calendar."

"Some things never change," Billy smiled. "If it's not broke, why fix it?" Billy rubbed his hands together with satisfaction. "Griff figures that the few times we came close to grabbing his ass, he got away with it so why not stick to the plan? Dumb cops that we are, we couldn't possibly figure out the mastermind's schedule. Never thought the Janitor would give up any details." He frowned. "What I don't understand is why LaPoshio hasn't got word to him through Mo China. Makes me wonder if LaPoshio's had him knocked off already."

"Let's go see," Johnny said.

"What are you talking 'bout? We don't know –"

Johnny grinned. "Round up Fang and his guys. One of my stoolies came across with a tip where he might be. We still have a few days before Griff hits the harbor."

Billy wasn't buying it. "Do you really think Mo China would hang around with all the heat coming down?"

"How the fuck would I know what Mo China would do? He knows the devil he has here compared to the demons he dealt with in China. Where would he go? Think about that. Old habits never die."

A Good Thing That Seemed Bad At First

CHAPTER 111

The "gang of five" was on the move. Johnny, Billy, Fang, Pan, and Chang wound their way swiftly through the crowded streets of Chinatown on foot. Johnny was betting his snitch's lead wasn't a wild goose chase. One thing Chinatown's residents knew was how to spot cops. Once spotted, you would hear *Jìngchá*[8] every hundred feet or so, keeping track of the direction they were heading. At an intersection, the call went out each way. The area was rife with corruption; spotters were on duty 24 hours a day.

The detectives' destination was the opium den they previously raided. According to Johnny's snitch, Mo China felt the cops would assume he wouldn't be stupid enough to return there.

Johnny and Billy stationed themselves in the back alley where Mo China escaped the last time. Fang, Pan, and Chang would – if all went well – flush him out of his private room through the escape door, leading him straight to Johnny and Billy.

By the time the echo of *Jìngchá* reached the den's wizened watchman, Fang, Pan, and Chang were at the top of the stairway. Immediately, shots were fired toward the door itself

---
[8]   Chinese for Police

in an effort to stop them. Fang was former military, an expert marksman. His first two rounds killed the gunman instantly. Chaos ensued. The men kept their focus, however, heading toward what they believed to be Mo China's room. People screamed and scurried every which way, a few tripping over the dead man in the middle of the floor.

The entire room emptied quickly, with the exception of the naked prostitutes too stoned to move. Fang moved toward Pan and Chang as they busted through the door. At the first sound of trouble, Mo China had climbed out the window and taken the fire escape … right into *Jìngchá's* trap.

CHAPTER 112

"Vero! You and Bradshaw get in here!" Captain Sullivan's wish was their command.

Sullivan had a lot to tell them. "You know that Detective Fang has to go through IA and all that bullshit. He'll be off for a few days, see the department shrink, go before the Grand Jury, back on desk duty for a while. I'll go to bat for him just like I did for you, Bradshaw. I'm with his captain and the chief, the PC, anyone and everyone I can, so he's cut loose as quickly as possible. In fact, I'm hoping we can bypass the desk duty altogether. We need good men like him – like all of you – out on the street where it counts."

Sullivan went on to explain that the opium den was closed, an active crime scene. The prostitutes who had been too out of it to escape were at Mother Cabrini Hospital. "They'll be given good care there," he said, making the sign of the cross. "All five of you will be getting commendations."

"You know as well as us, Captain, that even if that one's closed for good, another will open within 24 hours with more hookers and dope. Griff's not the only supplier, but he's still out there, too." Johnny said.

Sullivan nodded grimly. "We know it and expect it. Hell, if it didn't happen, we'd wonder why. We'll be fighting this battle forever. As long as there's big money to be made, there will be dirt bags willing to take a chance." He pulled something from his desk drawer. "Speaking of taking a chance, have you boys bought any of the Irish Sweepstakes tickets yet?" It wasn't a request.

Tickets sold in the US were smuggled in illegally, the men knew, but that was one crime they gave tacit approval to. It kept the captain happy, feeling he was helping out the motherland. Johnny and Billy each reached into their pockets with a sigh. Each, in turned, laid cash on the desk as Sullivan ripped their tickets from the book.

"Thank you boys. And the hospitals in Ireland thank you." He returned the book to his desk. "But back to business. Where are we with the Chinatown murders?"

"With the Janitor and now, Mo China, in custody, there haven't been any more ads. The feds are setting up LaPoshio with a sting and we have an APB out for Carol Lynne. We do not yet know who killed Monica in France," Johnny reported.

"We also have a reliable tip on Griff's next drop in the harbor," Billy added.

"Good work, men. You're dismissed," Sullivan said with a wave of his hand.

CHAPTER 113

Mo China smirked in his seat in the interrogation room. Molly and Dr. Amirc Masik stood watching through the two-way mirror. A uniformed officer stood in one corner, the usual precaution.

"He is trying to convince everyone he speaks no English," Dr. Masik explained to Molly. "Look at his body, how he is sitting, aloof, speaking Chinese. He's trying to create doubt."

The Chinese boss kept repeating solemnly, "Bù jiǎng yīngyǔ, Bù jiǎng yīngyǔ,[9]" until Detectives Jimmy Pan and Ru Chang entered the room suddenly, and loudly. Mo China's demeanor went from the divine, with the inscrutable countenance of Buddha to that of a man haunted by demons.

Using a pre-determined strategy, Chang bellowed, "FUCK YOU MO CHINA."

Pan yelled at the same time. "YOU ARE ONE STUPID SON-OF-A-BITCH!"

Shaken and caught off guard, Mo China responded as they had anticipated. "Fuck you, Detective and your fuck partner, and the other fuck detective. He killed friend. All to be ashamed. You disgrace to China." His eyes narrowed. "You come work me. I pay good. I Monarch of China. Mo

---

[9] No speak English, No speak English

China." The bastard had the presence of mind to actually seem proud.

"There is no more China, you stupid fuck," Chang barked. "It's now the People's Republic of China! Don't you listen to Chinese radio? The Communists took over the mainland. The government retreated to Taiwan."

"You and your friends dirty. You take money from shopkeepers and me, pay too for Fafi numbers." In a moment of panic, he realized that his cover had vanished into thin air.

Watching intently, Dr. Masik asked Molly if that was the usual way police interrogated suspects.

"Maybe we should go, Doctor." Molly was concerned the detectives would cross a line. Not that she minded, but she didn't want Masik to see it if they did.

"No, no. This is most interesting," he said. "I am learning something new here. I will stay and observe, if that's acceptable?"

Molly was glad he was enjoying himself. "Of course."

"Your detectives are using psychological manipulation in a most effective manner. Quite wonderful."

Across from Mo China, the detectives fired questions like bullets, moving back and forth between English and Chinese. "Ah!" observed Dr. Masik. "By quickly asking questions in both languages, your criminal must engage both sides of his brain. While the right side of his brain remembers the gist of an experience or the big picture, the left side of the brain recalls the details. I imagine he is answering the details in Chinese. Very good, Miss Penett."

"Alvise LaPoshio senior person," Mo China was saying. "Must respect to live. I know no one above him. He bad man.

Equal to Shanghai Du Yesheng[10] in China. I pay him to let Griff bring shipments of women and opium. He runs docks all illegal in New York City and Chinatown. Everything to him. He boss-man, if you live. See I tell you. Now I go home."

"Not just yet," Pan said, playing on Mo China's hopes. In reality, he would not be going anywhere any time soon.

Molly sensed a lull. "This could go on for hours, Doctor. They'll wear him down until they're satisfied with the information. They'll process it, check for accuracy. It all takes time. Let's go upstairs to Captain Sullivan's office."

---

[10]   Shanghai Du Yuesheng is notorious crime boss in China.

Even Accurate Information Can Run Awry

CHAPTER 114

"Johnny, today's the day. Bollinger called and it's a go for LaPoshio's sting."

This was the message he'd been waiting for. "I'd like to be there when it all goes down, Molly. Surely Bollinger won't object. We won't interfere."

"It will be very satisfying, I know. I already cleared all five of you to be there. You, Billy, Pan, Chang, Fang too. As of this morning, he's back on regular duty. We pulled some strings. It's a go."

Johnny was grateful. "What about you? Will you be there?"

"I thought it best for me not to be there, Johnny," she said, giving him all the details. They were to meet across the street from LaPoshio's Café at 3 that afternoon, with agents set up in the bakery. Her office had contacted the other detectives. "We're all set, Johnny. This should be smooth sailing. LaPoshio will be going away for a long time." She sighed. "And you're right – we probably *will* be retired by the time he's turned over to us on the murder charges."

"I'm good with it, Molly. It's the cost of doing business, you know, *quid pro quo* with the feds as Gra- well, as they say. We're getting our just desserts. I do want the last two, Griff and the Lynne woman. She's as bad, if not worse, than all the others."

Molly had news in that regard as well, opening a folder on her desk. "Her dossier just turned up, thanks to Paul's information. He gave her up in a heartbeat for a lighter sentence. Born Carolyn Navonni, in Francofonte, Sicily. Graduated from the University of Naples with a mortuary science degree. From there, she was recruited into Italy's most notorious mob, the Camorra.[11] Recruited by none other than her charming fiancé...."

Johnny ran his fingers through his hair. Things were finally coming together. "You know what they say, Molly – 'birds of a feather.' Of course, we don't really know him. He could still be manipulating us, giving her more time to get away."

"Maybe, maybe not. These birds were doing more than flocking together. The Camorra uses women because they're not generally as suspicious looking, because they fit in more places than men. They use their prowess to seduce and murder," Molly closed the folder. "The Camorra pays very well for their hits. LaPoshio had both 'birds' on his payroll. They didn't stop at anything or anyone that got in their way. Not the police, certainly."

Johnny remembered the sight of the dead officer in the cell. "Navonni. That's the passport that was missing when we hit her house in Yonkers the second time, where she headed after killing the Port Authority cop. It has her real name on it. It might be too late to put out an APB on her with that information."

---

[11] Camorra is Italy's most powerful crime organization

"It's never too late, Johnny, Molly said with a smile. "I'll take care of it right now. Don't be late for the dance!" Unspoken, she breathed a prayer. *Be careful.*

CHAPTER 115

It was a lovely afternoon in New York City. Early May, bright sunshine, flowers in planters filling the street with even more color. Everyone was in place for the "dance," as Molly had called it; they were just waiting for the music to start. The FBI and visiting law enforcement formed the orchestra, with Bollinger as conductor. The bakery was the perfect place to watch as the curtain was about to rise on the performance, across from LaPoshio's Café. "This is like a ballet," Johnny commented to Bollinger. "You guys have choreographed this thing to a T."

"Everyone is in place," Agent Bollinger repeated the plan one more time, leaving no room for misunderstanding. "LaPoshio's car is out front, so he's inside with his two henchmen. Our undercover agent is inside with them. If all goes well, they'll leave together and get into his car. That's when our agents will block him in and make the arrest. And that's when we go."

Johnny approved. "We're glad to be here to see it."

"Hold tight men, it's show time," Bollinger ordered the various agents through his radio.

Just as Benny Roberts had given the downbeat for his orchestra to hit that first note of "Auld Lang Syne" on New

Year's Eve, Bollinger prepared for the right moment. "Wait for my signal," Bollinger said quietly into the radio.

First to exit the Café was Bobby Hoffman, followed by Alvise LaPoshio. Behind them came Joey Tremont and a woman. From their position, neither Johnny nor Billy could see her face, but they assumed it was the same mystery woman who'd been spotted with LaPoshio several times. LaPoshio and the woman got into the back seat of the beautiful, black Cadillac Fleetwood sedan. Bobby Hoffman and Joey Tremont handed the briefcases filled with the counterfeit money into the back seat before getting into their usual positions, with Joey driving and Bobby riding shotgun.

"Green light," Bollinger signaled.

Three FBI vehicles carrying agents on the outside runner boards, appeared from nowhere, surrounding LaPoshio's car. The vehicles weren't even at a complete stop when the agents jumped onto the pavement. All weapons, hand guns, shotguns, and machine guns were pointed at LaPoshio's Cadillac. Bollinger, followed by the NYPD detectives, ran out to bring what would surely be a peaceful surrender, to its final, satisfying conclusion.

"Let me see your hands!" one of the agents yelled. LaPoshio's hands were held high in plain view. Joey's came off the steering wheel, compliant.

But Bobby blurted out, "I'm not going to prison," as he drew out his revolver.

"What the fuck are you doing Bobby?" Joey hissed nervously as the agents neared the car. "Don't do this. You'll get us all killed! We'll be okay! Put the gun away. Remember what they promised us."

Hearing Joey's pleadings, LaPoshio sat bolt upright.

"No," Bobby said calmly, slowly lifting the door handle. It wasn't much of an idea – ease his way out, undetected – but it was his only chance. "These bastards are going down."

The moment the door latch clicked opened, an ear-piercing gunshot cracked into the air as a blast of thunder emanated from the back seat. The car instantly filled with the odor of gunshot residue. Bobby's body slumped over, a good portion of the back of his head now gone. Brain particles and blood were splattered everywhere.

Storming the Cadillac, the agents and detectives pulled LaPoshio and Tremont out and to the ground, handcuffing them. No one bothered to check Bobby Hoffman's pulse.

Lying beside Joey on the sidewalk, LaPoshio spat in his face. "You son-of-a-bitch! You sold me out. You can't hide. You would've been better off like Bobby. We'll find you. You're a dead man, Joey! A dead man!"

"Shut the fuck up," an agent ordered LaPoshio, stepping on the back of his neck for emphasis.

"Are you alright?" Bollinger asked the woman, still sitting calmly in the back seat.

She nodded, looking down at the spatter of human tissue on her dress. "I'm fine. Hoffman was getting out with a gun; you'll find it with him. He said, 'These bastards are going down' right before I shot him. Get me out of here."

"Over here!" Bollinger directed one of his agents. "Get her to clearance now!"

Stunned, Johnny and Billy gazed in wonderment. This was out of their jurisdiction. There was nothing they could do but watch it unfold. "Jesus Christ, I can't believe what I'm seeing," Johnny mumbled as he and Billy watched Leelee Gaye being escorted to a waiting car.

"Now you *know it all,* detectives," Bollinger said, smiling at his own cleverness. Leelee Gaye is Operation Orchid and one of our top undercover agents. The FBI has been operating the No-It-Awl Jazz Club. End of story for you two, but this is as far as it goes," he said, dismissing them. "Our deal still stands."

What a day. What a fucking day. "Billy, let's get a drink at the Nostalgia Café."

"I'm right behind you, Johnny."

CHAPTER 116

Molly poured Johnny his two fingers of Old Crow, neat, and herself a vodka martini.

"That's a new one for you Molly," Johnny said.

"You're right. Charly introduced me to it when she was here, and I've been meaning to try it at home. Two olives," she said, "and, of course, an old favorite, our friend." She lowered the needle onto the latest Coleman Hawkins record. The air filled with its smooth melodic notes and unstressed rhythm.

Johnny studied each graceful movement. "Molly, you are beautiful inside and out. I can't tell you enough. I want you to know that I –"

Placing a single finger over Johnny's lips, Molly said, "Shhhhhh" as she replacing her finger with soft, full, welcoming lips. After all the kisses they had shared, her lips still sent thrill through him. *The best kisses. She has the best kisses.*

Molly sat down beside him, looking into his eyes. *Should I have let him finish what he wanted to say? Was he going to say "I love you"* – just the thought quickened her heartbeat. *We look at one another with love in our eyes, but the words never come out. Our hearts know, though. Our hearts know.*

fred berri

Nestled against him, she felt comforted in his arms. He nuzzled her neck with slow kisses. *If this isn't love, I don't know what is.* With gentle nudges and shifts, she directed to where she wanted his kisses to move in slow, passionate succession. Molly knew exactly what she wanted, where she wanted it, and when she wanted it.

Her wish would always be his command.

Don't Count Your Chickens Before They Hatch!

CHAPTER 117

Stepping from the tub where Molly was still slathering herself with soap, Johnny wiped steam from the mirror so that he could see to shave. Taking his brush from its little stand, he wet it, and swirled it in the mug of sandalwood scented shaving soap. He hadn't yet moved all of his things from his apartment, but a few. When Angie came home next month, he planned to tell her about Molly, and see if she wanted to find a roommate. *What if she's got her own fellow?* Molly's lover was okay with that; Angie's father frowned, almost nicking his chin.

"Molly, we got additional information that coincides with what you were telling me the other day."

"Which part?" she said as she shut off the water. "Hand me a towel?"

"For one, Griff's original schedule for a delivery," he said, pulling the curtain back. "The Janitor's still singing pretty, although it's nothing we didn't know already. But it does confirm that LaPoshio, Carol Lynne, and himself played a huge part in all this." Shaving as he talked, he could still enjoy her reflection in the mirror behind him as she dried herself. Even in that ridiculous shower cap, she was a sight to behold.

"Dr. Dean Paul," she said, as if introducing a celebrity. "He and Lynne were the 'murder for hire' right under the nose of New York City government."

"He still hasn't given us any ideas of where she's hiding, or who's helping her, dammit."

Molly dropped the towel and reached her arms around Johnny, pressing her breasts into his bare back. "LaPoshio isn't giving anything to the feds, either, from what I hear. Code of honor bullshit. It looks like he's willing to go all the way with his silence, but we'll have to wait and see what his attorney's going to pull," she said, moving her hands down to tug at his manhood. "I know what I would suggest if he were *my* client. "They'd just made love in the shower, but she was gratified to detect further interest.

Johnny moved her hand back to his stomach. "Do you want me to cut myself?" he chuckled. "What would you tell him, Madame District Attorney?"

Molly turned around to put on her robe, and pulled off the shower cap. "I'd tell him to make a deal. He could avoid the electric chair."

"You would want to help him?" Johnny asked, surprised.

"If he was my client and I was ethically bound to represent him, I would. Attorneys have to act in their clients' best interests. But," she continued, "I would also seek justice where justice is deserved. I'd want him to give the police information to help solve any open investigations or cold cases that he's tied to. For the families' sake, if nothing else. We might get some remains for a proper burial. I'm sure some of the victims were innocent bystanders that just got in the way. Wrong place, wrong time." Molly began brushing her hair. "So, what's your next move Johnny?"

"My next move is right here, Molly." He turned around, his interest obvious ... and growing under her admiring gaze.

"Not this morning," she said with an air of apology, and regret. "I'm already running late. But hold that thought for tonight!" she called as she ran down the hall, laughing, before he could stop her.

CHAPTER 118

Friday morning, Captain Sullivan bellowed, "Vero, Bradshaw! My office."

"Captain?" Johnny asked. "What's up?"

Sullivan put down the newspaper he'd been reading. "As you know, the brass has eased up on the Chinatown murders since you handed them the two top gangsters in New York City. All smiles at the press conferences, letting our fair city know it's safe under *their* watchful eyes. You both will probably have another commendation added to your file." Sullivan put his elbows on the desk and leaned forward a little, signaling the end to the fluffy stuff. "Now tell me, Lieutenant, the nitty gritty. Where are you with the rest of the hoodlums?"

Johnny sighed. "Hoodlums is putting it mildly, Captain. We have no idea where Carol Lynne is, and she is one bad ass lady. She'll slit your throat with a smile; she has a real way about her. After the APB went out, we've gotten sightings from all over. I'm convinced that Monica's murder in France wasn't random. Someone had her killed, someone who knew she'd helped us. I'm thinking that Carol Lynne might've used her real name to get by us and may be in Europe. I've gotten reports that she's been sighted in New Jersey, North Carolina, and Florida, but nothing's been solid. I believe she's either right here under our nose, or far away. She and her cohorts have their secret society connections there."

Sullivan had been waiting for an appropriate opening. "We have our secret society too. The Chief has them on call, and they're digging deep," he bragged.

"SABSO?"[12] Billy asked. He and Johnny shared a look of excitement.

"Yes, and so far as you said, Vero, you're correct. SABSO reports that she's in Sicily traveling back and forth between there, Italy, and France, connecting with her partners in crime wherever she goes." Sullivan knew what his men were thinking. "The department cannot and will not send you two there. SABSO works their detail, we work ours here. I contacted Inspector Laurènt to be on notice, just to be sure."

Johnny was not happy to have been kept out of the loop until now; his countenance said it all.

Sullivan sat back in his chair. "I see you're upset, but this is nothing personal. Captains can still occasionally do a little police work of their own. You know how this shit works. As a matter of fact, you both should consider being part of SABSO – they'd love to have both of you, I was told." He knew them enough to know that they would at least calm any pugnaciousness. "It's a holiday weekend. We're having a family cookout in the backyard, boys, if you want to stop by." Sullivan picked the paper back up, their cue to leave.

"That's great news. SABSO. Sure, we'll take all the help we can get," Johnny said, nudging Billy to leave with him. "We have an appointment to get to, *Captain*."

---

[12] SABSO; Saber Blue Society. See reference page.

CHAPTER 119

In reality, their "appointment" was three days away, with Commander Cunningham and the US Coast Guard. With any luck at all, they would capture Griff at last. Johnny felt that if the brass wanted to play the "keep information under wraps" game, he damn well could, too.

Tips from Dr. Dean Paul and Mo China confirmed Griff's originally scheduled drop of opium and women had been planned for Memorial Day, and although he had tried to disrupt, distract and outmaneuver with a couple of earlier drops, the word was that Memorial Day was a "go." The city's annual celebration would be in full swing on top of the usual cruise ships and sightseeing boats. The Navy would dock a ship and offer public tours. Tug boats and the fire department would host a display of shooting water cannons spewing hundreds of feet into the air. The celebration would be all day and into the night, when fireworks from the Coast Guard would be set off from barges anchored on the Hudson River.

With the Coast Guard and Harbor Police busy trying to keep a proper patrol on everyone and everything, it would be the perfect time for a smuggling operation to pull into the harbor undetected. Catching Griff would be an arduous task.

fred berri

All involved had been briefed. Early Monday morning, Detectives Vero, Bradshaw, Fang, Pan, and Chang joined Cunningham and his men on the ship for one last meeting. Ru Chang pointed to the bullet holes and ricochet marks from their last encounter with Griff, which only intensified the already formidable situation. This would not be a relaxing holiday on the water. The risks they were about to take, not only for themselves but for everyone in the vicinity of Griff's capture, weighed heavily. What had begun five months before would finally be over, they hoped.

Cunningham scanned the men's eyes, guessing their somber thoughts. "This is going to be a long day and a possibility a long night. I know if I were Griff, I'd wait for the shadow of darkness to pull into the harbor. I believe this man knows his shit, so he damn well knows how many boats, hands, and eyes will be on the fireworks barges. The availability of back-up, should we need it, is compromised. I've done this day for the past 25 years, and I'm telling you, it will be between him and us, that's it," Cunningham explained.

"Won't your ship be a dead give-a-way with all the Coast Guard markings?" Johnny asked.

"We don't really have a choice, given his fire power from our last encounter. Our unmarked vessels are too small to carry us all, and we need to carry more firepower. This is the same vessel we used the last time, but since there will be so many of our vessels on the water, it may actually work to our advantage," Cunningham responded firmly. Military through and through, he respected what the NYPD had been able to accomplish and was looking forward to playing a more active, successful role in taking down Griff. "I suspect, however, that

Griff will have a different vessel. And bring more fire power, so be prepared."

"Somehow, I'm feeling … diminished, Commander," Billy said.

"I understand, Detective. Sort of like being a boy in a men's locker room shower?" Cunningham said, his eyes dancing.

The men were grateful for a bit of humor to lighten the mood. The spell of impending doom was broken, at least for the moment. Cunningham grabbed the microphone to make an announcement over that all of his men could hear. "We'll be anchored here for a while, but don't get comfortable. All eyes on the harbor and waterways. Every once in a while, look at the horizon to help keep your balance, those of you without your sea legs. You're responsible to clean up your own mess – over and out!"

Time passed slowly as the men scoped the area, looking for anything unusual. Since he was standing close enough to his childhood friend to be more personal, Johnny said, "We've been bobbing up and down for a few of hours, Fred. What's your take on our mission?"

The commander shrugged. "Your guess is as good as mine. Johnny. *I'd* wait until it gets dark but he might use that thinking against us and try to get in right under our noses. This is just like one of your stakeouts, only on the water. Better view, anyway."

Johnny's stomach rumbled, and the commander heard it. "Can we send someone for coffee?"

"Coffee and food down in the galley. Help yourself."

Johnny had moved barely two feet when a cry came from the crow's nest. "Unidentified vessel approaching starboard!"

"Radio patrol to intercept," Cunningham yelled to a guardsman nearby.

"Aye aye, Commander."

Billy walked over to join him. "What if that's him?" he asked.

"Steady, Detective. It's way too small to carry the loads he'd have on board. But it could be a decoy. We'll check it out," Cunningham answered.

The boat carried a family of six, out on the water to enjoy the festivities. The boat was new and hadn't been fitted out properly yet with the necessary ID. The owner was given a warning. The men's adrenaline adjusted once more as the hours ticked off without incident.

Daylight started to bleed slowly into the horizon. For Johnny, there always seemed to be a loneliness associated with that transition to purple dusk. *It's like being in a waiting room, anticipating the door to open for darkness, empowering you to whisper things you don't want the sun to hear.* He decided that he would go bonkers if he had to sit on the water much longer.

And then, almost at once, the sun was gone. Cityscape lights came on – first a few, then many. The harbor lit up like the marquee for the premier of a Broadway play. Spotlights from hundreds of boats scoured the skies. As stars twinkled overhead, the fireworks barges exploded their version into the night sky, filling it with wondrous colors. The men could not enjoy them, however, ever vigilant to their task.

"Stand by!" Cunningham's voice was terse. "I see what might be him. Man your stations, man your stations!"

Johnny didn't have time to wonder how Cunningham had spotted Griff's boat in the midst of all the controlled chaos in the harbor. Not that it mattered; Griff's arrival came swiftly, out of nowhere. In the time it took Cunningham to maneuver the one-hundred-foot beast of a patrol boat into position to block Griff, they could already see the silhouettes of human cargo holding bags over their heads in the water, attempting to reach the shoreline.

The fireworks illuminated the sky, giving all those on Cunningham's mission a clear view. The choice was also clear – they would leave the cargo, the women and the opium headed for shore. Griff's boat had already turned, headed back to sea.

"Goddamn it! He did it again! He's a fucking magician," Johnny screamed. "Commander, your weapons! He's getting away! FIRE! FIRE! FIRE!"

Cunningham, however, had to wait for the right moment before giving the command. He had to be sure Griff's boat would not endanger others on the waterway, at the precise moment before Griff was able to mingle in with other vessels, blending in, ensuring his safety and escape. But Griff's boat did not turn in the direction he anticipated. Instead, it was heading straight for one of the fireworks barges.

"What the fuck...?" Cunningham was not able to finish his thought before a huge explosion sent shock waves throughout the harbor. Griff's boat went up in flames. Spectators assumed it was part of the fireworks display, the grand finale, but the Harbor Patrol and Coast Guard rushed to the scene, hoping to rescue survivors.

Cunningham's vessel was so close that the explosion knocked a few men off their feet. All five detectives lined the deck, shocked at the sight. Emergency vessels scoured the water with their powerful search lights, cutting their engines to an idle, virtually tip-toeing their way in fear that a survivor might succumb to a propeller. The air filled with the smell of charred wood and gasoline as the resulting oil slick burned on the surface.

"What the fuck just happened? Is Griff really dead after all this?" Johnny didn't expect anyone to answer.

CHAPTER 120

The mayor was probably not happy with her for missing the big celebration, but Molly had been too tired, too concerned about the mission. She'd planned to wait up for him to celebrate Griff's arrest, but she'd fallen asleep. Sometime during the night, he joined her in bed, freshly showered and smelling incredible but not wanting to talk.

Molly grinned to herself now, grateful she'd napped earlier. He had been particularly lively. In the morning, she slipped out of bed and opened her door to grab the newspaper, always there without fail, a reliable friend.

The headline hit her like a hangover:

Mysterious Memorial Day Blast in New York Harbor

Coast Guard Claims Unidentified Boat with NO SURVIVORS!

More on page 2

Byline: Grace Tilly

"Jesus Christ! Johnny! Why didn't you tell me!" Molly yelled as she marched back into the bedroom.

He saw the headline and grimaced. "I was going to tell you this morning. I didn't want to upset you. You would have waited, too, before telling me you might've been in danger," he said, pulling her down on the bed. "Besides, didn't we have our own fireworks?"

Molly snuggled next to him. "You're right. I just got scared, reading the headline, knowing you were out there. You could have been killed!" She looked up at him, her eyes starting to tear up.

"Shh, shh. Listen. I'll tell you everything ..." The two lay holding each other as he relayed the Memorial Day events, giving more time to the boredom and less to the horrific explosion.

"So you're telling me that Griff rigged his boat to go on its own? That he may have been with the people you saw in the water, scrambling for shore?"

"That's my theory. Cunningham says there's a self-steering mechanism known as wind vane."

"Jesus, what will they think of next?"

"There's no evidence anyone was on the boat when it exploded. Just bits of boat. No sign of survivors. Cunningham has three crews still searching, but if there were survivors, or even body parts, they'd be floating. There's nothing." Johnny explained. "Our first priority was Griff and Griff alone. We ignored the people heading for shore to catch him. And lost him."

Overwhelmed with gratitude that he was safe, Molly rolled on top of him. "I overreacted. Sooooo, let me make it up to you," she cooed as she lifted herself onto her knees, so that he could see her better. "It's early. We have plenty of time before we have to leave."

CHAPTER 121

A press conference was due to be held on the steps of the federal courthouse in an hour, and Johnny had some explaining to do. For the Chief to show up at Captain Sullivan's office only underscored the seriousness. "The bottom line is this – we've wrapped up eleven murders wrapped up, thanks to information we've received from those in custody. With the exception of Alvise LaPoshio, everyone's talked."

Molly spoke up. "He says he'd die before he gave us anything so much as a shoe size." *And he probably will.*

Johnny continued. "Chief, expand on that fact that you have one of the biggest crime bosses in New York City in custody, along with one of his under bosses, a notorious murderer for hire. Nobody needs to know LaPoshio's not talking. If the public thinks he *is*, all the better. Brag on the eleven solves, and misdirect the press from the missing duo, Carol Lynne and Griff. None of the reporters know anything about those two, not even Grace Tilly, and she's the best."

Molly's hostile glance when Johnny mentioned Grace Tilly did not go unnoticed by him. "The Lieutenant's suggestions are sound, Chief," she said. "LaPoshio isn't giving up anyone, but it will get back to his bosses in Italy that he's done just that, if we word things a certain way. It might scare him into a deal, rather than be killed in prison. Those hands reach across the ocean."

Johnny was gratified that she supported him in front of the brass. He hoped to show that same support to her, wherever her ambitions lay. "The same information will eventually reach Carol Lynne, too, no matter where she is. It'll either drive her deeper into hiding, or push her out. No one's going to hide her with a price on her head. That one's a crap shoot," he admitted ruefully. "Only time will tell."

"Let's get this dog-and-pony show on the road, Captain. The mayor and the PC are waiting. Lieutenant, Miss Penett, you're welcome to join us," the Chief said.

Molly smiled innocently but shook her head. "With all due respect, Detective Vero and I have some work to do on the Carol Lynne file and the updates from SABSO. Shall we go, Lieutenant?" She wanted to make a graceful exit before their presence was demanded.

"I'm glad you conjured up that excuse," Johnny whispered on their way out.

"Not really an excuse, Johnny. We're going to Rikers.[13]"

Johnny was puzzled. "Rat Island? What am I missing, Molly?"

"We have an interview with the Janitor," she said. "He's still trying to make a deal. He knows he's in deep shit and it's starting to wear on him." She glanced back to make sure no one else might be approaching who could hear. "I'm letting him believe his flirtations are softening me up; he's working on a transfer out of gen pop."

---

[13] Rikers Island; New York City's main jail complex.

"Let him think anything he wants," Johnny mused. "Let him believe he'll have a private cell with room service and all the hookers he wants at the city's expense."

Molly smirked. "Men. Is that *all* you think about?"

CHAPTER 122

"Right this way," directed a grim-faced guard at Rikers. "Your prisoner is waiting. Do you want a guard present?"

"No," Molly said. "It's fine.

"Yes Ma'am," he politely nodded. "We'll be right outside if you change your mind. Just tap on the door."

Dr. Paul glared at Johnny as they entered the room. "What's this prick doing here?" His Van Dyke was no longer neatly trimmed, and he had lost some weight.

"We're both here to help you," Johnny said calmly. "Miss Penett always speaks so highly of you, Doctor. I can pull strings she can't, and she can pull strings I can't. We work together."

"That's not the impression I got that night in the morgue. When I got shot by one of your men."

"Dr. Paul," Molly interjected gently, patting his hands. He jumped a little, as if shocked by electricity, but he didn't move his hands away. He had to keep them on the table, seen at all times. But this was the first time she had touched him. Johnny was surprised as well, but his expression didn't waver.

Molly saw the Janitor's eyes soften. "Detective Vero volunteered to help, as we spoke about before. It all depends on your cooperation." Her tone of voice was soothing and sweet. "Haven't I kept our part of the bargain so far? You have your own cell now, don't you? We're working on some other comforts for you."

"I want to be transferred," Dr. Paul demanded. "These people are *crazy*."

"I'll make the requisition. It takes a while, though; you know that. You worked for the City. We have to cut through all the red tape, but we'll get there, Doctor."

Johnny was impressed. Molly's words and demeanor – not to mention her curves – were working their magic.

"What do you want from me?" Dr. Paul asked.

Johnny and Molly had discussed their wish list. "We need Carol Lynne," she said, with the merest hint of an eyelash flutter.

Dr. Paul's eyes darted back and forth from Molly to Johnny. Finally he exhaled loudly and nodded. "Okay. But you have to put in that requisition."

"As soon as we leave here, Doctor," Molly assured him.

The doctor studied the ceiling for a few seconds. "There's one passport you don't know about."

With some effort, Johnny maintained a blank expression. "Go on."

"Carol uses another name sometimes. Lorac Sreknoy."

"Sounds Slavic," Johnny suggested.

"Maybe, maybe not. It could be anywhere in the vicinity. Yugoslavia borders Italy." He smirked at Johnny. "Write it down, Lieutenant. I'll spell it for you. L-O-R-A-C. S-R-E-K-N-O-Y. Lorac's meaning is 'strong, happy, and graceful.'" He seemed pleased with himself. "Actually, it's just Carol backwards, but she's all of that and then some." He hummed a little. "I really had you going, though, didn't I? Slavic!" He chuckled.

Johnny stared at the letters on his notepad. "And Sreknoy is Yonkers spelled backwards. So Lorac Sreknoy's the name on her passport now?"

"Unless she's using yet another one. Lorac Sreknoy. Kind of brilliant, isn't it?" Dr. Paul asked rhetorically.

"Where do you think she is?"

"Guard!" the Janitor called loudly, never taking his eyes from Molly. "I'm done! Take me to my cell, please." He stood with a lecherous smile. "Miss Penett, I await our next visit bringing good news. Who knows what I may have for you then?"

Molly nodded, turning to Johnny as the guard came in. "Detective." It was the tone she used to both calm him, and to signal departure. Molly knew Johnny wanted to rip Paul limb from limb.

Back in the car, Johnny called in an APB for female suspect Lorac Sreknoy, as well asking Billy to pass along the information via the proper chain to Laurènt and SABSO. Then he took a moment to just look at Molly, slowly shaking his head.

"Good work, Molly. That was a very nice touch, putting your hand on his. I hated it, but it worked."

Laughing, Molly said, "You haven't forgotten my campaign slogan, have you?"

Johnny laughed with her. "Of course! ' New York's hands-on District Attorney.'" Risking someone seeing, he leaned over and planted a kiss on her lips. You can put your hands on me any time, Miss Penett."

CHAPTER 123

Billy couldn't hide his exuberance as he read the teletype. Ripping off the paper, he fairly danced into the office he shared with Johnny. "Johnny, you gotta read this! I grabbed this wire before anyone else could get their mitts on it."

"Jesus, Billy, I'm busy right now. I'm trying to figure out how to get those last two perps behind bars and piece the murders together. I want to close this fucking case." Angie would be arriving that night, and there was much to discuss. It would be great to have this all behind him.

Billy grinned. "Trust me, you'll want to see what just fell into our laps." He handed the wire to Johnny.

I HAVE SOMETHING YOU WANT... STOP   FOUND IN MONICA ROOM...   STOP   MY INSURANCE POLICY STOP...   GOOD NEWS TRAVELS FAST A L... STOP

                                                                    C L

Johnny and Billy looked at one another. Carol Lynne had the ledger. Johnny's thoughts rushed overtop of one another. *She killed Monica. Eleventh murder solved. But what is A L ?* "Shit! Alvise LaPoshio. *What* good news?" he blurted out loud. Johnny dialed Bollinger's number.

"Agent Bollinger."

"Vero here, calling to confirm good news about LaPoshio...?" Now that he heard the question out loud, it sounded odd.

Bollinger's hearty laugh confirmed that his question *sounded* odd to him as well. "You can't be serious, Lieutenant. Alvise LaPoshio was found hanging in his cell at Alcatraz last night. We're releasing it to the press shortly, but first we had to tie up some loose ends. He kept true to the code of silence, so I guess you could consider it good news, in a way," Bollinger said. "Someone will take his place, all just a matter of time. But you and your detectives contributed a great deal in getting LaPoshio behind bars. You should be proud." Almost as an afterthought, Bollinger said, "One thing we *did* find out for sure. The real bosses behind all this were, Jimmy the Rat Enrizzi and his cousin Ralph Mariozo. Even though they're dead, their hands keep extending from the grave. We may be working together sooner than you think! Good luck, Lieutenant!" *Click.*

Son. Of. A. Bitch. *Will this never end?* Without hanging up the receiver first, he dialed another number. *At least some good things will never end either.*

"Molly...?"

The End – Sort of

Thank you for reading. I look forward to becoming one of your favorite authors. Please post a review on Amazon.com.

fred berri

For the reader:

• *AKA:* Also known as

• *"Auld Lang Syne"* is the title of the Scottish tune that translates to "times gone by." It's about remembering friends from the past and not letting them be forgotten. Despite its strong association with New Year's Eve, the song, written by Robert Burns in the 1700s, was never intended to connected to that, or any, holiday.

• *"Good Morning Heartache"* Written by Irene Higginbotham, Ervin Drake, and Dan Fisher.

• *Billie Holiday* (April 7, 1915-July 17, 1959) born Eleanora Fagan; an American jazz musician and singer-songwriter.

• *Coleman Randolph Hawkins* (November 21, 1904 – May 19, 1969), was an American jazz tenor saxophonist.

• *Florsheim Shoes* were recognized as being of high quality. They came to symbolize success for those wearing them costing around $10-12 in the 1940s while other shoes cost approximately $6-8. Florsheim still offers high quality shoes today, and happen to be the author's brand.

• *Gen pop:* the general population of a prison, as opposed to more restricted, safer areas

• *Jack Dempsey:* William Harrison "Jack" Dempsey was a cultural icon of the 1920's. Dempsey's aggressive fighting style and exceptional punching power made him one of the most popular boxers in history.

• *James Joseph "Gene" Tunney: Tunney* was a thinking fighter who preferred to make a boxing match into a game of chess, which was not popular during the times when he fought.

• *KA:* Known Associates

• *On Leong Tong* and *Hip Sing Tong:* Chinese-American criminal organizations based in New York's Chinatown during the early 20th century. They were involved in the violent Tong Wars for control of Chinatown during the early 1900s. During the 1930s and 1940s, they were involved in drug trafficking, opium, prostitution, and gambling operations. The *On Leong Tong* represented the interest of the elite in Chinatown. Its power lay in the social, economic, and political status of its leaders. The *Hip Sing Tong* was the power syndicate in Chinatown. Its power lay in the sizable number of professional criminals within its ranks. The word *tong* means "hall" or "gathering place."

• *Patron Saint Benedict Joseph Labre:* Although Saint Labre is considered an authentic Patron Saint (of those suffering from mental illness) in Catholicism, the Labre Island mentioned in this book is fictitious. However, there was a building on Welfare Island in New York City that was a condemned government building. It was once active as New York City's chronic health care facility for the insane. At one point, the War Department conducted research on malaria and human tolerance for food starvation. These studies were conducted in the same building on Welfare Island.

• *SABSO:* Saber Blue Society is a fictitious group of elite police, created by author, fred berri.

• *Schofield Barracks* is a US. Army installation located in Hawaii. The barracks was built in 1909, and its main purpose was to provide a base for the Army dedicated to the mobile defense of Hawaii, particularly Pearl Harbor.

• *"Smoke Gets in Your Eyes"* is a show tune written by American composer Jerome Kern and lyricist Otto Harbach for their 1933 musical *Roberta*.

• *The Shadow Radio program:* The Shadow was developed into a distinctive literary character, later to become a pop culture icon, by writer Walter B. Gibson in 1931. The introduction from *The Shadow* radio program: "Who knows what evil lurks in the hearts of men? The Shadow knows!" The words were narrated by actor Frank Readick Jr. who had replaced the original, but short-lived, James LaCurto. The Shadow operated mainly after dark as a vigilante in the name of justice, terrifying criminals into vulnerability. The Shadow's character name was Kent Allard, a famed aviator who fought for the French during World War I. One of the identities Allard assumes (the best known) is that of Lamont Cranston, a wealthy young man-about-town. Cranston is a separate character, but Allard frequently disguises himself as Cranston and adopts his identity.

• *The Student's Cantonese-English Dictionary* by Bernard F. Meyer and Theodore F. Wempe of Maryknoll. First edition, 1935 St. Louis Industrial School Printing Press, Hong Kong.

• *TOD:* Time of Death

About the Author

Berri was born in the Bronx, New York. After many years, his family moved to Yonkers, New York where he finished high school. After graduation, he relocated back to the Bronx with his family to an area called 'Little Italy' within the section known as Fordham. He married his high school sweetheart, Louisa, and together, raised their children.

Early on, he worked various jobs from shining shoes, grocer, butcher, owning a lunch truck, as well as owning a successful contract cleaning janitorial service, employing over 100 individuals. He sold his business and relocated to Florida. After graduating from Columbia State University with an online degree, he became a banking specialist with one of the largest banking institutions in the nation.

Retired now, he enjoys writing and spending time with his grandson, Carmelo.

Mr. Berri has volunteered teaching Junior Achievement in the Florida public school district and has also done public speaking. He has had the opportunity to be in a few T.V. commercials, including voiceovers. Berri has also created the website www.retirementusa.com.

He began writing while working full-time, but had his first novel published after retirement and believes the mind can imagine and create what you let it. An example he uses is the children's story we are all familiar with...'Humpty Dumpty'...

Berri claims he was *pushed!*

Of Interest, Perhaps

Previously published books:

Cousins' Bad Blood: **ISBN 1508567298**
Michael Pellegrino came from humble beginnings from Italy to America-the son of immigrant parents seeking the American dream. He far exceeded his parents' expectations building for himself a powerful and lucrative criminal empire becoming one of the most powerful men in America.

Ten Cents a Dance: ISBN 978-1506-902-82-1
Set in the late 1940's, homicide detective, Johnny Vero, hunts a serial killer who targets dance hall women that charge ten cents for a 3 minute dance at The Flamingo Room. They are murdered in the Budapest Hotel. The killer chooses certain room numbers because they have Biblical meaning to him. Detective Vero tracks this serial killer to France where Interpol joins the hunt.

Radio Interviews:

Boomer Times:
https://www.youtube.com/watch?v=dpZhhdG7RnQ
https://www.youtube.com/watch?v=v1csJDLTiiQ&t=18s
https://www.youtube.com/watch?v=TtQWxruKpog&t=35s

You may contact the author at fredberri@gmail.com
Author of Cousins' Bad Blood And Ten Cents a Dance

CPSIA information can be obtained
at www.ICGtesting.com
Printed in the USA
FFHW021349310119
50349578-55433FF